You're Breaking My Heart

You're Breaking My Heart

**OLUGBEMISOLA
RHUDAY - PERKOVICH**

Montclair | Amsterdam | Hoboken

This is an Arthur A. Levine book
Published by Levine Querido

LEVINE QUERIDO

www.levinequerido.com • info@levinequerido.com

Levine Querido is distributed by Chronicle Books, LLC

Library of Congress Control Number: 2023931855
ISBN 978-1-64614-181-4

Printed and bound in China

Published in January 2024

First Printing

To my parents, and Adedayo:
thank you for the stories that make everything all right,
even when I remember them wrong.

At 7:26 on Thursday morning, Harriet Adu and her older brother Tunde had a fight. This happened regularly; he was sixteen and she was thirteen (almost fourteen!). Voices were raised, doors slammed, and as her brother tossed off a body-shaming "joke" on his way out of the door, she muttered, "I wish you were dead."

By 3:00 p.m. that day, he was.

1

She used to read books about portals. Vehicles of spectacle, wonder, shock, and *ohhhh shhh* in films. The unlikely band of nerds would unexpectedly be transported to a place that was beautiful and better, and—after a series of character-building trials and challenges, revealing strengths no one, not even they, had known they had—they would be better too. Portals were doors and mirrors and wardrobes, places of possibility, even if the possibilities were of danger. Portals were not school bathrooms. School bathrooms were centers of humiliation. The story always went that way. But still, she held her breath every time she pushed open a school bathroom door, and not just because she was anticipating the smell. School bathrooms could surprise you, with a crying girl or a kissing couple, or a glance in the mirror that told you you looked good that day.

Or something much, much worse.

It had only been a month since she'd transferred to this school, but Harriet already knew that the bathroom on the third floor had a stall with a working lock. If she was lucky (haha), it would be empty. She sprinted up the stairs, holding a couple of textbooks to her chest.

She pushed the heavy door open and scanned the floor under each of the stall doors. It was empty. *Deserted* feeling, really. Harriet, who never felt alone these days but was always lonely, let out a long breath. Not much had gotten better here; after Tunde, she'd finished out the year "surrounded by friends and family," as Reverend Samuel had said, not taking into account the fact that she hadn't had any friends at her old school; not even being The Girl Whose Brother Died had changed that. A month into the new school year, her mother had worked out the transfer without telling Harriet; Nikka had just shown up one morning, apparently ready to skip to school arm-in-arm as though they could have fun together. Harriet had closed the door in her cousin's face and spent the day figuring out her own route to her new school, which turned out to be closer to the pool than her old one. Reverend Samuel would have called that undeserved grace. And she would have called him a fraud, in her head, just because.

She dropped her books on the sink ledge and locked herself in the last stall, the one where the portal jokes landed and stuck. She'd heard some kids talking about it on her first day; they called it the Troll Tunnel and stuffed all manner of contraband inside, from chewed gum to lighters to love notes. It led, they said, to a school of magic with more funding and no homework. Airy, freshly painted, and bright; the kind filled with cushioned seating and white kids who went on vacations to Black places.

Faint laughter and shouts floated in from the hallway as people rushed to class, to lunch, to the normal, thick places where she didn't belong. She tugged at her jeans; she'd *known* the faded yellow one-piece would be trouble; it was probably more than a size too small at this point, which meant that it worked its way up her butt every hour or so. (Her cousin Nikka, who liked to ask Harriet what she had up her butt all the time, would enjoy this.) But Harriet had woken up that morning gripping a wet pillow, and she'd continued to cry silently in the shower, where her tears could disappear into the water. *That doesn't count as crying.* She'd known that she would need the security blanket of her favorite swimsuit under her clothes all day.

Harriet leaned forward, away from the toilet and the ever-widening hole in the wall behind it. She gave the suit another quick tug and was rebuttoning her jeans just as the second bell rang. She started to leave the stall—then heard the bathroom door open. She locked herself back in.

"Oh my God, did you see the way he was looking at me?" Harriet didn't recognize the voice. She wondered if she should just make a quick exit now, but . . . should she flush? If she didn't, would they think she was gross?

This was awkward.

Better to stay hidden and be late for class. She slowly squatted on top of the toilet seat so that her legs wouldn't give her away.

"But . . . you don't think he's cute, right?" said another unfamiliar voice.

"Oh, yeah, of course, I know. I'm just saying . . . Ew, it smells gross in here, hurry up. Your hair looks fine. We're gonna be late."

"Let me borrow your lip gloss, then we can leave . . . I don't even know how people can go at school. I just hold it until I get home. It's always so nasty in here."

It's the clientele, thought Harriet. Then she grimaced. *Oh wait, I'm in here too.* She turned and noticed a crumpled piece of paper sticking out of the Troll Tunnel. It was silver, like slick wrapping paper, and she could make out something like a diagram or a map on one side, like fancy physics homework.

"This shirt makes me look ginormous. I can't believe I wore it. Look at me."

"Um, no. Everyone looks at you, I don't have to join in. Did you hear about The Ratings?"

"I want to know where they put me. As long as I'm not at the bottom of the list or something, I'm OK."

Harriet had pretended not to care when Nikka told her about the school's elaborate ratings system, but she hoped that even with Weird New Girl status, she'd been ranked higher than Corey "Yeti" Hayne.

"It's so sexist. We should do one for the guys, though."

"Wouldn't that be like reverse sexism or something?"

"Nah, it would be feminist. Completely different. I mean, I'm not a feminist, but . . ."

Harriet held back a snort.

"You know that weird new girl's got to be at the bottom of the list. She is so creepy. I heard she's Nikka Soy— whatever's cousin, but I don't believe it. Nikka is normal, even though she thinks she's all that."

"You'd be weird too if you had all that drama."

"That is so sad . . . Wasn't she like right there or something?"

Harriet wanted to tear off her ears, but she had to hear this. Later she'd replay it in her mind, over and over, like a penitential prayer.

"Supposedly. The whole school was there . . . I heard it happened in the lunch room. Just like one of those messed-up stories on the news. My mom joined one of those 'moms against guns' groups right after, like *that's* going to do anything."

"All I know is, New Girl gets side-eye from me, I don't care how tragic she is. You have to watch out for the weird ones . . . what if she goes all wacked out here and starts popping people off for revenge or something?"

"True . . . she's so obviously damaged."

"And she is *not* cute . . . I'd be mad too if I looked like that and my brother got shot." Snickering.

Harriet gasped.

She wondered if she'd given herself away, but they continued.

"You're stupid." Laughter. "Anyway, everyone here is normal. Freaks can't survive. Come on, we are *so* late. That was the last bell."

"Somebody left their books here."

"Not my problem. Let's *go*, Charisse. I do *not* want another detention."

"OK, OK, calm down . . ." The voices faded.

Harriet heard the door close. Silence. As she pulled the stall door open, she stumbled back and the crumpled paper fell out of the Tunnel. She pushed it forward with her foot, and a trick of light from the tiny bathroom window made it shimmer. She didn't want to touch it, but since she couldn't just leave it on the floor, she pulled a length of toilet paper and wrapped it around her hand to pick it up.

It was smooth and almost fabric-like, like an express mail envelope. She looked at it; a delicate line drawing of a subway car floating across waves. It was an exquisite piece of art, forgotten in a bathroom stall. Oh well. She gently pushed it back into the hole in the wall. As she finally left the stall, it dislodged and fell into the toilet. Of course. She sighed, and walked to the sinks. After she washed her hands, Harriet stood in front of the sink for a minute, listening to her own breathing. When she looked in the mirror, she was surprised to see that she was shaking. She gripped the sink for a few seconds and then picked up her books.

She heard a toilet flush from a stall behind her and the fleeting memory that she was sure she'd been alone in the bathroom shoved her out as though it had hands.

The bathing suit continued to bother her all day, but she didn't go back to the bathroom. She decided to let it be a reminder that she'd be in the water soon. Her real breathing—not just the shallow necessary-for-survival breaths—began as soon as she got to the pool.

Nikka's click-clacking platform heels broadcasted her arrival a full minute before she actually appeared at Harriet's locker. Harriet looked from her work boots to her cousin's feet and wondered how Nikka managed to wear shoes like that and still look so perky at the end of the school day.

Harriet looked up; "What," she said, declaring the word and turning back to her locker. "What can I do to make you feel superior today?"

"I don't need any help, ha, you know I'm all that," Nikka said. But her giggle trailed off quickly. "Are you going to swim? I have yoga, I can walk with you."

"Yes, I'm swimming, and yes, I guess that even in those shoes you're capable of walking there with me. Congratulations." Harriet started toward the school exit; Nikka stood at the locker for a moment, then sighed and followed, shoes clicking determinedly.

"Wait up . . . you don't have to walk so fast."

Harriet stopped and waited for Nikka to get alongside her. "I do, actually," she said. "This is like my warm-up." Her body needed to hit the water.

"My *shoes*," Nikka whined.

Harriet slowed; she wondered if Nikka was waiting for an opening. She remained silent as they walked up Amsterdam Avenue, past the busloads of tourists gathering their cameras for tours of the Cathedral of St. John the Divine, and the hospital, where a woman in a hopeful red coat sobbed loudly next to a hot-dog cart.

Nikka tried out a few heavy sighs, and then: "You should come to yoga. People think they can't lose weight doing yoga, but that's a myth. You should totally try it."

Harriet stopped. *You don't want to say something you'll regret, Harriet.* Also, Nikka's mom, Harriet's Auntie

Marguerite, who taught an under-enrolled undergraduate course at the university, was the reason Harriet had access to the pool. So she needed to watch her step before she lost the only thing that loved her back.

"Oh, of course I didn't mean it like that . . . Anyway, Charisse Clark was bragging about how she does vinyasa yoga all the time, which I know can't possibly be true because—"

"Charisse?" Harriet stopped abruptly.

"Yeah, do you know her? She's in my grade, but just barely. She should have been left back at least twice."

"I don't know her." Harriet started walking again.

"Um, OK . . . So anyway, what an idiot. She thinks she's popular, but she has no idea. I have nothing to do with that trash."

Nikka droned on like an evil stepsister, as they walked. The small Teachers College campus slid from stately into shabby more quickly than its rich cousin, Columbia University, a few blocks away. Harriet made a quick right and stopped in front of Trell Hall. There was a strip of CAUTION tape across one of the doors, covering an ugly crack.

"Was that it?" she asked Nikka, who was dropping a gold dollar coin into a man's cup. "I need to go downstairs. And I seriously can't believe you still have one of those coins."

Nikka smiled. "You know I save stuff like that. Remember our sticker collection?" She sighed again. "No, actually. I . . . wanted to know if you . . . Do you want to hang out with me and my girls this weekend?"

"My mom or your mom?" Harriet asked, rolling her eyes.

"Huh?"

"Who put you up to this? My mom or yours?" Their mothers were sisters who fussed at each other regularly, but always managed to tag-team when it came to their daughters. Harriet pushed open the working heavy door. Nikka slipped in behind her, smiling at the security guard walking out. He smiled back, then gave Harriet a short nod. She lifted a hand in recognition.

"Oh . . . they both suggested it but—"

"Tell them . . . oh, forget it. Thanks for the offer, Nik, but don't worry, I won't accept. You and your racist money and your *girls* are safe from me."

Nikka smirked. "Being difficult doesn't make you better, cuz. It just makes you difficult."

Harriet closed her eyes and wondered if clicking her heels three times might transport Nikka away.

Her cousin continued: "Being better makes you better. Take it from someone who knows."

Harriet clicked her sneakers lightly and opened her eyes.

Nikka was still there. No dice.

"Ooh, you should have a podcast," Harriet said slowly, sighing out the words. "I bet tens of people want to hear the pearls you're dropping. Why are you bothering me, Nikka? What's so urgent now?"

After that first day, Nikka came to the door a few more times, then she'd stopped. They'd been binary stars, orbiting each other for nine months.

It was better that way.

Nikka didn't reply. Harriet waited for her cousin to leave for the fitness center upstairs, but Nikka continued to follow her down to the basement.

Harriet pushed her way into the locker room, which was empty. As the faint sounds of splashing wafted toward them, Harriet panicked; no way was she changing in front of her cousin.

"What time does yoga start?" she asked, as Nikka began to change.

"Now. I have to hurry, so let's meet up later." Nikka pulled her thick twists up and clipped them into a high bun. The clip was shaped like a small crown, dotted with rhinestones. Harriet noted with satisfaction that a few of the stones were missing. "I'm supposed to pick up some bodega candles, you can come with me before we go home."

When Harriet's Auntie Marguerite and (real African!) Uncle Jidé had moved with their daughter into an apartment just down the block from her own, her mother *had* rolled her eyes and grumbled repeatedly before toting a six-year-old Harriet and a Dutch oven filled with baked chicken, tangy yellow rice dotted with a rainbow of vegetables, and sweet plantains over to welcome them. "She can't stop copying me, even now," muttered her mother as she pressed down the tops of the Tupperware that she later made Harriet retrieve. "I got here first." Harriet had wondered if her mother really had been the first person in all of New York City; it wasn't a difficult thing to imagine. "They call plantains 'dodo' where your uncle's from, in Nigeria," her mother had said, and that had made Harriet giggle more than the way her mother started pronouncing it "planTAYNS" did.

Tunde said more than once that it was weird that Auntie Marguerite was the one who had actually married a Nigerian when her sister had spent her whole life trying to tether herself to "the Motherland," but still could only snag a shadow—another kente-clad New Yorker who called other adults of no relation "Brother" and "Sister."

"Like why is my name even Tunde," he would say, rolling his eyes. "I can't even say it right. It's embarrassing. At least you got a regular name."

But as Harriet grew older, she wondered why *she* had been given such an old-timey, non-Nigerian name; her mother's certainty that *her* ancestors were Nigerian remained strong even though she'd never made an effort to verify her claims. It was as though the story she told herself, and her children, was proof enough. Auntie Marguerite had suggested African Ancestry, but her mother just sucked her teeth, saying that those things were government scams.

The next time her mother had sent her to the African and Caribbean market on 145th Street to buy black soap, she'd smiled widely at the auntie behind the register, just in case they were related.

On that first visit to Auntie Marguerite and Uncle Jidé's, the children had been sent off to "play." Nikka, after explaining that she didn't play with "babies," had demanded that Harriet fix her a plate. Tunde threatened to report Harriet's rudeness if she refused. When she'd gone to ask the adults for help with the plate, she'd gotten in trouble for trying to bring food into the bedroom.

They'd played "royal kingdom" for two hours that day; Harriet had been a guard and a bench. Tunde was the king. Nikka explained that only beautiful girls get to be princesses.

"You can be the witch later," she'd added, clearly believing she was offering a reward. Tunde had laughed and whispered that Harriet already was a *witch-with-a-b*, which was something he'd just learned but already said with relish and ease, and Harriet kept quiet, then played her assigned parts with apparent gusto. All the while, she imagined an alternate story in which she, the true princess, knocked Nikka and Tunde over and into a vat of foul-smelling goo.

"What do you need bodega candles for?" Harriet asked.

Nikka shrugged. "There was one of those emergency preparedness block association meetings last night, didn't your mom tell you? The candles are on the list."

"Aren't they religious, though? Seems kind of like blasphemy or something, just using prayer candles in an emergency."

Nikka shrugged again. "Seems like it would be the perfect time to me, but whatever. Anyway, I'm supposed to get some for your mom too—thank goodness, y'all live in a cave these days. What's with the mood lighting? Is she just being cheap?"

"Ha, ha," said Harriet. "I don't know how long I'll be here. Can't we just talk at my house? Bring a flashlight or something if it's too dark for you." The water was calling her; she tried not to fidget.

Nikka let out another of her seemingly endless supply of sighs. Harriet almost asked if they were part of some new social media workout.

"Swimming makes you flat-chested," said Nikka, raising her eyebrows.

"Oh yeah?" Harriet looked straight ahead, determined not to glance down at her chest. She thought about the cool water swooshing between her fingers and toes.

Nikka smiled without showing any teeth.

Harriet bared hers. "Good to know. Thanks for the tip."

Nikka sat down on the wooden bench next to Harriet, ignoring the two women with identical blonde messy buns who jumped up from the bench in an exaggerated huff. "I was just trying to be nice."

"Keep trying," muttered Harriet. "You'll get the hang of it."

Nikka shrugged. "See you later." She left the locker room, her slim back straight, not glancing once at the large mirror near the door.

There was a large X of CAUTION tape blocking the open doorway to the pool. Harriet looked left, then right, and quickly slipped under the tape and inside the chlorine-scented room. The lights were out, and the pool itself was empty. The regular magazine-reading lifeguard was nowhere to be found. It was against the rules, but Harriet dropped into the pool anyway. The water welcomed her home. As soon as her fingertips hit the cool counterfeit ocean-blue water, her entire body relaxed, the way it always did. She moved slowly to the bottom. She started swimming, a strong crawl, until she got to the ladder on the other side. She pulled herself up out of the water, and, heavy again, sat at the concrete edge of the pool. She glanced around, then tentatively patted her chest. She tumbled back into the water.

She swam her laps, graceful and weightless, and long; she swam as the true self she was in the water and her dreams. Sometimes, on her bed in the dark, Harriet would reenact her backstroke, stretching out on her bed and reaching up and around until her arms hit the pillow with a muffled thud.

The blue-green sea waters of Negril, Jamaica were the first she'd ever swum. The family vacation (courtesy of Auntie Marguerite, who had shared the first of many bonuses) to visit Sister Gwendolyn and Sister Harriet, was her first airplane ride, and at four, she'd thought that the magic of air travel was better than birthday presents. Even the foil-wrapped smushed sandwich that her mother handed her as she looked longingly at the shiny bags of candy and chips at the airport newsstand hadn't dampened her enthusiasm for the trip.

She didn't know much about her mother's former teachers who'd left the U.S. to found a school in Lagos, Nigeria, then built another in Negril, but could sense that Daddy's "conveniently pleasant choice," was the muttering of a man who'd been hurt by people who claimed to pray. Harriet hadn't fully understood, but she'd squeezed his hand anyway; he'd squeezed back, even as he said, "I'm sure it was *God* who directed them here. Phonies."

Years later, when she realized that her father had not been born Oluwatosin Adu, but had instead grown up as Michael Johnstone with Saturdays filled with Freedom School and community Kwanzaa celebrations, Harriet remembered how he'd spit out the word "phonies" as though it burned his mouth. When he sat stony-faced in holiday services, she and her mom would sit on either side of him, squeezing his hands; she'd wonder if maybe the patina of liberation theology at their current church was enough to convince him that God was good, all the time.

After Tunde died, they kept their hands in their laps. And her father only went back to church twice.

But in Jamaica, the hot bright sun and the fantasy-colored vistas overcame any sulks, and Harriet had ran to the water's edge, exploding with anticipation. Sister Gwendolyn had taken her hand; together they'd dashed into the waves and Harriet had known even then that this sort of joy was rare and precious.

She'd begged for swimming lessons as soon as the plane touched down back in New York, and had zoomed from Pike to Starfish in a couple of months at the Y. She'd idolized "Coach" George, leaving him cards crudely cut in the shape of fish for two years, and celebrated her tenth birthday by swimming twenty laps without stopping or breaking her smile.

Now she was almost fifteen, and after a long, self-imposed exile, she was in the water, home again. She'd just keep swimming, just keep swimming, like that cartoon fish. She wouldn't think about anything. She wouldn't feel. She'd just keep swimming.

Today, sapped by the bathroom conversation and Nikka's "niceness," she was exhausted after only a few lengths. She tread water slowly, and watched as the lights suddenly flickered on, signaling another malfunction in this creaky old building. She realized the lion's head fountain that usually spouted streams of water into the pool was turned off. This quiet was . . . disquieting.

WHAM!
Strong hands, impossibly large, pulled her under.
Harriet heard a *whoosh* just before her ears, nose, and throat
    filled with water . . .
She looked up for the water's surface and saw the hole that
    her body had made get smaller, saw it close over her head
    as though something had ended.

she couldn't get back up
she was drowning,
she was dying,
she
was
coming apart.
It really was going to be
Over.

Last swim, little sis.
Was it her turn to die?

Was it really that dream come true?
Be careful what you wish for.

Harriet bit her tongue as the hands pulled HARD.

Even though the hands were around her legs, squeezing the shape out of her calves, it was her throat that closed. She knew nothing except that she could stop fighting, right now, and stay under. The hands (were they hands? They were so BIG) yanked harder. She could just stop. Everything.

It will all be over.

She relaxed into the vortex a little, and a distant thought that it was like being flushed down a toilet tickled the back of her brain.

Just let go. Let it all stop.

But as much as she'd thought she'd wanted that . . .

Reflex, instinct, *something* made her fight.

She fought back.

Harriet kicked and pulled and tugged, but the hands held fast. She battled upward, fighting the angry whirlpool that surrounded her.

She was so small.

just keep swimming

Breaking through to the surface for a brief moment, she managed some gurgling *Help!*s.

No one came.

WHAM!

Harriet fought harder, her arms flailing as she tried to pull free. The grip on her legs hurt—burned even—and she sobbed and coughed.

Harriet paused for a moment; the grip relaxed momentarily, and she used her whole soul and ripped away, sobbing harder.

She must have left bits of herself behind, but she didn't look back until she'd reached the dingy pale blue tiles of the pool wall, marked 3FT. Trying to catch her breath before it was stolen from her again, she stood, facing the off-white wall with the red-lettered NO RUNNING sign that at least one person ignored every day. Her purple flip-flops lay upside down where she'd kicked them off without thinking, facing the locker room as though they were poised to leave without her.

She closed her eyes. Then, still crying, fists raised, she opened them and turned to face it.

There was nothing in the water.

There was nothing there.

She gripped the ladder's metal bar and hoisted herself out of the pool.

The water lay calm, without a memory of Harriet or that . . . THING, whatever it was. Wherever it was. She shivered and looked around.

She was alone.

She tried to stop crying, and waited.

She made a conscious effort to hold her body (and soul) together. She wondered if she'd ever catch her breath again.

Quiet. Deep, heavy quiet.

For a moment, everything shimmered, and the entire building seemed about to melt away from her. She would be left standing, ugly-crying in a too-tight yellow bathing suit, with a wedgie and leftover screams tickling the back of her throat.

"I thought you were all that in the water!" said a deep voice that she recognized in an instant. "That didn't look like much."

There were so many reasons why Harriet rarely looked Luke directly in the eye; one of them was that he was about a foot taller than she was.

"What are you doing here?" she asked. She stumbled up, trying not to squirm. "How long have you been watching me? Did you see that? Why didn't you help me?"

"I'm up here," Luke said, smiling as she pulled her eyes up from his black jeans and faded Notorious B.I.G. T-shirt to his face. "What kind of hello is that? Did I see what?"

She stared at him. "You didn't see what just happened? I almost—" *Almost what?* She saw a shadow pass across his face but didn't acknowledge it. "I almost . . . drowned."

"What are you talking about?" he asked, frowning. "I saw you doing some slow-motion swimming. You weren't drowning, right? You didn't look like it. Kind of weird, you in there all alone, though. Isn't it lap swim time? Did you scare everyone else away with your attitude?"

She glanced toward the bleachers, and . . . the lifeguard was there, reading his magazine like he'd been there all along, and he looked up at her and smiled. *What is going on*?

Harriet wanted to stop shuddering. But her body would not cooperate. She looked down at her legs; no marks, no bruises, nothing had changed.

What had happened?

"Seriously," said Luke, putting both hands on her shoulders. "Are you OK? You look like you've been crying, but we all know that you're a modern scientific miracle who doesn't produce tears."

This was it. She had officially lost it.

"Water. Chlorine. I was in the swimming pool, stupid," she muttered.

But she could still taste the terror she'd felt. And it had really hurt—it hurt so much. But then . . . *how*?

"I've got to go dry off and change," she continued, looking down again. Standing there exposed, in the yellow bathing suit, was excruciating.

"Where's your towel?" he asked, looking around. "I'll get it."

She gave the back of her bathing suit a quick tug as he turned away. He brought over her bright yellow towel, and she snatched it from him and wrapped herself in it. Now she looked him in the eye. "Thanks. So, what do you want? And why are you all the way uptown? Isn't this kind of a trip for you?"

"I came to see you, shorty, and I'm already asking myself why," he replied.

"OK, that makes two of us. Again: What. Do. You. Want?"

There was a long pause; Harriet watched the water droplets fall from her braids.

"It's something . . . for T," Luke said, using one of her brother Tunde's nicknames. "Something he . . . he wanted me to do."

Voices approached; seconds later, two old ladies marched in. Water Aerobics. They looked at Harriet and Luke; one smiled, the other didn't.

Harriet looked back at the water.

Were those bubbles?

What was *in* there?

She closed her eyes; opened them again, slowly.

It must have been a trick of the light. A bad cramp. The water was still and clear.

What was in *here*—in her head?

"You leaving?" asked Luke. "Or you waiting for those first few notes of old-school music, so you can do some aquatic electric slide with your friends over there?" He started doing a little uncle two-step, and Harriet had to hold down a smile. Right on cue, the first few notes of Luther Vandross' "Never Too Much" poured out of the loudspeakers, and the energized old ladies threw their hands up, yelling, "Ayyyye!"

Luke inclined his head and laughed.

Harriet turned away and started walking to the women's locker room. "Meet me by the vending machines," she called to Luke. "Just give me a few minutes." She slid into the locker room, wondering if he had something of Tunde's to give her, and if he did, why he'd waited eight months to hand it over. She looked at her reflection in the mirror by the locker room door and wondered if she could break into a nearby locker and borrow a lip-gloss, thanking Someone, once again, that no one could read the mess that was her mind.

"T wanted me to look out for you," said Luke immediately, as Harriet emerged from the locker room, wondering if there was ever a way to leave a locker room gracefully. "Here I am, knight with a shining fade."

She waited, expressionless. She wasn't going to give him anything. She had texted Luke, she had even called. For three months after. He'd never responded.

Harriet was trembling, and told herself it was the aggressive AC.

Harriet and Luke walked side by side, past the messy bun blondes from the bench earlier; they stared in silence now.

"I'm serious, Little One. Your new bodyguard, at your service."

"Give me a break," muttered Harriet. "You sound stupid."

"Some things never change," said Luke, easily. "You must be at the top of your class in Advanced Angry Black Woman. Congratulations."

She didn't get a retort in before he blurted out an apology. "Sorry. I'm sorry. That was unnecessary."

"Yes, misogynoir, so sweet," Harriet said. He shot her a pleading look, and she turned away. He'd left her messages on READ. He'd *wanted* her to know that he *chose* not to respond. She wanted him to know what he could do with his sorrys.

"Also, I'm at the top of all of my classes." School was a distraction; she'd been careful about her grades. She had read enough teen novels and health center pamphlets to know that slipping grades were a tell—a broadcast of depression or other "causes for concern" that could mean people asking questions and *getting involved.* So, she stayed quiet and maintained the A average with the occasional B+ just to keep it realistic. Of course, in her parents' estimation, anything lower than a B was a sign of the Apocalypse.

The Apocalypse wouldn't be coming only for her, though, right? And she'd always heard that horses were involved, not . . . invisible pool monsters. Maybe she *was* losing it . . . but she wasn't hearing hoofbeats yet.

"Nah," Luke continued with a new urgency in his tone. "I know I owe *you* the apology. I'm sorry. Seriously."

They'd watched an old movie together once; well not exactly together, but she'd been watching it and he came in and sat on the edge of the couch while he'd waited for Tunde. It was called *Love Story*, and the intense girl with the long, long hair had said, "Love means never having to say you're sorry." And Luke had nodded, grunting, "That's tight, that's right," like the chorus on a corny hip-hop song.

But he doesn't love you, Harriet.

Luke did not have eyes that saw, or ears that heard. Everything Luke was, was there, on the surface. Luke, like her brother, didn't know enough about true princesses to not believe in them.

He tripped over nothing and cleared his throat. "Like I said, your brother wanted me to look out for you and I haven't been doing my job. It's my bad. Things have been . . . tough."

A siren screamed, and an ambulance blew past them, racing down Amsterdam Avenue, narrowly avoiding the need for more ambulances.

"Remember when you used to pray the Our Father every time an ambulance went by?" asked Luke.

"No," replied Harriet. She'd recently learned the Hail Mary prayer too. And then: "What do you mean, 'look out for me'?"

Did Tunde know that he was going to die? Did he have some kind of suicide pact with the shooter? Was it not her fault? Was there really a way that it wasn't her fault?

She held her breath.

"Nothing . . . you know, we used to chill and one night, we were . . . um, like, talking . . . and anyway, he was talking about when we got all old and whatever . . . but he made me promise to look out for you if anything ever happened to him." He cleared his throat again, and pulled a pack of gum from his pocket.

Harriet closed her eyes and let out her breath. *Stupid, stupid, stupid.* She wasn't sure why she'd thought that she could escape the guilt that threatened (promised) to smother (drown?) her. Sometimes hope snuck up on her, and she forgot for a moment that it was her duty to bludgeon it back.

"I like how you guys assumed that I'd need to be looked out for. I'm not the one who . . ." *Who what?* She trailed off, and walked a little faster, tripping on the uneven sidewalk. Luke held out a piece of cinnamon gum that she pretended not to see.

"How's Auntie doing? My mom said your dad is still traveling a lot . . ."

"That's what travel doctors do," said Harriet sharply. "It's literally in the job description."

Luke went on as though she'd said nothing, popping the gum into his own mouth. "So I know how you are about surprises. I came by to plan. I was thinking we could meet up once a week. Mondays are good. I'll take you to lunch after school."

"People eat lunch at lunchtime," said Harriet after a pause, not knowing what else to say.

"Y'all girls never eat at school," said Luke, smiling. "Don't front."

"I'm not 'y'all girls,'" replied Harriet. She frowned; she didn't want to sound like she was auditioning for his friendship.

Luke sighed. "A snack, all right? An after-school snack. You and me. We'll eat and we'll talk. I'll have you home before dinner."

They'd reached the 110th Street subway station, which smelled like sweat and fried foods, and was comfortingly normal in its mild afternoon chaos. High school students clutching Styrofoam containers of greasy french fries screeched and ran as though they hadn't been sitting in neat rows, silent and sullen, only a little while earlier.

"I don't need an after-school snack," said Harriet. "Or a babysitter." Luke didn't look at her as he fished his debit card from his back pocket. "How do you think you can stroll up after eight months of silence talking about body-guarding and Monday afternoon snack time?

"And anyway," she went on without taking a breath, "Momma is not going to go for that. I don't know what you're thinking, but she hasn't changed that much. It'll sound like a date." She hadn't meant to talk. She'd wanted to stay but-toned up and coldly regal, but she'd unraveled. She'd failed. She looked down at her sneakers. "Even though it's not."

Luke grinned. "It'll be fine. See you Monday" With a swift, graceful movement, he was on the other side of the turnstiles. "You can pick me up at work. Four o'clock." He started walking away.

"I didn't say yes!" called Harriet. *Not out loud, anyway.* "And what do you mean, pick you up at work? Who was clueless enough to give you a job?"

"Ask your mom," Luke said. "See you then. And don't be late. And then you can tell me what you were crying about."

"I didn't say yes," said Harriet again, to his retreating back. He lifted an arm without turning around and disappeared into a crowd of early bird commuters and girls in ridiculously short school uniform skirts.

I'm scared, thought Harriet. She only realized that she'd stopped shaking when she started again. She couldn't go home just yet. She knew where she had to go. As she walked up the hill, passing the Cathedral of St. John the Divine, a peacock screamed.

"I'm really scared," she whispered.

You should be.

When she'd first started going to Confession, Harriet had stayed far out of her own neighborhood, for fear of being spotted by some friend of her mother's who thought Catholic churches were worse than juju. Her mother, despite her fond memories of the Sisters at the tiny Catholic school in Queens where Harriet's namesakes had taught, kept her mouth shut when her father would grumble about the *institution*, and nodded vaguely when her friends laughed at the old ladies in thick rubber-soled shoes who handed out bilingual prayer cards featuring an alabaster-skinned, auburn-haired Mary.

Then Harriet found a dusty little church on 114th, often padlocked shut and seemingly without a congregation, but open for Confession whenever she passed by.

She'd tested it a few times already, arriving at different times, and on different days; the door was always open to her. She'd never even seen the resident clergy, but judging by the sounds of the voices on the other side of the confessional, she imagined a desultory team of chalky old white men who probably ate bread and soup for dinner every night, wondering how they'd ended up in this city surrounded by Brown people who called them "Father." Harriet never said "Father." She always slid into the booth, said "Bless me for I have sinned" fast and breathless, without the Father/Son/Holy Ghost preamble, then said the same words she always said, and got out before anything real could happen. She did not wait for the official response:

May God, who has enlightened every heart, help you to know your sins and trust in His mercy.

She wasn't there for mercy. She could hear her father's voice. *Anyway, Catholics need to deal with their own problems, of which there are many.*

Nor did she wait for these old white men to explain what she could do for "penance." What was the appropriate sentence for murder by words? For speaking something into existence so terrible that it made you feel frighteningly powerful and infinitely small at the same time?

She didn't understand why she kept going back. Why it felt so necessary to take herself to the brink and back before the tears could start. She always made it out before the tears could start.

As Harriet turned onto her block, she saw Nikka leaving the bodega on the corner. It was too late to turn around, so she fell into step beside her cousin.

"How was your workout?" asked Nikka. Harriet shrugged. A girl who looked about their age and vaguely familiar was walking toward them. Her long locs swung as she nodded in Harriet's direction; Harriet frowned.

"Can you put these in your backpack?" asked Nikka, holding out a black plastic bag. "I got like fifty candles. They had some funny ones, like Beyoncé and Rihanna as Statues of Liberty. I'm thinking about starting a collection."

"You bought them, you carry them," Harriet snapped. It was almost comforting, this bickering with Nikka— like idly picking at a scab.

Nikka stopped, stomping her ridiculous heels on the sidewalk. "You make everything a fight. Everything."

"I know you are, but what am I," Harriet muttered in a low voice. A sharp laugh behind them startled her; the girl had stopped walking, and was clearly watching them.

"What are you looking at?" Nikka asked sharply, narrowing her eyes and glaring like the Nikka that Harriet had first seen when she started middle school. "Do you have a problem? I mean, other than your outfit."

What was the girl staring at? If Harriet had been alone, she would have glared back too. Instead, she turned the full force of her feelings onto her cousin. "You make everything an opportunity to try to make other people feel small," she snapped. "Maybe she's looking at the real you. Maybe she knows that you wear stupid shoes and raggedy crown clips so you can seem big and disguise your pettiness, but it's hopeless. You can run, but you can't hide, *cuz*."

Nikka gasped, and thrust the black plastic bag of prayer candles into Harriet's arms. "I give up," she said. Harriet saw the tears pooling in Nikka's eyes as she turned away, but Nikka half-galloped, half-stumbled away before Harriet could say anything else.

The girl laughed again, and tilted her head in Harriet's direction. "Nice," she said. "The freaks come out at night, huh? And they wear platform heels to yoga." Before Harriet could respond, she turned and walked away slowly, whistling. She was actually whistling.

"Hey," Harriet called. But the girl kept walking.

"Well, excuse you," Harriet muttered. She looked in the bag; there were the usual white and pink candles, and a big one with someone who she thought was supposed to be Beyoncé, wearing a veil, her head bowed. *How did she know Nikka went to yoga?* Harriet approached her building, but then swerved, and headed back to the B train. She'd popped into the church early that morning, but this was obviously a day to double up somewhere else.

The confessional smelled of disinfectant and cigarettes, as though a diligent cleaner had lingered for a quick smoke and quicker prayer.

You know the routine, Harriet told herself. *You started it.*

She walked in, hearing her own voice asking, *"Seems kind of like blasphemy or something?"* She always held her breath when she entered, expecting to be grabbed by her collar and hauled out as an impostor. But no one ever noticed her.

Harriet tried to take shallow breaths as she waited for the priest to speak first.

"Do you need to confess?" said the voice on the other side of the screen. It sounded familiar, like someone she knew, and for a second Harriet wondered if she were being tracked, followed by some secret Catholic Confession Corps who wanted to remind her that she really couldn't get away with murder.

"I snapped at Luke," she began. "And Nikka. Again." She breathed in and gathered herself to prepare for a fast exit. "And I killed my brother and I'm sorry and I'm sorry and I can't ever make it go away."

Then she got up and ran, knowing by now that it would be at least a full two minutes before the priest would recover enough to move.

Outside, she took off her bright orange "decoy" hoodie to reveal a navy-blue T-shirt, just in case anyone from the church made it onto the sidewalk with her description in tow. When she'd first begun all this six months earlier, she wondered if her parents would somehow smell the household heresy on her.

But the cool stillness, the ostentatious *practice of the presence of God* in these sanctuaries kept drawing her in. She never waited for a response, as something told her that would be cheating. One day she realized that it was all part of the punishment—that she was like the rich man in the parable, peering up out of the Pit, with no more access to Love, but the joke (haha) was that she didn't have any brothers left to warn.

And she lived scrappily ever after, Harriet thought to herself as she walked through the Rockefeller Center plaza. She felt a hard shove from behind and almost lost her balance. She turned to glare.

Three guys, posturing like actors playing "thugs" in a school play, stood behind her.

They were grinning, eyes narrowed, daring her to push back.

"Watch where you're going," she made herself say, not realizing that her fists were clenched until she unrolled her fingers.

She moved slowly now, hitting each step squarely, feeling their eyes on her back and hoping they noticed its muscles.

And suddenly, she smelled chlorine.

4

"A little late," murmured her mother as Harriet walked into the kitchen. Mrs. Adu pointed to a bowl of fresh greens sitting on the table waiting to be shredded. She didn't look up from the whole chicken she was dismembering. Harriet murmured a "Hello" and went to wash her hands.

"Soap," her mother called.

Harriet bit back a retort as she dried her soapy hands without rinsing them. So there. In the kitchen, she stood next to the round wooden table, and traced the lines where Tunde had carved his name a year before. Her mother put the chicken into a large cast iron pot where onions, dried shrimp, and greens were already simmering.

"Pepper soup?" Harriet asked. She'd been planning to make burgers, piled high with cheese, lettuce, pickles, fried onions . . . to remind her mother of the days when she'd pretend to have a restaurant. She opened the fridge; the patties sat in full view, thawed and waiting. Her mother would have had to push past them to get anything else. *OK. So you didn't want my food.*

Her mother nodded and poured a little more of the chopped chilies into the pot for emphasis. She had started a few years ago, making Nigerian "soups," insisting on calling them *soups* when Tunde said "Yoooo, the stew again?" She'd invite Auntie Marguerite and Nikka over to try them out; after some moments of sisterhood when the two of them would sing lyrics about *starfish and coffee* and *love getting left behind* and lament in unison about *back in the day* and how the city used to be, they'd go back to opposing sides. Auntie Marguerite would lean over the pot, and sniff, then raise her eyebrows and bustle out quickly as Nikka bragged that they'd be ordering Korean BBQ again.

Her mother's headwrap was loosening, and Harriet moved in to tighten it. She stood beside her mother, remembering long ago days on the playground, when a little girl would come over and grab her toys every day. And every day, Harriet would say nothing; she'd return to the bench where her mother sat watching, and they'd sit quietly together watching squirrels until the girl abandoned Harriet's toys for greener pastures.

Harriet blinked. Even this close, it was hard to read her mother's expression. Nikka was right; the apartment felt shrouded and charcoal gray. Shadows threatened to take over in the kitchen, and the blinds were permanently halfway down—her mother claimed that made them easier to clean. The silence was long and empty, as though the room had no memory of the days when a steady stream of music played underneath constant conversation. *This is what I used to think a black hole meant. But we wouldn't be alive in a real black hole.* The row of succulents on the windowsill were about to surrender; even they couldn't survive the perpetual gloom. Nothing seemed to fully acknowledge her presence. *I might be haunting my own house.*

Harriet turned on the overhead light, ignored her mother's grimace, and moved to the table and began tearing the leaves; she saw now that they were precious bitter-leaf greens, likely from the shelves of the West African market where plastic squeeze bottles of red palm oil and Nollywood DVDs sat in narrow aisles beside almost-stale Ovaltine biscuits and cans of Milo, right across from the giant glass jars full of dried fish bits. Pepper soup would be warm. Maybe they could light some of the candles too.

"Your father's traveling," her mother said, as though he wasn't away so much these days that it was like he was on a trip to visit them when he was there. Except he didn't bring presents.

Her father used to make her write "permission speeches"; since Tunde had been gone, he hadn't been home long enough to dole out an assignment. And she didn't have anything to ask for anyway. The last one was a Jack & Jill party that ninth-grade Nikka had been invited to; she'd wrangled an invitation for Harriet too, as though her eighth-grade cousin's presence would boost her stock in the eyes of the bourgie.

Harriet had agreed, because Nikka was going to pay twenty dollars, and that would buy some nice yarn. Tunde walked into her room as she was practicing her speech.

"Add in something about how those kids all go to elite schools, talk about college aspirations and stuff like that," he'd said, dodging the pillow she'd thrown his way.

"Daddy's not going to fall for that, he's not stupid," she replied.

"Of course not, but he'll hope that just saying it will make you aspire to new academic heights, blah blah blah."

She had shrugged and stayed silent. Her brother was right.

"And don't worry, I'll be there," Tunde said. "Missy's mom invited all of us from Key Club. It gives them a chance to show off." He rolled his eyes. "Black people who play golf and go to dude ranches are just as dumb as white people who do that stuff."

"Dude ranch," she said, giggling for no reason.

"*Duuuuuuuuude ranch,*" *he said again, picking up the joke and drawing it out to make her laugh more. Then he'd pretended to be their father while she practiced.*

The party ended up being as boring as she'd expected it to be. Nikka and Tunde had mostly ignored her, but every once in a while, he'd catch Harriet's eye and mouth, "*Duuuuuuuuude.*"

Her phone buzzed in her pocket.

i'm sorry, cuzzee.

Nikka. Harriet rolled her eyes. She thought that adding an *ee* sound to anything made it cuter.

i was out of pocket. forgive me?

Harriet tapped back the ultimate in petty: *k*, which she knew would infuriate her cousin, let her know that she wasn't truly forgiven just yet. An unwelcome wave of remorse threatened to rise; it wasn't lost on Harriet that she'd been out of pocket too. A little. But still. Harriet pushed it back.

Another Confession in the morning.

Her mom hadn't even made a requisite *put your phone away* comment. She knew that she should offer a tidbit about her day at school; she wondered if she should bring up Luke's surprise visit and his cryptic remarks. If Tunde were here, he'd have made her laugh with mean-spirited impressions of his teachers that their mother would excuse as charming. *If Tunde were here.* It was a game she played sometimes. If Tunde were here, I'd be doing his math homework. *If Tunde were here, he'd tell me to change my outfit. If Tunde were here, he'd say, "Hey Pizzaface," as he passed me the pepperoni he'd saved from his own slices.* Once in a while, she wondered: *if Tunde were here, who would I be?* What would he have done to change this precise moment in her life? Or would she still be lonely, no matter what? If Tunde were here, she wouldn't have to fear the undertow. There would be no monsters in the water.

And sometimes there'd be extra pepperoni.

This thing of helping her mother with cooking was a new routine, one that Harriet didn't much enjoy or understand, but it felt like penance so she didn't question it. Just like the open church doors whenever she arrived, her mother was always at the kitchen counter, chopping, stirring, kneading something, no matter when Harriet got home. Before, she'd spent the hours before dinner in her room knitting, having finished her homework at school. Faint laughter would float toward her as her mother and Tunde played one of their endless afternoon games of chess. Harriet didn't have to look to know that the chess board still sat as it had been for almost a year, the pieces unmoved. Harriet had never had the patience for chess, she couldn't remember who did what—did the bishop move zigzaggy? The horse guy slanted? So she'd pretended that she hated it. She had a sudden impulse to ask her mother, who used to throw her head back and erupt with laughter when they'd played Scrabble and dominoes, if she wanted to set up the Ludo board after dinner. But when she looked up, her mother was gone.

"Talk to you later," said Harriet softly, and she tore a handful of bitterleaf into shreds.

Then she made her burgers anyway, and ate them standing at the kitchen counter. As she placed her dishes in the sink, she told herself that she'd clean up later, knowing full well that her mother would return and scrub the kitchen spotless as soon as Harriet left. When she wasn't cooking, her mother was forever cleaning, scrubbing, and making things gleam in the dim light of their apartment. *But I'm still here*, Harriet thought. *Can't get this place clean enough, I guess.*

In her room, there had never been any rainbows, unicorns, or hints of pink-purpleness. Harriet's poster of crocheted hyperbolic models and the signed yellowing headshot from astrophysics celebrity Neil DeGrasse Tyson were the only real decoration, unless she counted the multicolored balls of yarn and blue glass vase of abandoned aluminum knitting needles that she couldn't bear to toss.

She sat on the bed, picked up her in-progress double helix scarf, and started knitting. For most, the cabled pattern of DNA might not be considered "mindless knitting," but Harriet had been knitting since she was five; she'd made herself a multicolored Fair Isle sweater when she was seven. She'd already done fifty-seven prayer shawls this year, dropping them off in small paper-bagged batches at the Clothing Closet attached to the touristy Episcopal cathedral. She leaned back and knitted without looking; she'd learned to knit by watching YouTubers who'd talked to the camera as they worked, and sometimes she pretended to be one of them, late at night in her room. She wondered if Nikka was going to drop by with the rest of the candles. Her mother did keep the apartment decidedly . . . dim. They didn't get much natural light, and ever since Harriet could remember, her father had walked through their home reminding them all of the ever-rising costs of electricity.

Why hadn't Luke seen anything?

Why hadn't she seen anything?

No. It was just a leg cramp. Nikka's fault; she'd ruined the walk to the gym.

Why had Luke chosen that precise moment to appear? Did he also have some unfinished business, some guilty secret that he needed to atone for? Harriet doubted it. Luke's soul was probably as clean and solid as his name and his shoulders. He didn't believe in anything other than the people that he loved, and he was able to love his best friend Tunde unreservedly, in the way only naturally and perpetually cool people do. No, he'd just remembered to feel sorry for his dead friend's little sister. Harriet let out a hiss as she pricked herself with the cable needle.

After Tunde, she'd wondered if she should continue to allow herself the pleasure of needlework, the relief that came from fiber and textiles, patterns made by her own hands. But the Fiber Fanatics, her loyal and mostly anonymous online best friends, had posted links to a variety of organizations in need of apparel, toys, and other handmade hugs, so that made it OK. She was allowed to do something she enjoyed as long as she wasn't doing it because she enjoyed it. That was one of the basic rules.

She decided that the incident in the pool was already morphing into something forced and false, like an urban legend or a spam email with lots of capital letters and exclamation points. Even the memory of intense pain was beginning to be overshadowed by the familiar shame she fell back on daily, like a poisoned pillow.

But she dropped stitches every few rows; her hands still weren't steady yet.

There *had* been something in the water. She was trying to hold it down, but there it was, just under the surface. Even at her worst—even if that's where she still was—Harriet knew that she was not a hallucinator. It had been real. She wasn't as shocked as she should be. OK, some invisible pool demon had tried to drown her. Uh-huh. Yeah, that sounds about right. Totally normal. Her wrists already hurt; she put the knitting down and massaged them angrily.

What else have you got for me, huh? Give me your worst. I wish you would, because I want it bad. Just let me have it so that this can stop. Just make it stop.

And the reply was a harsh whisper, like a frozen breeze, in her ear.

She could feel her hair move.

Be careful what you wish for.

5

For the next few days, thinking about swimming and avoiding the pool kept her occupied. But when there wasn't the *crack* of the water splitting open to look forward to, school was almost unbearable. Walking through the halls with her head down and her books up, without screaming, was harder. Existing was more exhausting.

In English, Mrs. Barclay spoke with a faintly British accent even though she was from New Jersey. She told anyone who'd listen and everyone who didn't that *Dead Poets Society* was her inspiration; every year, her classes spent the first few days of school watching the film. It was one of the first jokes Harriet heard when she'd arrived at the school: Barclay's obsession with those white boys being tragically sad and misunderstood. Harriet had watched it on her tablet, with dry popcorn and drier eyes, late one night in her room. She didn't like it. It made her embarrassed for Barclay, and angry. Couldn't she tell she was a joke?

They were studying Tennyson now, and when no one volunteered to read aloud from "The Lady of Shalott," Mrs. Barclay read herself, as they all knew she wanted to do from the start.

She climbed on her desk and threw her arms wide, crying:

> *Out flew the web and floated wide—*
> *The mirror crack'd from side to side*

There were snorts when she almost threw herself off the desk during "side to side."

"*She'd* crack a mirror," whispered someone in the back row. Mrs. Barclay didn't seem to hear. But Harriet did and she knew who it was; she dropped her daily *do not engage* policy to turn around and cast one of her most ferocious hard stares. Mrs. Barclay was ridiculous, but she went hard at it, like she had nothing to lose. To her own surprise, Harriet teared up, and turned her eyes back to the smartboard, where Tennyson's words were written in Barclay's enthusiastic and illegible script.

Harriet knew this poem. *"The curse is come upon me"* she thought. *I'm the Lady of Shalott.*

Nights were not so good. It helped that she usually hovered on the edges of sleep; no disruptive alarm needed to wake her at 3:12 a.m. She slipped out of bed and into the familiar darkness of the hallway easily and quickly for this late-night sentinel routine. Schrödinger fell into step beside her, watching her instead of his path forward. His eyes shone yellow-green in the dark. In her alpaca slippers, a knitted sock project gone wrong, Harriet padded to her parents' room. Deep silence radiated through the closed door, and Harriet tried to stuff the panic back down her throat. She paused and listened; the air seemed to be waiting with her, clutching her hand as though it wanted her to protect it. Her mother didn't seem to be puttering, organizing and reorganizing the giant wooden wardrobe that five-year-old Harriet had been sure concealed a loving lion behind the coats. Once she'd closed herself inside, underestimating the terror of being pressed on all sides by heavy winter items that never seemed to be in use. When the doors had clicked shut, she'd burst into frightened screams. Tunde hadn't laughed at her that time; *he'd* been the avenging lion of the stories he'd shared, swiftly unlocking the door and hugging her out of the wardrobe before her mother even left the kitchen. She shoved that memory down too.

Harriet slid into the room and tiptoed to the bed, easing herself onto the Yoruba stool meant to carry the weight of royalty. None of them were supposed to sit on it, and her mother polished it lovingly each morning; at night, it gleamed as if lit from within.

Her eyes adjusted to the different dark of her parents' room; she watched, waiting to feel the rise and fall of her mother's breathing. *Once. Twice. There.* Still alive, even if not really living. She relaxed against the wall, ready for her Night Watch, ready to battle with whatever made her mother wake up with her eyes dry and red every morning.

If I'm the Angel of Death, she thought, *I'm going to fight myself like the Devil.*

She leaned over the bed again, wanting to rest her cheek against her mother's smooth one. Her mother murmured; Harriet drew even closer—*how does she not feel my breath*—but couldn't make out the words. She made her own chest rise and fall in concert with her mother's; a sweet, almost silent duet. Harriet sat, waiting for the first slivers of sunlight that would come through the window to offer those first, fleeting moments of a new day.

As her classmates pretended to listen to a rapturous ode to polynomials, Harriet stared out at the empty schoolyard, where the ragged basketball net fluttered in the breeze. What Luke? She hadn't really thought about him at all. Luke who?

There were other, much more pressing matters. Ducking Nikka for one thing, who'd ditched the heels for equally loud platform boots that heralded her approach like a palace guard. Cobbling together whole conversations with her mother from scraps of greeting and murmured instructions. Sure, it was Monday, but she'd barely noticed. So much to do. No time to think about Luke. Luke who?

"Pssst. Did you do the homework problems?" whispered a voice from behind during math. Harriet looked up. It was a somber girl she'd noticed a few times; Harriet didn't remember her name, but she'd arrived at the school after Harriet, was also in Honors English, and she'd worn a dark-gray Katara T-shirt on her first day, with the quote "I'm making my own water!" across the back. Harriet had been impressed. Showing love for animated characters was *not hot* at this school, and anyone willing to advertise their love for *Avatar: The Last Airbender* and ignore the giggles of derision as she walked the halls got props.

Wait a minute. She was *that* girl. The one from the sidewalk fight with Nikka. Who knew about yoga. The one who'd laughed. And now, she was smiling. Harriet blinked a few times, then nodded back.

"We need absolute silence," said the teacher sharply, glancing their way because apparently nodding made noise. Kentler was the only teacher here who didn't let Harriet be the Quiet Grieving Girl. He'd pulled her aside on her first day and told her that he'd heard about her "mathematical prowess," and that he hoped she'd consider joining the math team "at an appropriate time." Tried to make her talk every day, and probably prided himself on it. If Harriet made herself visible, Kentler would definitely pounce.

Harriet felt an insistent tap on her shoulder and saw a tightly folded piece of lined paper fall to the floor. *Old school note-passing, so retro*—like a montage in a teen movie. Harriet slid the note toward herself with her foot and leaned down to pick it up. She unfolded it discreetly under her desk.

I'm not asking for your answers, don't worry. Just some help? I'm gonna have to hand this in late bc I didn't get it at all. But I bet you did? I know we both have 4th period free, I've seen you in the library. And I know we both think Katara is a boss. Tomorrow? Help a sister out? I'm Alisia, btw. Hi Harriet.

She'd been noticed. Not as the One Whose Brother Died, but as someone who could be useful—as a kindred spirit? The girl knew her name. This time Harriet turned around fully and nodded again.

"Ms. Adu? I assume that whatever is occupying your mind is more important than quadratic equations? Care to share?"

Jackass.

"You're right, it is," she muttered back. A couple of girls giggled, and a boy Harriet knew only as Wiz whispered, "Ohhhh."

Kentler's eyes held hers for a moment as she faced him; Harriet scowled, and the teacher turned back to the board. Harriet scanned the equation, answered it quickly in her head, and turned to the window, wondering if she could call this one a win.

She heard the smile in the whisper from behind. "Nice."

"Ms. . . . Barnes, perhaps you can enlighten us with the answer here," said Kentler tightly.

"Uh," Alisia started.

"X equals negative five," whispered Harriet under her breath.

"X equals negative five," said Alisia loudly. "Thanks, Harriet," she added, without lowering her voice. The rest of the class laughed.

Yeah. It was a win.

She knew she'd be late; she also knew that her mother wouldn't say anything about it. This detour down to Riverside Park wasn't giving the quiet she'd hoped for. A few nannies and their charges, tight-lipped joggers in expensive leggings, strolling tourists, and coffee-drinking laptop holders crowded the outdoor space on the grey autumn afternoon. Not exactly the best circumstances for quiet alone time. But Harriet found herself walking across West 110th Street anyway, passing the industrial chic of the newest high-rise, and tripping on the uneven sidewalk near Riverside Drive, as a dog and its owner ran past her into the park.

"Her" bench was taken, so she walked a bit, pretending to have a purpose. A little girl was collecting large, smooth stones, holding them in a battered Yankees cap. She looked up and ran over before Harriet could put on a forbidding face.

"I'm going to put these in my rock collection," she said solemnly. Harriet realized that the girl wasn't that little. Maybe seven, or even eight. They stared at each other for a few moments; Harriet broke first.

"You have a rock collection?" she murmured politely. "That's cool."

"Do you?"

"No," replied Harriet. "But I used to collect shells."

"Oh! I wish I could find some shells here," the girl said.

"Well, we're not at the beach," said Harriet apologetically. She glanced around, wondering where this solemn little girl's parents were.

"The ocean's in Brooklyn," said the girl. "I used to live near it."

"I . . . yeah, we're in Manhattan now," fumbled Harriet. "You probably found shells near your house, then."

"Yeah. I have some," the girl said. "But it would be awesome to find some here."

"Why?" asked Harriet.

"Do you want to see my work?" asked the girl, saying "work" as though she'd completed a masterpiece. Harriet checked the time on her phone. She was on the brink of being more than just a little late. She stood.

"Sure," she said, half-expecting a parent to jump out and snatch this strangely serene little girl away.

The girl held out a hand, carefully holding her hat full of rocks in the other. They walked to the place where the letters LUV were carefully spelled out in rocks. Some had already been kicked out of place by careless passersby; Harriet helped the girl realign them, then stood.

"Do you want help with this?" asked Harriet, remembering her own humiliation when she'd learned that her own "invented spelling" had no value in the real world.

"No," replied the girl. "I like it the way it is. I'm done." She smiled, revealing a partially grown-in bottom tooth.

Harriet turned and offered the girl her first genuine smile of the day. "There's a good one," she murmured, pointing to a small, almost blue stone. "Let's get it before someone kicks it away."

"I said I'm done," said the girl, not pleasant, but not hostile either.

"I know, now I want to do one, is that OK?" Harriet said. "You can help me now." She spotted a light-gray stone, flecked with gold. "Look at that one! It could be a jewel from a crown." She picked it up, and started looking for more. The little girl watched, silent and skeptical, for a moment.

"What are you doing?" the girl asked, as Harriet squatted over a patch of grass along the walkway.

"I want to make a crown for you," said Harriet. "So you can be a princess." She started lining up the stones on the pavement in the shape of a simple, three-pointed crown.

"But how will we pick it up?" asked the girl, leaning over until she was on the tips of her toes. "I can't wear it."

"We can pretend, right? We can play a story." Harriet finished the crown. "What do you think?"

"What's our story gonna be?" asked the girl.

Harriet didn't answer; she sighed and stood; then, losing her balance, she fell onto the rocks she'd just arranged. "Ouch," she muttered. She shrugged and smiled. "Figures," she said, jumping up, scattering the stones. "That was a dumb idea. Let's go back to what you were doing, I'll help with that."

"You want to write love too?" asked the girl, sounding like she'd sooner believe that Harriet had just flown in from Mars. "You have to just make a heart. I already did the letters."

They searched the ground for appropriate pebbles, but the girl rejected them all like a particularly zealous inspector. Finally, Harriet sighed.

"I've gotta go. I guess I don't get to make a heart," she said.

"Not yet," said the girl, pressing a rock into Harriet's hand. She lifted her own hand in a slow, solemn wave as Harriet said goodbye.

She'd planned to open with a gentle inquiry on her mother's day, but her body had other plans. She walked in with a scowl and without a greeting. "Mom, Luke Vincent told me something about a job?" She stepped around a carton of eco-unfriendly cheap copy paper, a staple in her parents' unimaginatively named "Pack & Ship" store. Incongruous items had slowly crept in over the years: off-brand snack bags in flavors like prawn jalapeño, sickly sweet car air fresheners, travel pillows, and artificial mini terrariums were on the shelves today. The out-of-season scented candles made the whole place smell somewhat like a cathedral. "He said you'd know what he's talking about. He was just messing with me, right?" she continued, as she dropped her jacket and backpack behind the counter. She took a deep breath, exhaling the tension of the school day. Time to summon her "Thank you, have a nice day" energy for chatty Brown immigrants and entitled but not-desperate-enough-for-the-post-office white people for three hours until dinnertime.

"Luke Vincent messes with no one," said that dangerous bass. Luke stepped out of the supply closet and dropped a tower of boxes on the counter. "I resent that."

Harriet took in his sharply pressed khakis. She turned to her mother. "He's working *here*? With *us*?"

Harriet's chest tightened as she watched her mother and Luke exchange smiles.

"Don't be rude," said her mother, glancing at Harriet. "Say hello. And please pick your jacket up from the floor."

Harriet used the act of retrieving her coat to compose herself. "Sorry," she mumbled to the floor.

Her mother walked over and squeezed her shoulders, and Harriet started at the motherly touch, almost falling to the floor in surprise. Everyone pretended not to notice, and she went to the tiny bathroom to wash her hands.

"Ow," she muttered as she pricked her chest with her employee pin. When she was eight, it had felt cool, wearing the pin proudly on her chest and doing her homework alongside Tunde at the back counter, letting customers know that she belonged. Now it just felt silly, wearing a uniform in the tiny, dusty, unfocused shop. She pulled the little girl's rock, warm and dry, from her backpack and stuck it in her pocket. She'd picked up a cherry ChapStick at the corner store the day before, telling herself that it was for purely medicinal reasons; she resisted applying it now. Harriet bit her lip and left the bathroom quickly.

Luke was wearing his jacket now, pin high up on the collar, and carrying more boxes. Harriet tried not to look like she cared that he was leaving. But his return had nourished her, briefly, she realized; now, the loss of his gently annoying cheer could release the regrets she kept pressed down and shaken together. The Harriet she never meant to be could . . . runneth over. It was a scary thought.

"Help Luke bring that over to the university," said Mrs. Adu. "Somebody bought out our entire stock of shekeres for her class. You can swim afterward if you want, you don't need to return here. We're not busy today."

"I didn't even know we sold shekeres," she muttered. Suddenly, as much as she wanted to prolong the practice of the presence of Luke, she didn't want to leave her mom alone in the store.

"We don't both have to go, Momma. Luke knows where Robeson Hall is," she said. "I'll stay here. We can . . . go downstairs and organize the storage room. We still don't know what it looks like in there. Should I get the key from . . . somewhere?"

"Tomorrow," her mother said, not looking up. She'd said "tomorrow" for months. "Go."

Harriet bit her lip; Tunde had claimed the storage room when he was twelve, calling it a clubhouse and claiming that only those who instinctively knew the secret password could enter. Of course, Nikka and Luke had been welcomed in; Harriet had hurt her foot the first time she'd kicked the closed door, and then pretended to ignore it until the day Tunde invited her in to help him draw constellations on the walls with fluorescent markers. They'd scrubbed for hours after their mother had found out. No one else in the family had gone down there since his death; as supplies and stock came in, she and her mother had silently agreed to keep everything in the closet upstairs and the main room of the already cluttered shop. After the funeral, Harriet had seen her mother gripping the supply room key as she'd accepted condolences and covered dishes that later filled the freezer; then, the key disappeared and her mother's face closed every time Harriet mentioned it. *I get it,* Harriet thought. *Not worthy yet.*

"There are a couple more boxes right there," Luke said after a pause, pointing. "I thought you'd help me out, being that you're so strong and all."

"*Being* that you're obviously *not,*" she retorted, and picked up the boxes.

"I've got hidden strengths," he replied, dropping another box on top of the ones in her arms. "And I believe in equal opportunity—can't call me a chauvinist."

"Or chivalrous," Harriet said, easily managing the boxes and opening the door. "Let me get that for you," she added, stepping back so that Luke could exit, and taking another step away so that their bodies wouldn't touch.

She turned to tell her mother goodbye, but Mrs. Adu, her usually ruler-straight back curved into a C, was not looking at them. She wasn't looking at anything. Her eyes were closed, and she was smiling.

"How are things at that school?" Luke asked, as they waited to cross the busy street. "Must be good to have Nikka there, show you around and everything."

"If by 'good,' you mean veering between debilitat-
ing and inconsequential, then yes, it's all good," said Harriet.
Luke laughed.

"You'll get a college scholarship with that vocabu-
lary," he said. "Your parents will be happy."

"Yeah, right," Harriet muttered, but didn't continue.
They walked in silence for a few minutes, then Harriet blurted
out, "I thought you were supposed to feed me. Where's the
afternoon snack?"

Luke laughed again and pulled a crumpled white
paper bag out of his pocket. "Voila," he said, and it sounded
like "Voyla"; Harriet didn't crack a smile when he showed
her two slightly squashed croissants. But when he pulled a
jar of Nutella from his backpack, saying "Payn oh chocolate,
your favorite," she couldn't hide a tiny grin at his faux "bad
French," something he'd once told her was a display of sol-
idarity with his Senegalese father. Harriet had loved Saturday morning breakfasts at Luke's apartment, when his
mother would hand them *pain au chocolate*, chunks of
baguette and chocolate, and reminisce about the Left Bank
while his Senegalese father grumbled about "imperialist
affectations" and dipped his bread into a large mug of milky
tea.

"We can chill at the pool if you want; I can hang out
in the bleachers and do homework while you swim."

After a pause, Harriet replied, "I'm not swimming."
Ever again. But even as she thought the words, her throat

closed; she didn't want to face whatever was in the pool, but she knew she couldn't face anything else without it.

They'd reached the Hall, and Harriet worked hard to keep her breathing even and her face impassive; she'd never have said it, but she wouldn't have been able to return here alone. After Luke tried holding both the door and his boxes without success, a well-manicured hand grabbed the door and held it while Harriet and Luke passed through.

"Well, well, well," said Nikka's high, sharp voice. "Now I know why you've been avoiding me."

Inside, Luke dropped his boxes and held his arms out; Nikka jumped into them and Harriet wanted to laugh at how much they looked like a pairs figure-skating team, but she didn't. She looked away.

"Where have you been?" Nikka asked Luke, grabbing his arms in that rough but cute way conventionally pretty girls could get away with. "I *called* you. A *lot*."

"I know," said Luke, looking down. "I just . . ."

Nikka touched his arm again, more gently. "It's OK. I know."

Wait, he hadn't replied to Nikka either? Of course she'd thought about mentioning the black hole of Luke's absence to her cousin . . . but never did, not wanting to give Nikka the satisfaction. For a moment, she wondered what she might have given herself by sharing, and how much it would have cost. Harriet cleared her throat to stop the tears from welling up. "Ahem. Luke, we need to drop this stuff off."

"I'll wait until you're done," said Nikka. "And then Luke and I can catch up while you swim."

"I'm not going swimming," she said again, heading up the stairs with her boxes. "So please, give it up. I have."

1

"What kind of class needed all those shekeres anyway?" asked Luke, after they'd been thanked profusely and sere- naded by a small group of three-year-olds. "I thought she was going to hug us or something." As they took the stairs down to the main floor, he pointed to Nikka, delicately lounging in one of those surprisingly uncomfortable plush lobby chairs. "Look who waited for us," he said. "Maybe we could all go get some tea or something? Or a falafel. Maybe both; I could go for a good green tea. We can hang at the Peace Fountain."

"What's with you and the tea?" Harriet asked, as they approached Nikka. "And she's a preschool teacher. It's kind of their job description to be like that."

"Tea?" asked Nikka. "Sounds good. So what's up, cuz? Are you really not swimming first?"

"Why are you two trying to push me into the pool anyway?" asked Harriet. "I just don't feel like it. End of story."

"Was it whatever freaked you out that day?" asked Luke. "I mean, I thought you were just . . . I mean, I don't know, but . . ."

"Fine!" Harriet almost shouted. "I'm swimming. Satisfied? Just stop nagging me!"

Nikka blinked, and Luke flinched, but just barely, as though he was holding himself together by sheer will. Harriet was suspended between clinging to them for dear life and running far, far away, screaming. "Please," she added, quietly. Maybe she could do it if they were there. She didn't have to tell them anything. They didn't have to know that maybe she needed them there a little bit, because the idea that she might always be too afraid to do the thing that was her heart would break it. She couldn't be afraid of the thing that she loved more than herself; the water that had loved her all her life. She remembered a verse etched on a plaque under a church window: PERFECT LOVE CASTS OUT FEAR, and tried repeating it to herself in a whisper, like a magic spell, even though she knew no amount of magic could bring perfect love into her life.

Harriet stayed in the locker room for almost fifteen minutes and flinched when the door creaked as she pushed it open.

The pool was empty and seemed recently still, as though a party had just ended. All the lights were on, harsh and artificially bright, and she could see straight to the bottom. She could hear herself breathe; she rubbed the goose pimples on her arms. The playful lion sculpture was still dry and humorless, waiting to close its jaws on something. A stray pair of small yellow flip-flops and a matching swim cap were neatly placed on the first row of bleachers. She told herself that the presence of the same lifeguard, sitting on the bleachers and seemingly reading the same magazine, didn't give her the heebie jeebies. She took a deep breath, and paused to listen for the Voice.

Nothing.

She closed her eyes and stepped closer to the edge—and stopped. She was truly scared.

"We'll be right here, take your time!" Nikka's voice rang out in the stillness and broke the silence like a hammer. They were in the corner to the right.

Harriet started and almost fell into the pool, her toes grabbing at the concrete edge, her arms flailing.

"Wow, that was graceful," called Luke. Nikka giggled.

Harriet looked over at the lifeguard, and was disconcerted to find him already focused on her.

"Hey! Mermaid! What's up? You OK?"

"I'm fine," she called. "Just . . . nothing."

She turned her back on them all and focused on the water. *Is anyone down there? Don't hurt me, please. Or if you must, just do it in front of these guys, and then they'll be sorry. I want somebody else to be sorry for a change.*

The water seemed to smile at her. But she was still scared.

Two boys shuffled in a few moments later, early for their after-school class, swim caps perched high on their heads. They walked over to the lifeguard, and as Harriet watched him show them his magazine, she wondered briefly if they were stalling too. She sat next to Luke and kept looking at them.

"You're really not going in?" asked Luke, after a moment. "It looks like a class is about to start, I guess it will be filling up in here soon. Your lifeguard friend might have to do his job."

"OK, you're done," she said. "You can check me off of your daily good-guy list." She'd meant to sound playful, but the flash of hurt in his eyes told another story.

Will there ever be a day when I don't want to take something back? Harriet wondered.

The two boys suddenly jumped into the pool and started paddling ferociously, obviously favoring splash size over technique. The lifeguard blew a furious whistle, calling them out of the pool. More students trickled in, weary parents hustling them down to the pool's edge.

Then she saw her.

Harriet took a breath.

The little girl with the LUV rocks was here, and again, there was something fairy-like about her—it almost seemed as though her feet weren't touching the ground. As though she felt Harriet's eyes on her, she turned and waved without smiling, like the queen of a very serious parade. Harriet lifted a hand in return, squashing questions like *How did she get here?* and *Is she following me?* and *Is she actually a little girl or something . . . else?* ignoring Luke and Nikka's curious glances. The lifeguard, finished with his dressing down of the boys, came over.

"Hey," he said, smiling. "I've been meaning to ask if you'd be interested in helping out with the Guppy classes. You've got lifeguard certification, right? I mean, I hope I'm remembering that right, because it's why I let you come in here when nobody's around."

He knew? "I . . . what . . . um," Harriet nodded, because she didn't know what else to do. He knew she was a rule breaker—a violator? What kind of lifeguard was he? She was mildly offended by his disregard for her safety.

"So maybe there's some community service credit or something you can get from your school?" he went on. "We're piloting an assistant program, you know, to have extra eyes in the water when we do these Community Swims. You'd help out during lessons and stuff. We actually have one kid in this group who needs some extra attention . . ."

He pointed to the Little Girl, who was sitting on the concrete at the pool's edge. She didn't look afraid or unhappy, Harriet thought. She was just . . . there . . . but not there.

"You look like you've taught before, yeah?"

Harriet nodded slowly. The summer after sixth grade, Momma had volunteered her as a neighborhood swim coach, and she'd walk to the Jackie Robinson Pool every day, with at least two whiny neighbors in tow, so that she could see what they'd learned in their free city swimming lessons and "help them practice." Never mind that city pools were for discreet horseplay and general splashing around. Momma had seemed to think she'd be leading little kids in a lap swim every day. What really happened was that Harriet stood in the three-feet depth with them and mimed a couple of strokes, then watched as other people had fun. But as long as they went to the Mister Softee truck every day, the kids kept their mouths shut, and so did she.

"So, uh . . . think about it, let me know. I'll hook you up with Mr. Escalante, the director."

Harriet shrugged and kind of nodded, because she didn't know what else to do.

After the lifeguard left, Harriet avoided Nikka's and Luke's interested eyes. The three of them watched the swim classes in silence, and Harriet wondered if they were thinking the same thing she was: *Tunde should be here, not me.* She was so used to watching the three of them sit in companionable silence—that is, until she picked a fight with Tunde or

Nikka. Turning her eyes back to the class, Harriet noticed that no one had been able to convince the Little Girl to get into the pool. If she'd been alone, Harriet might have gone over and talked to her, but in the company of Nikka and Luke, she felt silly. Would they laugh at her very young new best friend?

Only, said the Voice. *Only friend.*

No! There was maybe one other. Right?

When the classes ended, Harriet rose to follow the kids to the locker room. "Bye," she muttered. "I'm going to change."

"We'll meet you by the vending machine," Nikka called.

Harriet didn't answer, letting the door slam on her way out. She dressed quickly, and ran out of the locker room, before they could get there.

"Hope you aren't trying to ditch us," said Luke, leaning against the exit door, while Nikka collected her things and stood.

"No worries, I called Auntie already," said Nikka, holding up her cell phone. "She's cool with it. I've decided we should go over to Eton. I could go for a honeydew bubble tea. Do you want to split an order of dumplings?"

Harriet shrugged. She was tired. And they were implacable.

"We can split *two* orders." Then, she smiled.

"Oh no, not a smile—it's like the sun is coming out!" said Luke. And the three of them laughed, and Harriet knew that if they didn't get out of there soon, she might hug them, or cry, or both, so she pushed the heavy door open quickly.

"Or the moon," said Nikka. "The full moon on a clear night."

"Not Niks with the poetic language," said Luke, high-fiving her.

"You guys . . ." Harriet whispered. On the sidewalk, she blinked. The sun was setting, but it was still light.

Nikka put in their dumpling order, lingering at the counter to chat up the cashier, while Harriet and Luke sat at the larger of the two tables in the tiny restaurant, directly across from each other.

Nikka cleared her throat, sitting back down. "So . . . it turns out that we both really want to talk to you, even though you've been making it harder than AP Calc, and forcing us to hang out by that janky old pool. There have got to be a million violations going on over there. Is that lifeguard even real?"

"He's absolutely real, and *very* good at his job," Harriet blurted out. "And you can say the same for me. You heard how they want me on staff."

"Uh-huh, I heard. Didn't know you were so cozy with the people here. You don't tell me anything. We grew up together, we're *family,* and you make me work so hard just to get a hello out of you."

"You're breaking my heart," said Harriet. "You must be exhausted with all of that effort. So. You keep telling me that you want to talk? Just talk, then, if you've got something to say."

Nikka opened and closed her mouth.

"I thought so," said Harriet, looking over at the counter. "Also, our dumplings are ready."

"Why don't we just hang out and eat," said Luke. "Now that we're . . . reunited . . . we've got plenty of time for sharing and caring. Let's just relax together, enjoy each other's company." He grinned and grabbed a dumpling and ate it whole, but Harriet didn't miss the warning glance he gave Nikka.

After they ate, Harriet waited for more questions about the pool, and her mood, but they didn't come. She tried to tell herself that it was because they didn't *really* care. The three of them stepped outside to a fine mist that fell gently onto their faces, while blaring car horns reminded everyone that it was still New York City.

"I hate this kind of weather," said Nikka. "I'm always afraid that it will make my hair frizzy."

"But somehow those fears are never realized, thank Jehovah God Almigh-TEE!" said Harriet, punctuating the "tee" with a soft smile to Nikka. Throwing her a bone. The mist felt like tiny kisses on Harriet's cheeks.

Nikka kissed her on the cheek lightly. To Harriet, it felt hot, as though someone had lit a match and held it against her face. "Bye, cuz. I have some errands to run so I'll come by your place later." She hugged Luke and walked away quickly.

Harriet and Luke stood staring at each other. Harriet resisted the urge to wipe her face.

"If the rain doesn't get too bad, I'll even have time to shoot some hoops before it gets too dark," said Luke.

"Don't you have homework to do?" she asked.

"Worried about my grades?" Luke smiled. "Don't worry, I'll still give you a run for your honor roll money."

Harriet didn't answer, thinking about her rising pile of unfinished assignments. "Whatever," she said finally.

"I know how to get you," replied Luke, grinning and hugging her shoulders. "You think I don't remember, but I do. The Pig thing."

Harriet's lips twitched.

"You know you can't resist it," he went on, clearing his throat and singing:

If I had a way to make your day for you

He was off-key and croaking and silly and goofy.
It was beautiful.

I'd sing you a day shiny and blue.

Harriet blinked rapidly and pulled away. "Stop," she
whispered. "You play too much." She elbowed him gently.
"And those aren't the right words anyway."

Luke laughed and hugged her shoulders again, like
a teammate. She pulled herself out of his grasp and began
walking.

"I would too, you know that, right?" he said, jogging
to keep up with her. "You're so fraudulent, playing it like
you're some kind of Tin Girl in the Land of Oz, but a corny
song from an old kids' movie about a pig melts your heart.
And it's not even *Charlotte's Web*!"

"Leave me *alone*, Luke," said Harriet, glad that her
voice didn't break. It *was* corny, but every time she thought of
Farmer Hoggett trying to cheer up his sheep-pig Babe in her
all-time favorite film, she wanted to laugh and cry at the same
time. Luke *would* have to show up and trouble the waters.

"I would," said Luke, suddenly serious. "But I can't."
They stood near the subway station entrance, as weary,
damp commuters brushed past. Harriet knew that some girls
would have drawn out a moment like this, leaning into him
and giggling, asking "Would what?" from beneath their
lashes. Harriet had never been Some Girls.

"Thanks for walking me," Luke said.

"See you," she said, touching his arm and turning away quickly. The mist had turned to rain, and she almost-ran all the way home.

INTRUSIVE INTERLUDE

3:33 a.m.

She'd forgotten to pull down her window blinds, and the city lights demanded her attention. She flipped the blinds closed and let them fall all the way down; blanketing herself in the darkness usually helped.

This time, it didn't.

She fluffed her pillow and tossed and turned. Neil DeGrasse Tyson gave her a smug smile from her wall.

Was there something special about threes?

Oh yeah. Harriet sat up slowly. *So which one was here now? Father? Son? Holy Spirit? Which one was supposed to keep her from crying in her sleep?* Maybe she'd ask that at her next Confession Session. She wondered what would happen if she did ask a question. Did that happen? The thing about going to Confession without actually being in the club was that you weren't sure what the rules were. But then again, that was familiar territory for her.

As she tiptoed through the cool darkness of the hallway to her parents' room, Harriet took in the unusually deep quiet of the night. The air was close and heavy, and she resisted the urge to touch her neck even though she was afraid the invisible hands would first.

Father? Son? Definitely Holy Spirit. Slowly, she put her hand on the closed bedroom door.

Maybe they could sit up together and have a secret middle-of-the-night snack. She could crawl into her mother's bed, like she hadn't in years, under cover of nightmares or even better, exam anxiety. The old Momma would have loved anything academic, even stress.

Or you could let your mother see who you really are.

"Go back to bed, Harriet" whispered her mother from inside, causing Harriet to jump.

No Night Watch tonight.

Wordlessly, Harriet turned and stumbled back to her room. Father, Son, Holy Spirit. Any of the Three could see her, whether she believed in them or not, isn't that what they said?

Still, she sat on her bed and held in her tears until sunrise. Then she got in the shower, and sobbed quietly until the water ran cold and her mother was calling her for breakfast.

LUNCH IN THE LIBRARY WILL SAVE YOU

"Anyone sitting here?"

Harriet looked up from *Yoruba Girl Dancing* to see Alisia standing next to her table. She realized that the library had filled up quickly today. The usual suspects were there, enjoying their thirty minutes of respite from the teasing that hung around their lives like greasy hair. A few scattered loners like Harriet hogged whole tables, their books spread out to lend an illusion of soon-to-return companionship that fooled no one. Harriet shoved her books to one side and nodded without smiling. "Sure."

Alisia sat lightly, almost floating down into the chair. "Thanks," she murmured.

Harriet watched as she pulled out a book—Harriet couldn't see the title—and began to read, moving her finger along the page. Annoying. Harriet surreptitiously crunched on a celery stalk, wondering if her tablemate found *that* annoying.

"I didn't realize we could eat in here," said Alisia. "I'm Alisia, remember?" she added, as though Harriet had so many friends, she might not be able to keep track.

Harriet shrugged and looked pointedly at the precious minutes ticking by on the wall clock. Alisia kept looking at her, so she added, "You know, there are a bunch of special rules for the die-hards. It's the same at every school. I think the librarians feel sorry for us. Or they used to *be* us." She cleared her throat.

"Oh yeah," said Alisia. "I know all about secret geek perks. At my old school, if you wore glasses, braces, and got As, you were invited to the pizza party in the nurse's office on the last day of school. The principal comes, and twerks to some nineties New Jack Swing."

Harriet's mouth dropped open.

"Um, I'm kidding," said Alisia, raising her eyebrows.

Harriet reopened her book and crunched hard on a stalk of celery.

After a pause, Alisia went on, "You're in my English class too, right?"

Harriet nodded without looking up.

"So about those polynomials . . ."

"Um, yeah, these are my notes," said Harriet, pulling a notebook out of her bag. "I have some examples there, you'll probably be able to figure it out in a couple of minutes." Harriet hoped that Alisia didn't notice that the notebook was brand-new. She'd sat at her desk the night before, carefully making this mini textbook for such a time as this . . . for Alisia, her friend.

Alisia took the notebook with an expectant smile. "I knew you'd hook me up. Thanks. So . . . Harriet. For the spy or the freedom fighter?"

"Neither," said Harriet, looking up. "Or both." It was not the first time she'd got that question, and she always tried to answer in a way that ended the conversation there.

"Got it," said Alisia. And, Harriet realized, she did. They both lowered themselves into their books (now that she saw it was *The Thing Around Your Neck*, Harriet was impressed), and after a minute or two, Harriet pushed her container of baby carrots to the center of the table.

"These are really good," Alisia said, now reading over Harriet's notes. "You could teach that class better than Kentler."

"This table could teach that class better than Kentler," Harriet replied. It made no sense, but they both giggled.

Along with a carrot, Alisia picked up Harriet's other book: *The Works: Anatomy of a City.* "This looks cool."

"I've been waiting for it to come in," said Harriet quickly. "It's about all of the invisible systems in the city."

"Invisible?"

"Like underground behind-the-scenes stuff. And the weird jobs that we need that no one knows about."

"Anything on subways? I'm going to drive a train before I'm twenty-one," said Alisia, eyes shining. "Maybe before I'm eighteen."

"I don't know," replied Harriet, trying not to sound too intrigued.

"Did you ever read *The Mole People*?" asked Alisia. "About those people living in the subway tunnels? Tunnels that go to what you might call Other Places?"

Harriet nodded carefully, trying to muffle her joy. Someone else knew about *her* book. "Most of that book was discredited, you know," she said, eyeing Alisia. "Probably fantasy." She held her breath, waiting for a bark of laughter—or worse, dismissal.

"That makes it more true, right?" murmured Alisia. She raised her eyebrows, and smiled.

This . . . casual conversation . . . this felt like fantasy too. *Too good to be true?* Harriet considered the other girl for a moment, then nodded and passed *The Works* over. "Page twenty-six," she said. "She even talks about abandoned stations, and you might like the part about retired subway cars."

"Thanks." Alisia didn't look at the book. "Do you read graphic novels?"

Harriet nodded. "I mean, yeah, like any books," she said. "Are you talking about one in particular?"

"You heard of *Night Man*?" Alisia leaned forward. "With the guy running the underground magic school?"

"No . . . who's the author?"

Alisia ignored the question. "I heard that it's based on the insane asylum under Columbia."

"Huh?" Suddenly Harriet flashed back to that piece of paper in the wall behind the toilet. Maybe it had been left there by someone on . . . the other side.

"She's talking about Trell Hall," said a familiar voice. A stack of books and a large mustard purse with YOU FAKE LIKE THIS BIRKIN painted on it fell to the table in front of Harriet with a loud thud.

"What's up?" said Nikka, sitting down. "Are we talking about the secret tunnels under the university that everyone knows about?" She wrinkled her nose like she smelled something rotten. "It's been a long time since I've heard someone use the term 'insane asylum.' Not exactly cool."

"This is my cousin Nikka," said Harriet to Alisia. "Self-proclaimed royalty."

"You're the one always proclaiming it," Nikka retorted.

"I know who you are," said Alisia to Nikka, without expression.

"Hey," said Nikka, flashing a smile that expected a warm welcome. Then she narrowed her eyes. "I know you, right?"

"I don't think so," said Alisia. "Maybe your mind's playing tricks on you."

Nikka smirked. "Oh. Um. So what are you guys doing? Homework?"

Alisia shrugged. "Easier to concentrate in here."

"Good," said Nikka. "That's what I was hoping for." She lifted a book and settled back in her chair.

"What are you doing?" asked Harriet, mimicking Nikka's falsely bright tone. "Homework?"

Nikka looked up and said, "No."

The three sat in silence after that, and Harriet wondered if she was the only one pretending to read.

"Don't look up," whispered Nikka a few minutes later.

"What?" said Harriet, looking up. She smiled when Alisia grinned into her book.

"It's that ridiculous Amy Lee," muttered Nikka.

"You mean 'Amélie,'" said Alisia, rolling her eyes.

"Whatever," said Nikka. "I think I mean *Amy Lee* Johnson. Being The Artistic One on a stupid teen reality show doesn't change anything in my book. She's always trying to talk to me about a makeup tutorial collab. Not happening."

Alisia gave Nikka an appraising look, and Harriet's heart sank before she'd realized how much she'd already begun thinking of Alisia as her own.

"Watch. She's going to walk over here and start pretending that she likes us," said Nikka.

"That she likes *you*, you mean," said Alisia, looking over at Harriet. She tilted her head toward Nikka, as if to say, *Get a load of this one.*

I do, thought Harriet. *All the time.* But she didn't meet Alisia's eyes.

Then the library door slammed shut, loud and hard. All three girls jumped in their seats, and Harriet had to force herself not to dive under the table.

A trio of boys came in, hoodies up, long-limbed and laughing, ignoring the almost-visible waves of dismay at their arrival, their swagger on full display.

Harriet was sure they were the boys who'd shoved her the other day. She could *feel* it.

She saw Nikka notice how tightly she held the table's edge and realized that Nikka was doing the same thing. A current of fear passed between them, as real and painful as an electric shock.

She hadn't recognized them before. But they were familiar now. These were the boys who made fun of her clothes when she was wearing the same thing as the other girls. The ones whose eyes slid over her when they had to pick teams for gym, and sneered when they caught your eye. The ones who pushed past you a little too hard for it to be accidental. Not these exact boys, of course, but their type was everywhere. And sometimes they were your brother and then they got shot.

One smiled at Nikka, and Nikka's cool stare in return was a departure—Harriet hadn't known that her cousin could look so . . . closed. Harriet glanced at the boys again—*careful, don't let them catch you looking*—and frowned. There was something more menacing about their confidence than the usual "I Rule This School" attitude that guys like this wore carelessly, like a loosely tied cloak. These boys were . . . dangerous. They spoke briefly with the librarian, who said, "Oh! *The Works*! Someone else just picked that one up. I can put it on hold for you if you'd like. But please, keep it down next time."

And then all three stared at Harriet. And they smiled. And it was mean. And it was like this smile spoke; she heard: *You can't hide in here forever, Little Sis. Don't think you're safe because the number on the school door is different. It doesn't matter where you are. Your number is up. And lunch in the library won't save you.*

LUNCH IN THE LIBRARY COULD HAVE SAVED HIM

She hadn't even been there that day, in the cafeteria. And all the versions of the story of That Moment were slightly different; some said that Tunde had actually grabbed for the gun, others said that his back had been turned, and the surprise in his eyes had been the saddest part of the whole deal.

"You seriously don't deserve to live," she'd muttered that morning. She hadn't put enough force behind it, though; Tunde didn't react. As usual, he couldn't even expend energy on caring about what she said.

"I wish you were dead," she'd said, spitting each word out, punctuating the ending *d*.

"OK," he'd said, not even looking at her.

She'd walked three subway stops to make sure they wouldn't ride the same train to school.

Harriet had been in the library as usual, still nursing her anger from the morning fight, feeding on it instead of the cheese-and-tomato sandwich she'd brought for lunch, planning her after school payback. Maybe she'd tell Simone that he'd been out with Johanna last Friday when he'd pretended that he was sick. Or maybe she'd just tell her mother, because even though Tunde was clearly her favorite, she never tolerated "disRESPECT of these young ladies, Tunde! That is NOT how you were raised."

Harriet's mental revenge planning was interrupted by the crackling of the PA system and the slam of the library door as a skinny, breathless, wide-eyed sixth-grader had run in babbling about a gun and shots and school shooter and FREAKING OUT, and there'd been commotion and yelling and running and still Harriet didn't begin to think, until she'd wandered out on the basketball court with hundreds of other students, as more and more police cars screamed and skidded into view, as an ambulance siren blared in the distance, as the principal was running toward her, that this could have anything to do with her.

The End.

"Hel-*lo*," said Nikka. "Wake up, cuz, it's time to get out of here."

Harriet wondered how long she'd been sitting there with her eyes squeezed shut. The boys were gone, and Nikka's stare was now on *her*. She cleared her throat and gathered her things inefficiently, dropping an item every time she tried to pick up another. The other two helped her in silence, until Alisia broke it with an urgent whisper.

"So I heard the Mole People never left after the eighties. They just went . . . deeper." She deliberately turned her back to Nikka. "Like there's a whole community down there, kind of like an upside-down projects."

"Projects?" asked Nikka, in a low, tight voice. "Like, why? If you're going to set up a secret underground society, wouldn't you, I don't know, build fancy subterranean castles or something? And yeah, OK, there's a whole world underground that the city has somehow missed." She snorted. "Talk about the definition of talking out the side of your neck."

Alisia flicked a glance her way. "Ooh, 'subterranean.' *Big* word."

Are they fighting over me? Harriet wondered, feeling a small and precious frisson of joy at the prospect.

Alisia went on. "Anyway, I heard they can do that too," she says. "Like something out of a really good horror movie. The story is that a guy got his throat slit and—"

"Stop!" yelled Nikka.

And then all three of them got kicked out of the library.

They stood in the hallway as the first bell rang. Harriet didn't realize that she was rubbing her neck until she saw that Nikka was doing it too.

"I'll see you after school, cuz." Her voice took on a frosty edge, as she started to walk away. "Cool stories, Alisia."

"By the way," drawled Alisia. "You know Charisse Clark?"

Nikka stopped, and nodded. "Uh, yeah, why?"

"Oh nothing, she's in my physics class and I heard her talking about something in your group chat—"

Harriet stiffened. "You're in a group chat with Charisse? I thought you had nothing to do with her . . . with 'that trash,' I think you said." Of course, Nikka didn't know about the scene in the bathroom. Or maybe she did. Maybe they'd all laughed about it in the chat, with memes and emojis and lots of in-joke shorthand.

Nikka looked away. "I mean . . . it's a big group, I don't—I'm not . . ." She tugged at a curl, twirling it around her finger, stalling and awkward as if she'd forgotten a line in her script.

Alisia's lips curled into the kind of smile that Harriet thought only Mean Girls made. "That's so funny, she was talking about how the two of you were cool and saying that you told her about some great yoga class?" She went on, smoothly: "You and her got some amazing bubble tea or something together?"

Harriet raised her eyebrows. "From trash to BFF. Cute."

"I don't know what your point is," Nikka snapped at Alisia. "But it's whatever. I was just being polite, which maybe you don't understand, but it's really none of your business."

Alisia shrugged. "I'm not trying to get in your business, I was . . . just trying to place you. She smiled. "I think I have now."

Nikka turned and marched away quickly and stiffly, like someone else was controlling her movements. Harriet stayed where she was, looking at Alisia's shoes.

"So Nikka's your cousin," said Alisia.

"Yeah," Harriet made a point of rolling her eyes.

"It's cool how you're so real with her. Which way? I'll walk with you."

Harriet was silent as she fell into step beside Alisia. Then she blurted out: "Nikka would say by 'real' you mean 'rud—"

"It's not always about being polite," interrupted Alisia, with another quick, tight smile. "Sometimes rude is protection. I'm like that too."

As they approached Harriet's classroom and she mentally practiced how to say "See you" lightly, and without expectation, Alisia stopped.

"We should hang out sometime. For real." She ripped a piece of looseleaf paper from a notebook and scribbled on it. "I know this place in the Heights, we can get maduros, they're my favorite. Ooh, and the roast chicken is amazing. Or we can go for bubble tea," she added, with a smirk.

Harriet smiled back.

"Text me later, or whatever," Alisia finished, dropping the paper into Harriet's roomy bag. "Or we'll probably see each other again in the library." She left without waiting for a response.

Or whatever.

Harriet hadn't texted Alisia. She'd thought about it when she and her mother "worked" another afternoon in the shop without customers, then again after dinner. But she wasn't ready to wait for the three dots in anticipation of a response. Even though Alisia had mentioned sweet plantains and chicken from Malecon, and—"*here are a group of my fav-o-rite things*" Harriet sang softly to herself. Something like that. *This* inner voice, a hopeful one, felt scratchy and unfamiliar.

That night, Harriet slept through the night, which, as she packed her knitting in her messenger bag the next morning, she attributed to Alisia. But Harriet the math nerd knew it was easier to imagine the possibility of friendship than face the probability that a few more encounters would show Alisia that Harriet wasn't someone to befriend. Or whatever.

At school, she was grateful for a double-dose of substitute teachers. The first one had advised the students to "read ahead" in preparation for the teacher's return; that had been in *gym*, and the level of community ennui was so extra that no one even laughed. Now, in the second class, the sub had said only, "I don't care what you do as long as you don't bother me and stay relatively quiet."

Harriet was starting to put her head down on the desk when she noticed the girl next to her pull out some knitting, and briefly considered stepping far enough out of herself to ask about it. What if? What if she just became the kind of person who made friends, who went out for coffee after school with another girl, who swapped knitting patterns with someone other than her online friends? What if she was that person, instead of one who didn't even use her real initials or a photo online? What if?

Anyway. She took out *The Works*; she was almost done, but not ready to return it quite yet, since she knew that those guys were waiting for it. She held the book open without reading until the bell rang, then she brushed past the girl and her knitting, out of the classroom.

"Cuz!" Nikka's shrill voice rang through the halls, cutting through the normal between-class chatter.

"Yeah, hurry up, I'm late," said Harriet as Nikka pulled up next to her. "And I need to get to my next class early."

"Make that make sense," said Nikka. Without waiting for an answer, she grabbed Harriet's hand like they were seven again and heading to the Mister Softee ice cream truck on the corner with a precious ten-dollar bill.

"We're going out to lunch later," said Nikka, and Harriet suddenly noticed the two girls on Nikka's other side. "We want you to come with; Stacy wants to learn to knit."

Stacy, who was wearing a crop top that said RESIST across the front, held up an unenthusiastic hand. "Hey," she said.

Knitting again. Was this some kind of sign? Would two sticks and some yarn be her saving grace—a way to belong?

"Yeah," said Stacy. "And I need help with geometry. This is my second time taking it. Nikka says you're like a champion math freak or something." She looked Harriet up and down.

Harriet glared at her cousin. "Um, math and physics actually. And yeah so, sorrynotsorry, today's not so great—"

Nikki actually stopped and stomped her foot in frustration. "Seriously?! Don't tell me you're busy eating in the library again," she blurted out. "Have you been in the cafeteria at all since . . . since you've been here?" When Stacy and the other girl snorted, Nikka glared at them too. "It's not a joke," she said.

Stacy rolled her eyes, and Harriet could feel the power dynamic shift; she knew Nikka felt it too. She'd never been part of one of these friend triangles, but she knew enough to know that they were never equilateral, and usually scalene. She smiled to herself as her mind slid into a vision of herself, growing until she was monster-sized, screaming, "AM I A JOKE TO YOU!" to these bored, wispy friends of her cousin, as they ran screaming down the hall. The idea made her laugh suddenly, and from the look on the other girls' faces, she was just confirming their freak suspicions.

And that was with keeping her geometry references to herself.

"Just come with us, it'll be fun," said Nikka softly. "And for the record, I didn't say anything about you being a freak."

"No, actually," said Harriet, stopping short herself. "It won't be fun. For *any* of us, but especially not for *me*."

"Oh, she *feisty*," said Stacy. "That's what's up."

The other girl raised her eyebrows and said, "Guess your cousin don't have time for you, Nikka." They both looked at Nikka, as though waiting for her next move.

Nikka shifted from one leg to the other. "She's just miserable. I mean, she's my cousin, but look at what I'm deal-ing with." She tried to laugh, but it was more of a strangled choking sound that Harriet recognized as *Regretting the words that come out of your mouth as soon as you said them.* "I mean, I—"

Harriet cut her off. *"There* she is. The Nikka I know and have to spend holidays with! Byeee. Enjoy your lunch, say hi to Charisse," she added. "And good luck with math." She turned and hurried away from them. Harriet knew she'd embarrassed Nikka. She didn't want to look back to see the expression on her cousin's face, but it was fun to imagine.

She was at the door of the third-floor bathroom before she realized that she was going there. She slipped in, forgetting to hold her breath, and immediately regretting that. "Did someone die in here?" she muttered under her breath. She did a quick check for feet under the stall doors. She was alone. There was new Sharpie grafitti under the dingy mirror with the words SUNKEN PLACE and an arrow pointing down toward the sink. She tried to turn the tap, but it was stuck, and uncomfortably warm, almost clammy. Now she wanted to wash her hands. She peeked into the last stall; no new slips of paper. She grabbed two lengths of toilet paper and used one to pull the hallway door open, then held it with her foot while she took a small bottle of hand sanitizer out of her front pocket; after she rubbed the remnants of the gel away, she dried her hands with the other sheet and tossed both wads of toilet paper into the empty trash can just inside the door. *And the crowd goes wild!* She let the door slam shut with a flourish. *Adu with another buzzer-beating shot!*

The door reopened suddenly with a loud creak. "Hey, long time no see!" announced Alisia, stepping out of the bathroom that Harriet had just left.

"Oh—hi," said Harriet, almost dropping the over-sized book. "I didn't see you in there." Had Alisia been perched on a toilet seat, having a silent cry? For a wild moment, Harriet imagined her hanging from the ceiling like a bat or a spiderly superhero, waiting to drop on an unsuspecting lipstick checker. *I need to get some sleep.*

"You know, thanks for letting me know about that book. I put my name down on the hold list, it sounded pretty cool," she said, ignoring Harriet's confusion. "There are three people ahead of me, though, so it'll be a while."

Harriet had to force herself not to look over her shoulder; she hadn't actually seen the three boys at school again, but they had gotten under her skin. And she had to keep reminding herself that she was just missing the pool—that had to be why everything smelled of chlorine.

"Your cousin is staring at you from all the way down the hall," said Alisia. "It's kind of freaky."

Harriet shrugged and didn't look. "She's all about the freaky," she said. "It's kind of her thing."

"I love how people think they can decide when you're worthy, you know? Like you should be grateful for their attention." When Harriet glanced at her, Alisia added, "I don't mean your cousin, of course," in a way that sounded like she *definitely* meant Nikka.

Harriet, feeling somewhat disloyal and liking it, just shrugged again. "I'm not worried about what you meant." Alisia gave her a long, almost challenging look.

"You know, you don't say much, but when you do, your words are pretty powerful."

Harriet held her breath and looked down. *If you only knew.*

"OK, you're probably going to laugh, but . . ." Alisia touched her arm lightly with icy hands that made Harriet shiver; she hoped Alisia hadn't noticed. "I think we're kindred spirits. Does that seem weird to you?"

"Weird is my thing," said Harriet. "I'm guessing you noticed." She put on a smile she hoped was convincing. "So I'm going with it."

Alisia laughed as the second bell rang. "*We're* going with it," she said, linking her arm through Harriet's as though they did it every day.

"Um, I can give you the book tomorrow. I'm almost done and I still have time left before I need to return it. You can even keep it late if you want. I don't mind." She was trying too hard, she knew, but she couldn't help it.

"Thanks!" replied Alisia. "What do you do after school? I know you don't go to the library because that's where I am . . . Do you have to work?"

"Um." Harriet was reluctant to mention the store, especially now that Luke and maybe Nikka had become a part of that life.

"It's just, I want to introduce you to some people, people I think you'd really connect with," Alisia said. There was something in her voice now that made Harriet frown.

"Connect with?" Harriet asked, her heart sinking. The light of other people would show Alisia just how out of sync she was. "Like I said, I'm pretty . . . disconnected around here."

"Oh, they're not from around here," said Alisia, waving an arm. "I know you don't know me, but . . . trust me? Something tells me that you'll like my crew."

Now Harriet saw Nikka waving at her from the other end of the hall. *Kindred spirits.*

"I need a guardian angel," she muttered under her breath.

"Huh?"

"Let's talk after last period," Harriet replied quickly. "I'll text you . . ." The late bell rang. Alisia didn't seem to be in a hurry to get to class. "I'm sorry, I have to go." As Harriet rushed to the nearest exit, she hoped that she hadn't burned a bridge before she'd built it.

10

She started the text three times as she walked down Amsterdam Avenue. Should she just say:

hey
let's link up
hey girl, it's your kindred spirit!

There was weird and then there was creepy. But . . . Alisia seemed like she'd been paying attention, and was still talking to Harriet, had talked about *we*, so . . .

A block away from the store, Harriet's phone beeped insistently, as though she'd been ignoring it. A text message from Momma, saying that she should go directly to the university campus to correct a mix-up on the order that she and Luke had dropped off the other day. *The Shekere Shake-Up.* Harriet briefly imagined herself getting to the bottom of it like an intrepid teen TV detective who had side-kick friends and a date for the prom. Again, she thought: *Sleep.*

When she got to campus, she sat on a stone bench near the edge of the quad, watching the students whose grim-faced, focused movements from building to building little resembled the sunny, head-thrown-back-with-laughter website photos that she'd seen as Tunde built his never-ending "college list."

Their parents had begun hounding him in the spring of ninth grade, saying those dreaded words "permanent rec-ord" and "extracurricular." He'd rolled his eyes at the end-less forwarded email articles about odds-beating Black children who'd won "full rides" to every Ivy League school, and the "little" ones too.

"What's a 'Little Ivy' anyway?" he'd said to Harriet one day as they'd shared a bag of Cool Ranch Doritos. "Like a tiny bit excellent?"

"Dollhouse-sized campus," Harriet said back with a snort. "And you'd be like a giant, not even able to fit in the classrooms. Like that movie—"

He snatched the bag of chips from her hands and poured the last crumbs into his mouth. "You'll never find out, anyway," he'd cut with a snort, jumping up and leaving her wondering why these moments seemed to get shorter and shorter.

Would he have ended up here—so close to home, and far from the opportunity to completely reinvent himself?

No one had asked about her college plans in a while. Her phone buzzed again, and she made her way to Trell Hall. She wasn't completely surprised to find Luke and Nikka, standing and unsmiling, just inside the entrance. *Mystery solved.*

"Me and Luke got a plan," said Nikka. "We still don't know why you're not doing the one thing you've loved since kindergarten, but we're going to get to the bottom of it."

Harriet eyed them both, wondering how Nikka once again seemed to have been inside her head. Standoff. For a minute, she wanted to giggle, imagining the three of them stone-faced and in cowboy hats with tumbleweed rolling by.

"OK. So what?" she snapped finally. "I'm here. What's next? More tea and dumplings? Questions that I won't answer? Meaningful looks and tense silences?"

Luke stepped next to her, so close that his body heat warmed her like an actual hug.

"We're all going swimming," he said simply.

Harriet opened her mouth, but Nikka held up a hand.

"*We're* swimming, OK?" she said. "You can watch, or sulk, or whatever. You don't have to get in the water. But you have to stay." Harriet tried again, but Nikka continued: "If you try to leave, I call Auntie and tell her what's been going on."

"The pool's closed. And what do you mean, 'what's been going on'?" asked Harriet. The brief warmth from her conversation with Alisia was now leaving her. "Just because I don't feel like going swimming right now?" She thought she'd succeeded in keeping her voice level.

"I don't know what exactly, but I know *something's* up. Things are . . . weird. And I think you know it too."

"And the pool's not closed," says Luke. "I think I hear a baby class splashing around."

Harriet looked around and hoped they didn't notice that she was shivering.

"All right," she said, not quite pulling off a casual shrug. "You swim. I'll watch. But not for long. I have home-work to do." Nikka and Luke were perpetually untouched by Trouble. She was sure that whatever was in the pool, she told herself, wouldn't bother them.

Once, last year, they'd gone to Nikka's after school. Luke had met them at the corner, dapping up Tunde and grabbing Nikka and Harriet in one-armed hugs on either side. Inside, Harriet had kept quiet, watching their easy wordplay and inside jokes, trying to remember exactly when it had started feeling like she couldn't join in. Like she could only just watch.

Yeah, you better watch.

Harriet shivered again.

"Let's go change," said Nikka. "You know you have to wear your suit, even if you only sit in the bleachers. And by the way—you should really get a new one. That yellow thing is like, really thrift shop . . . and not in a good way."

Harriet sat, stiff-backed, on the damp bleachers, while Luke and Nikka deliberated over the easiest way to get into the freezing water. The doors to the pool had swung open easily, but it turned out there was no baby class and no lifeguard on duty today. And this time, there were actually signs. Angry, bright, ominous signs that had never been there before.

DO NOT ENTER, UNDER ANY CIRCUMSTANCES.

NO UNAUTHORIZED ENTRY.

KEEP OUT.

They could get in real trouble for this.

The temperature seemed to be dropping in the usually warm and humid room with every second they were in there; Harriet clamped her lips to keep her teeth from chattering. The chlorine was so strong that it stung her eyes, but at least here, that made sense.

As Luke and Nikka argued about who would dive in first, the lifeguard, *her* lifeguard, finally walked in. Oh. OK. So everything was normal. He was going to get up on his perch and make everyone feel safe.

"Hey, Mermaid," he called. "You OK?"

"Fine," she answered, not looking at him. "But it's kind of cold in here . . . what's up with that? And all those signs? Is it OK for me to—"

"I've been waiting for you to come back," he persisted urgently, ignoring her question. "You know, to talk about you working here. Mr. Escalante really liked the idea of getting someone new involved—I been hyping you up and he wants to meet you, he really wants to meet you." He was talking fast, like they'd been in the middle of a conversation just a moment earlier, and he was rushing to finish it. "There's something here for you."

What was wrong with this guy? Harriet felt obligated to look at him, and as she did, she watched his face change—*transform*, really—like a slick special effect in a scary movie that was slow and fast at the same time, with skin and teeth and everything moving and sliding and *metamorphosing* and suddenly it was her brother Tunde standing in front of her and she screamed and Luke and Nikka fell into the pool with a terrific splash.

Then it was quiet beyond any silence she'd ever known.

And then Luke and Nikka didn't come back up.

11

It's not until the water burns my skin (how is it *boiling hot?!*) that I realize that I've dived into the pool. I am full-out, swim-meet swimming, but it feels like a war; the water I know so well is pushing back, and I have to use every bit of my body to go deeper.

Luke and Nikka are down there, and I'm not going to mess things up again.

I kick fast, expecting those awful hands or paws or whatever they were to grab me again.

I can't do anything but push myself forward and down. I swivel around to find them. I see nothing but water and walls.

Lifeguards don't *transmogrify* into dead brothers.

People don't fall into pools and disappear.

I swim the entire length of the pool in an instant. They are not here. I don't have time to wonder, I don't have time to cry, I want to scream, but I just keep swimming, because *you are not going to beat me like this, whoever, whatever you are! Take me out, if you want to, but I won't lose anyone else.*

I zigzag and crisscross and scrape the bottom until I have to come up for a breath.

I am alone.

I tread water, not knowing what's coming next; there's only silence that makes my teeth chatter.

Tunde is gone. So is the lifeguard.

Luke and Nikka fell into the pool and now they're gone and it's my fault, and I want my mommy because I don't know what to do—

Giving up already, Adu? Why am I not surprised?

I scream out a curse; the Voice has nothing to give back. I fill my lungs with that cold, cold air and dive back under.

No matter what happens, I'm never swimming again.

And over at the deep end, next to the 9FT mark, there's a door.

Even though I know, I *know* that it wasn't there before, that it's *never* been there, that the closer I get to it,

YOU'RE BREAKING MY HEART   111

the hotter this unbearable water seems to get, I swim toward it.

The door glimmers and slowly clears until it's like a window. As I get closer I see him again—Tunde—on the other side.

I didn't know you could scream underwater, but when I put my hand to that crystal clear doorknob I scream, and my mouth doesn't fill with water, but it hurts so bad that I promise, I *promise* I will be the best daughter ever and I won't be mean to anyone and I'll make friends and smile and act nice every day and I'm sorry I'm so sorry just make it stop because I will not let go of this door even if my hand burns off, I will not turn back, I will not go away.

I will not give up.

I pull the door open and I'm whooshed in like I'm riding a wave. I fall onto dusty, dry ground. The water is gone. Large coins, like oversized vintage subway tokens, litter the floor. The door shuts behind me, and then it's gone too. I'm looking at a wall. I look up at Tunde, my dead brother Tunde, his eyes flashing like we just finished fighting, but he's looking through me like he doesn't see me in front of him. He stands perfectly still and straight, wearing the prom tuxedo he'd been buried in, like a Wedding Magic Ken Doll, his arms glued to his side. If he'd just reach out, I could . . .

I hear the rushing water again before I see it, tumbling down the winding hallway toward us, frothing and angry, just like a movie, and I stand up just as he dives *into* it. I try to follow, but the water pushes me backward and I know that in a second I am going to be crushed against that wall, and that Tunde is gone

and of course he's not going to save me
and I've failed
and this time I do feel the grip of those . . . hands
and the door is back, and I'm pulled through
and I'm back in the pool. At the gym. And I've failed
     I've failed.
     He's alive.
     He's dead.
     They're gone.
     I've failed.
     And there are more hands now, and I fight just because there's nothing else to do, and I keep fighting
     They're holding me
     Nikka and Luke are holding me
     And someone is crying.
     They carry me up out of the pool
     They're *here*
     And someone is crying
     I didn't save them.

They're *here*.

And there's my lifeguard
With his magazine.
Tunde's dead.
I'm not losing it
I'm already lost.
Someone is crying.
And Nikka hugs me tight.
And Luke squeezes my shoulders and says
"What is going on?"

12

Nikka's play-mommy tendencies are in full force; when we were kids, she was the one who'd always strapped her rag dolls to her back with a small strip of adire cloth stolen from her mother's stash, instead of using the toy stroller. I guess it's aftershock that's keeping my mouth shut while she leads Luke and me to our towels, because she's seriously clucking like a mama hen in Pretty Little Thing loungewear. I dry off in a daze, and pull on my black track pants and the red "Keep It Fake" T-shirt that actually made me laugh out loud when I got it at a street fair three years ago, half-listening to Luke cursing in French under his breath. Nikka is all business, and marches us outside and down Amsterdam Avenue, even waving to Mike, the cathedral security guard.

The three of us walk in silence, ignoring the tourists and their camera phones and the grouchy rumblings of rush-hour traffic. Nikka brings us inside of V&T, where the waiter grunts his usual greeting; Nikka places an order without consulting either Luke or me. I don't even try to get my head around the concept of a normal thing like pizza.

"What the—" Luke has switched to English cursing; it's less elegant, but still effective. I notice that his hands are shaking. Then I realize that mine are too. Then I remember Tunde's stiff, frozen arms that refused to reach out to me. Luke sees me notice and focuses on wringing his not-damp Wu-Tang Is For the Children T-shirt.

We stand there until Nikka goes back in and returns a short time later with a hot, fresh, down-to-earth cheese pizza. She hands Luke napkins and paper plates and starts walking over to the Peace Fountain without looking to make sure that we follow.

We do.

She picks a spot on the steps near the sculpture of Albert Einstein, and I take my slice and napkin from her like she's the mom in charge of the playdate. The three of us eat the whole pie without speaking. Finally, Luke says, "Again. What just happened?"

They both look at me. I focus on pulling my hoodie on, wondering if I'll ever stop shivering.

"How should I know?" I snap, and I'm grateful, thinking *Welcome back!* to my old cranky self. "What were you two doing? It wasn't funny, or cute. Falling into the pool? You scared me out of my mind. And you're lucky the lifeguard—" My voice breaks, but I go on, "You're lucky the lifeguard didn't kick you out."

He kicked you out, though, says the Voice, and I almost have to sit on my hands to keep from clapping them over my ears.

"I don't know what happened," Nikka starts slowly, "It was like someone shoved me—"

"I thought *you* shoved *me*," Luke interrupted. "Trying to be cute."

"So we both fell in . . . and it was so deep! We just kept going down . . ." Nikka trails off and hugs her own shoulders.

"It's only three feet where we were. It must . . . it must have just felt that way because we were surprised . . . I guess one of us just lost balance or something," Luke finishes in a low voice, not quite succeeding in sounding as sure of himself as usual.

I stare at them, wondering if I should tell them everything—well, not everything—but about the Hands, the Voice, the three boys at school—wondering if I can trust them

if they can trust me
even though I didn't save them.

You want to make up for the Terrible Thing that you did? You want to help your brother?

You want your mommy to love you?
Do you think you can handle it, Little Sis?
You want to make a deal?

I clear my throat. "I think there's something going on," I begin, and then stop.

"Yeah, so that's the understatement of the year," mumbles Luke, and Nikka lets out a snort, and I roll my eyes and try to continue . . . but instead I laugh, and suddenly we're all laughing—big, deep belly laughs that bring up tears and leave us gasping for a long time.

"OK," I say finally. "So yeah, something . . . weird is happening at the pool. Or to the pool."

Luke starts to say something, but Nikka grabs his arm; I look away from them both.

"I know it sounds . . . impossible, but I think the pool is . . . haunted. Or something." Should I tell them that I saw him? I wait for an assault from the Voice, and then realize that I'm waiting for the voice in my head to start talking and I'd better be careful because I'm seriously cracking up.

"*Haunted?* Or *something?*" Luke's voice rises with each word. A couple of passing tourists admiring the fountain stop and glance at him nervously. I glare at him.

"Were you not just there?" I ask. "Even you have to admit that was just a little bit weird! You can't just rationalize everything."

Now it's Luke's turn to look away while a bus creaks and groans as it leans down to let elderly passengers off nearby. A man takes pictures of himself at awkward angles underneath the fountain's self-satisfied sun.

"What do you mean, *even me*?" he asks.

I keep my mouth shut; no way am I saying anything about Tunde. They'll probably both run screaming, and return with a straitjacket.

Right now, just for a minute, so I can pretend, I want them to stay with me.

Nikka touches my arm. "There's more, isn't there?" she asks softly. "There's a Something Serious here."

I blink. She remembers. It's been years since we've talked about *Somethings Serious*. When Nikka and I were six and the older boys held that against us, we'd whisper "SS" and head for the nearest closet or huddle under a table to whisper about the latest happening that was monumental enough to require a meeting. Like finding out that there was going to be okra for dinner, or that the adults had been talking about money, or someone's divorce. As we got older, we perfected a "look" to exchange that meant the same thing—*this is something big*. Those were the days when we'd decide who was going to make the ice cream dessert request or make sure that our own parents' marriages were intact. The last time Nikka had whispered "SS," I'd called her a Nazi without looking up from my book until she'd stomped out of the room. Now I want to say that we don't have time for baby games, but the words stick in my throat. Instead, I start to cry.

And my cousin hugs me *(we used to pretend we were sisters; I forgot we wore matching outfits and everything sometimes)* until I stop enough to pull away and wipe my face with the bottom of my shirt. It feels like hours have gone by. I glance at Luke who is sitting there with his hand on his chin, like an uncomfortable and unhappy Rodin. As though he feels my eyes on him, he walks to the railing and leans, defiant, over the water.

Nikka draws me back into an awkward shoulder buddy-buddy hug, her eyes kind and dry, and I forget that she's the same cousin who always got to be the princess long enough to blurt out:

"Tunde—I saw him. He was *here*."

We hold each other's eyes for a long moment. I see something soft in her deep brown, almost black eyes that fill with her own tears as I stare, but she doesn't move to brush them away.

For a second, I want to grab her hand and play pretend

—maybe we can both be the witch for a little while—

"I know," she whispers. "I saw him too."

13

It's almost been long enough for the pizza and intermittent church bells to bring my heartbeat down to normal. Almost. I try repeating declarative statements to myself. *I am in New York City. We've just eaten pizza. I am still cold.*

Tour buses are still resting while their riders bustle in and out of the cathedral. Extra-fit white people jog past with AirPods in their ears, an oblivious couple makes out on the lawn, and the cathedral peacocks survey the three of us as we sit watching the light and shadows dance with the sculptures around the Ring of Freedom, where children sculpted hopeful animals that look just as good to me as the fountain sculpture itself.

Maybe now, I will wake up.

Luke is doing push-ups against the steps of the plaza, as though he's just getting in a quick workout after an innocuous dip in the pool.

I turn my gaze back to the fountain; the Archangel Michael looks tired and Satan's decapitated head looks not quite dead.

"'Peace Fountain celebrates the triumph of Good over Evil, and sets before us the world's opposing forces— violence and harmony, light and darkness, life and death— which God reconciles in his peace,'" Nikka reads. "No matter how many times I read this, I still don't get it," she says. "Or maybe I'm reading into it too much."

I haven't looked directly at Nikka since she said we'd had dead-Tunde-double-vision in the pool.

Because if we both saw a ghost, then . . . we both saw a ghost.

If you don't say anything, it's like it didn't happen.

If you don't step on the cracks, you will go home and your mother's back will be straight and intact.

"What do you think this is?" she asks, pointing to the small cottage-like building in the corner of the plaza.

I shrug.

"It wasn't a ghost," Nikka says suddenly, sitting down next to me as Luke lets out an extra-macho grunt. "I'm pretty sure of that."

"What did you see?" I ask quietly.

"I saw Tunde. And then he was gone. It was like a flash, really quick, but I know what I saw. I know what you saw too."

I don't bother asking how Nikka's so all-knowing. Even I have to admit that she's always had this *thing*—this way of seeing beyond reality. Long after I'd quit our fairy-tale play-acting in protest (did I mention the perpetual princess?), Nikka had kept up elaborate productions, staging one-woman shows for which she'd weave intricate storylines, like a tiny Scheherazade, who not only saved her own life but made everyone fall in love with her in the process.

"I need to go back," I say. "He's down there some-where, somehow. I have to tell him . . ." I trail off.

Luke plops down next to us, breathing hard.

"Ladies, I think we all got a little spooked. That dusty old pool is kind of creepy, actually. I'm pretty sure I caught a leg cramp, and I panicked, because . . . I was worried about you two . . ." Now it's his turn to trail off. He stands again, shaking his arms out. "Our minds playing tricks on us, that's all. It's dark. Let me get you two home."

I stare at him, and Nikka does too.

"Ladies?" says Nikka, rolling her eyes.

"A leg cramp?" I say, working hard to keep the screech out of my voice. "Are you kidding me? You *know* something weird happened back there!" I stand, facing Luke and Lucifer's severed head; the stained-glass cathe-dral windows gleam in the distance. "Whatever. I've got to go back," I continue. "I've got to go back." If I say it enough, I'll be able to do it.

Sure about that, Little Sis? Don't want to step on another crack, do you? Don't want to make things worse . . .

"You can't go back there," says Luke. He sits up straight and turns away from us, his back rigid.

"Why not?" Nikka says quickly. "There's nothing there, *right*?" They glare at each other; any other time, I'd be enjoying this.

"I am going back to the pool," I say. "I know what I saw."

"And I know what I saw nine months ago!" Luke barks back. "I saw my best friend being lowered into the ground in a box. Because he was *dead*. Because he got shot by some crazy kid who—"

"Shut up!" I scream. Now everyone looks. Passersby stop; only the kissing couple half-hidden and half-dressed remains undisturbed.

Nikka starts to cry. A part of me thinks, *Finally*, and another part of me wants to hug her like she hugged me.

Luke can hug her. It's his fault she's crying anyway. I inch away to make room for him to do it.

And he does—they huddle in guilt-free grief, and the lump in my throat gets so big that I think I might choke to death right then and there.

"I'm sorry," Luke says after a long moment, looking up. "I'm just—"

"It's OK," I say quickly. The show's over, and the strolling and stretching around us resumes. Someone even tries to snap a quick picture of our little trio, but my side eye shuts that down fast.

"Luke, we have to take this seriously," says Nikka, sniffling, coming to stand next to me. "We weren't both hallucinating."

"I'm about to be a grown man," replies Luke, and it's only fear of impending hysteria that keeps me from laughing at *that*. "I believe in six hundred sit-ups before breakfast now. I just don't have room for Impossible Things, or that Serious Something stuff anymore."

Nikka looks at Luke for a moment and then says simply: "I think you're going to have to make room."

We walk uptown in silence. Nikka stays close to me, not touching, just close, like she's guarding me. She catches my eye and smiles; her eyes are still red from crying. I can't figure this Nikka out.

"I'm on your side, you know . . . whether you believe that or not," she whispers.

I don't look at her as I speak.

"I know you mean well," I reply, "But . . . you saw him too! You should understand why I have to go back there!"

Not all of why, though, right? Do you want to tell her the whole story? Bet she'll let you go then. Ha, she'd probably throw you into the pool herself.

No! I can explain to Tunde, show him that I didn't mean it, prove to him that I'm not that person—

"*We* have to plan," says Nikka. "*We* have to . . . figure out what to do. We don't even know what's going on, what's really down there—"

"Yes, we do," interrupts Luke. "Nothing."

Nikka doesn't look his way. "Cuz, trust me. I will help you with this, whatever it is. Let's just go home tonight and talk. Auntie will be looking for you in a minute, and my mom has been on my back ever since she saw me talking to this cutie James . . . Let's do this right."

"Do *what* right?" asks Luke. "Do you not hear yourself, Nikka? I'm about to give you some real talk now. I won't let it happen. Harriet, I'm supposed to be looking out for you, and I . . . this . . ." He trails off.

"*Let* it happen?" Nikka asks, raising one eyebrow. She's so good at that.

I walk up to Luke and look him right in the eye. Nikka slips up beside me. "I don't have time to care about what you believe, Luke," I say slowly. "I know what I saw, I know what's been happening to me, and I don't care if you call me crazy, or if you think you're on a mission to save the little ladies from themselves." I move closer; there is negative space between us now, and I can see the faint scar on his cheek, a remnant from one of his more epic wrestling matches with Tunde. "I don't care. I am going back to the pool." I stop and look at Nikka. "As soon as I've got a plan."

As Luke literally puts his hand over his eyes, I go on, "And you can stand right here forever with your head in the sand or up your butt or wherever you want to stick it, but just don't get in my way. Because if you do, I will just Get. You. Out."

Nikka slings her arm over my shoulder. "I think that's clear enough. Don't you, Luke?"

Luke nods slowly, his hand gone, now not taking his eyes off me.

I don't blink.

"OK, let's go home."

14

Of course, this *would* be the time that Momma decides to interrogate me about where I've been. Even Nikka's cutesy hug-filled vagueness doesn't go very far.

"Open Swim ended at five p.m. It is now eight p.m. What have you been doing for three hours?" She slams a platter of fried fish on the table. Idiot Luke immediately reaches for the food like nothing's wrong, and she stops him cold with The Look.

She glares at him and Nikka. "You were supposed to—" She stops and clears her throat. *Supposed to what, Momma?*

"And explain to me again why your clothing is wet," she changes the subject. "I know you children think I don't know anything, but I do know that one doesn't swim in street clothes." She narrows her eyes and turns to Luke, arms folded. "Unless . . . did you take these girls to the river? If you in any way involved them in one of those foolish schemes . . ."

"No! No, no, Mrs. Adu," stammers Luke. "Absolutely not!"

I almost laugh, but I know that this is not the time. I allow myself a small smile, remembering how Luke and Tunde had once planned an "Urban Ironman" competition that involved swimming in the sludge that was officially called the East River. They had actually started collecting registration fees before the parents busted them. "Um, I should go call my parents and let them know that I'm here." Luke slides out of the room to the hallway.

"I don't get it," I say to Momma. "*You* told me to go there." I'm furious at myself for the pathetic whine I hear in my voice. *I thought you were worried about me.*

Nikka places a hand on Momma's arm. "Auntie, we're so sorry. We went swimming and then we went to the library and just lost track of time. Oh, we're wet . . . you know that fountain near the cathedral?" She waved her hand and let that be the extent of her explanation. Momma would never let me get away with that. "We did get a good start on our homework, though. Here, let me show you—" She rises as if to get her bag, and I stare, wondering how she's going to pull this off.

Momma grunts and pulls Nikka back as Luke returns. "Just eat," she says, nodding permission to sit down. The three of us sit right away, and we all have enough sense not to mention the pizza. Luke stares at the fish, but he waits until Momma says grace and passes me the platter. I pass it over him to Nikka, and Momma frowns but doesn't say anything. I tell myself that it will all be worth it when I fix things with Tunde. She'll love me so much. Maybe then I will too.

NO FAIR

"This is some *Pet Sematary* territory y'all are in right now, and it's not even funny," says Luke, shaking his head. "Hallucinations happen when you're tired. You need to get some sleep. I need sleep." He fake-yawns and gets up from the living room floor and paces. We'd decided not to even try to talk things over in my bedroom, at least not while Luke was still here. Momma and Auntie Marguerite would put us on lockdown for months. Luke was family, but at certain times, he became a Boy. In my bedroom after 7:00 would definitely be one of those times.

"Are you serious? Who exactly is laughing?" I ask. The goose bumps are still visible on my arms, and I rub them hard. We've lit some of Nikka's bodega candles, and the flickering light warms me more than it should. "Momma's not going to be happy that we're using the emergency candles," I say.

"On some level, I think she knows we're in an emergency," says Nikka. "You know how the mothers are."

"Look, I've got college apps to do," says Luke, rubbing his hands together like he'd finished fooling around and was ready to get down to real business. "So we need to stop with the scary movie stuff." He glares at me for a moment. "It's bringing back . . . memories, and none of us have time for that—"

Movie night memories? Is he mad that I was there, ruining their big kid fun?

"Why don't you go home and . . . make a list," says Nikka gently, patting him on the shoulder like he's an over-tired toddler. "Make a list of all of the logical reasons for what happened and then tomorrow we'll meet at the store and talk it over."

I open my mouth, but she raises an eyebrow at me, so I keep quiet.

Luke looks at both of us, then nods slowly, obviously relieved to have something "real" to do.

Momma materializes, looking all *It's Late*, and no one says anything while Luke stands there looking awkward. Then he waves, murmurs some goodbyes, and walks out.

"I don't know how you did that," I say. "Smooth. Some might say . . . snakelike."

Nikka grins. "He doesn't mean to be all"—she waves her hand—"whatever about all this. He's coping." At my warning look, she sneaks a glance at Momma. "Let me just grab some fruit. Meet you in your room."

I expect Momma to say something about eating in the bedroom, but she's already leaving, heading toward . . . Tunde's room?

For a wild second I wonder if he's in there. If I saw my dead brother in the pool today, who's to say he wasn't going to be laid out on his bed right now, with his sneakers on and that lazy smile?

"Momma!" I start, not sure what I'm going to say. She looks at me. "Um . . . where are you going?"

She doesn't answer, but comes over to me and touches my cheek gently, the way a mother on TV would.

Before the mother dies.

She walks away quickly and opens his door.

I don't want her to go into that room.

I run to the door, just as it slams in my face.

Nikka comes out of the kitchen and grabs my arm, babbling like it's Christmas morning and she just caught a glimpse of a pile of presents under the tree instead of my brother. *My dead brother.* "Come on," she whispers, "I'm going to have to go home soon, I may actually do some homework tonight, but I don't know how I'll focus. We should have a sleepover soon, yeah, because we have to plan, right? We'll leave Lil

Lukey out, he doesn't know the stories, so he doesn't get it."
She takes a breath. "What do you think? Do you think it was
a ghost? Oh my—wait, have you seen him before? Can you
touch him? Was he solid? I mean, I can't believe—"

I put my hand over her mouth mostly because I'm
listening for sounds from Tunde's room and a little bit
because I know how much she hates that. Silence. Nikka
brushes my hand away, her eyes snapping, but she shuts up.
Schrödinger whines a long meow, and Nikka picks him up
and closes my bedroom door behind us.

Nikka seems to take up a lot of space in my room,
but she stays quiet for a few minutes. I clench my fists as she
wordlessly examines my Klein bottle hat and the matching
plate tectonics scarf that I've almost finished.

"So," she says finally, sitting on my bed, "do you
think he was a ghost?" Schrödinger settles on the pillow and
begins to wash himself.

I'm not sure if I can take myself seriously at this point,
and part of me still can't trust Nikka's willingness to plant herself so firmly on my side. She's humoring me, the same way
she told Luke to go make a list. "No," I answer slowly. "He
seemed too . . . real, you know? Not . . . dead. But not . . .
undead." I can't believe I'm having this conversation. I don't
mention the lifeguard. I need to talk to someone I can trust.

Alisia? She knew about the Mole People. She'd
talked about a book with an underground magic school.
"That makes it more true, no?"

Alisia would take me seriously, no questions asked. For a brief moment I wonder: if I go to the third-floor bathroom right now, would I find Alisia there?

"Hmmm, so we'll rule out zombie too, then," Nikka mutters, like she's crossing things off a grocery list. "Are you sure he didn't say anything? Send some sort of message?"

"Of course I'm not sure!" I snap. "I was a little distracted, maybe?" Schrödinger jumps to the floor and walks over to me, meowing. I hold my breath, wondering if my cat is going to start talking. I wouldn't put it past him at this point.

"Are you sure he didn't give you some kind of message or something?"

"He kind of . . . there was some money there," I say. "Coins. He—we reached for them. But then they . . . were washed away." I glance up to see how she's taking this in. "I think he . . . needs my help."

"Coins!" she cries, a little too loudly. Now Schrödinger meows at her. "Sorry," she mutters to him. "That makes sense." She must see the confusion on my face and adds: "Maybe . . . maybe he hasn't crossed over yet."

"He was kind of standing in the water, next to a door," I say. I lower my voice to a whisper because I don't know if I even want to hear my next words. "So maybe I . . . If he hasn't crossed over, maybe I can help . . . bring him back."

Nikka looks at me like my skin has gone green and I'm carrying a broomstick. "Not that I agree with Luke, but . . . that's a little . . . Stephen King, don't you think, cuz?" she says gently. "And we know how that turned out. I'm thinking something different. The water, crossing over . . . ?"

I just stare at her.

"The River Styx? Charon? Did you really forget everything?"

Of course I remember, I just . . . I didn't think *she* did. I thought she'd stopped reading anything that didn't come on her phone and with a recommendation from an "influencer." It's been a long time since we acted out the stories of hidden princesses and monstrous boogeymen. How is she still *that* Nikka, and this one too? How are some people able to hold all these selves without dropping something? I think of that gruesome murdering baby in *Pet Sematary*. *No fair*, he said. *No fair*.

"What are you getting at?" I ask carefully.

"So . . . maybe Tunde hasn't paid his fare, to get to the Other Side," she continues slowly, adding, almost to herself: "Ha, you know how he was always borrowing money." She picks up the Klein bottle hat and puts it on. I won't tell her that it looks cute.

I need to look up that whole river thing again. But I'll go with it for now, if it means she'll help me go back to the pool.

"Um, OK . . ." I start, "so, maybe I can do it for him. Pay the fare, I mean."

And then maybe I can rest in peace.

We sit in silence until Schrödinger begins to whine again. Nikka rises.

"I'm sleeping over tomorrow. The mothers won't mind. See you in the morning," she whispers. "Don't leave without me for once."

"You're making a lot of declarative statements," I mutter. She picks up the cat and hugs him closer to her, and they both glare at me.

"I'll bring a treat for you next time," she coos at Schrödinger, and I swear my cat smiles. Traitor.

After Nikka leaves, Momma opens the door and comes out of Tunde's room. She doesn't look traumatized, and I almost feel silly. Almost.

"Has Nikka left?" she asks. "Your Auntie Marguerite was wondering what was keeping her. She'll be sleeping over tomorrow, I heard."

How did she know? "Oh," I say. "Were you on the phone? Because I—"

"Good night, Ayo," says my mother slowly, drawing out my pet name as though she's just learning it. "Go to bed."

"But—" I sputter.

She kisses me on the cheek; I try not to flinch at the current of electric shock that passes between us, even though it hurts a little more than it should.

"What were you . . . why did you go . . ." I don't know what to ask.

"To bed," she says firmly, walking toward the front door. I notice the gleaming gold store supply room key around her neck, and a small black plastic bag in her hands. "And stay there," she adds without turning around. She stops and smooths out her wrap as though she's on her way to the door to welcome a stranger. "Do not leave your room until morning."

I wake to a nudge from Schrödinger and I push him away gently as I reach for my phone. Two-thirty already! I can't believe I slept that long! I struggle to sit up; a hand on my shoulder stops me cold.

Momma is sitting by my bed.

"Sssh," she whispers, as if I've called out in my sleep. She strokes my cheek gently and I want to lean in so badly.

She leans down and kisses my forehead. This day has been filled with more Momma-love than I've had in a long time. "Rest tonight," she says, with a smile that doesn't quite reach her eyes. But she strokes my back so gently I want to cry tears of joy.

"But Momma," I whisper, suddenly wanting to tell her about the pool, about the daughter she might wish she'd never had, about the weight of my days. I sit up all the way, and she draws me into her arms. I have to squeeze my eyes tight to keep from losing this. Schrödinger has knocked down one of the ibeji figures on my nightstand. Momma breaks our hug, picks it up, and sighs. It's cracked and split.

"I should have gotten more of these when I had the chance," she says. "I'm surprised they've lasted this long."

"Maybe you can ask Auntie Bunmi," I say. My mother's college roommate was actually Nigerian-American, and had married a rich English guy who did something vague but apparently inappropriate in the oil industry, judging by the way Momma's lip curled when she mentioned his name. They'd moved to Banana Island in Nigeria, and when I was little, I could tell that Momma thought that Auntie Bunmi's vision of moving "back home" was less Marcus Garvey and more Real Housewives. Auntie Bunmi made occasional trips back to New York, claiming our city "over" and always asking Momma how she managed anything without house boys.

"Bunmi?! These are from Bed-Stuy, just like your Auntie Bunmi," Momma replied, taking both statues and putting them in a drawer. Auntie Bunmi, by moving to my parents' "spiritual motherland," had gone even further than Auntie Marguerite. When we pointed out that Auntie Bunmi did actually have a Nigerian parent, Momma just sucked her teeth, which Tunde and I agreed was one of the most Nigerian things she could do. She would always grumble under her breath, imitating Auntie Bunmi's apparently put-on "Continental" accent and letters using words spelled with "ou" and "ae." "Can't escape the colonizers," Momma would mutter, as she put on one of her Moshood dresses before a visit.

I never told her how, when I was six, Nikka gleefully told me that my parents were "fakers" themselves who had fallen in love over an agreement to construct a story of a back home that didn't really belong to them.

"My dad is a real Nigerian," she'd said proudly. "Like, *from* Nigeria. He should own that store, not your parents. *My* dad says they don't even know what they're *doing*."

Our dads had never been close; Uncle Jidé's tendency to laugh at my father and his affinity for all things Nigerian had put a bit of frost on things, even though they were married to sisters. Sometimes now, I wonder what my father had meant when he'd said "phonies." If it was mostly the frustration of knowing who you knew you could be, if they would just let you be great.

Once, I told my mom that one day I'd trace our roots back past our enslaved ancestors to our Yoruba family—the kings and queens who lived in palaces more spectacular than any Auntie Bunmi house.

"You don't have to bother with that," she'd said. "If you know in your heart who you are, that's enough. Our story is written in the stars."

Tunde had leaned over and quipped, "Plus, there's like eleventy billion Nigerians anyway. *All* Black people are basically Nigerian." We'd laughed at that, all three of us, but afterwards, I switched to eating my eba with a fork when we had soup for dinner.

Last year, as we'd walked home from the subway station, Tunde had said that he thought our parents were probably right about us being Nigerian. "Look at how they've scammed so many people into believing it. Even us—I really thought I was named after some great uncle or something when they just Googled."

"You can't say stuff like that," I replied. "It's . . . offensive."

"But it's OK because I'm Nigerian, remember? That's my point." And we'd laughed and fought over who would pay for an order of fries from the Chinese takeout place on the corner of our block.

Now, I look at Momma, holding the broken statue. "Do you remember the story of the little girl who sold palm oil?" I blurt out. She looks back at me blankly and doesn't respond.

I don't know why I think of that one now. Like so many of the stories she used to tell, it didn't exactly put me to sleep. Sisters who took turns following goblin tricksters into the woods. The good one makes it back home and receives riches. The selfish one ends up lion food. I used to want to be the good girl, but I knew I'd have a hard time just following some troll into the void without some assurances. Plus, it seemed to me that her sister got punished for doing exactly what her mother told her to do. They both just wanted to make their mommas proud.

When we shared a room, Tunde would read to me from his math textbooks after Momma had read some of the stories from our big book of blunt *West African Folktales*, or worse, told the ones she remembered from her grandmother, which were a diasporan mishmash of matter-of-fact violence and comeuppance for cheeky kids. Some of those stories needed to come with a warning.

My head hurts, but there are still more hours to the night. I'm going to sleep for an hour and then go sit on watch.

"Good night, Momma," I say.

"Good night, Ayo," she says. She starts to sing. It's a song I know, about river crossings and finding your way, but I can't quite remember. She used to play it on Sunday nights . . . I close my eyes.

I don't know when she leaves.

Don't Let the Bedbugs Bite

In the gray of the next morning, I wonder if I dreamed Momma's bedside song, but my head hurts, as though it spent hours keeping me from dreaming anything at all. I'm desperate to talk to Alisia at school—it can't be a coincidence that she was talking about the Mole People . . . the Underground . . . portals to Other Places . . . but she's absent. I want to tell her about the third-floor bathroom, about the hole, the piece of paper. *Kindred spirits,* she'd said. *Trust me.* Maybe if I'd been less afraid, maybe Alisia would have been with me at the pool instead of Nikka and Luke. Maybe then Tunde would have . . . stayed? *Am I really thinking like this?* It doesn't make sense, but something in the pit of my stomach is telling me that maybe we're tethered together in some weird way, and if I hold on, I won't fall completely away into whatever all of this is.

Or maybe I'm just hungry.

By last period, my body feels like a series of tangled wires, tight and confused. My head hurts, and I don't have the energy to spar with Nikka as we make our way home from school.

That must be why I don't say anything when she leads me to DIG for a chic healthy meal. She's paid for both of our little boxes of roasted veggies, starch, and protein before I even realize we've ordered. When we sit on the same bench in Riverside Park where I'd met that sad, solemn little girl, I open my box and eat every last bite without stopping.

"Thanks," I say, gathering my trash. "I didn't know how hungry I was." Then I wait for a joke, but Nikka just takes the trash from me and walks over to the garbage can, where a squirrel waits. She grabs my hand and we walk home.

In my room, Nikka flops down on the purple beanbag chair and lights a candle. "You know, I was wrong, I kinda like how dark it always is in here. It's . . . cozy."

"You know that's your bed," I say. "Might want to be gentle."

Nikka leans back. "Oh yeah, I forgot. It's been a minute since we've had a sleepover, Cuzzly Bear." She looks around the room. "Do you ever think about redecorating, though? How long have you had that space poster up there?"

"That *space poster* is the *Endeavour* and it's signed by Dr. Mae Jemison, thank you. Respect. Maybe you shouldn't worry about my walls."

"Oooh, now that's an opening for a meta-convo if I've ever heard one. I got a lot to say about your walls, boundaries, barriers . . . "

I ignore her and pull my knitting basket up onto the bed with me.

"What are you making?" she asks.

"A tardigrade," I say. When she raised her eyebrows, I sigh and add, "Also known as a water bear. Remember the *Octonauts* episode when we were babysitting Trina? Microscopic animals that can survive just about anything—even space travel." I show her the picture on the knitting pattern. "This is magnified, of course." Nikka actually looks interested.

"Huh," she says. "Weird." So much for interested. "So anyway, I brought some stuff too. Combination of sleepover fun and quest supplies." She opens her baby-blue weekend bag. "Gummy bears—chocolate-covered and plain—protein bars, mani/pedi kit, Swiss army knife, nunchaku, Doritos, mace, tissues . . ."

"Hold up," I say. "Did you say gummy bears and nunchucks? Does not compute."

"Actually, I said 'nunchaku,' and for your information I do remember the *Octonauts* episode—ooh, can we watch it tonight? I'm sure it's on YouTube."

"Can we go back to nunchaku and mace? What are you even talking about?" I drop my knitting and fold my arms. "And we are not going on a 'quest.' This is not a book."

Nikka mirrors my folded arms. "Are you really going to waste time arguing with me? You know I'll win. This thing is . . . we both agree that what happened was—"

"*My* business," I say. "It was . . ."

"It was Something Serious," interrupts Nikka. "And Something Serious means it's *our* business. Those are the rules, remember?" When we were little, we'd shared a yellow notebook for all of the Somethings Serious we were planning to investigate, like what happened to our shadows after we went to sleep, and what parents talking in hushed tones behind closed doors could mean.

After a pause, I start knitting again. "OK, yeah, this is Something Serious, but . . . it's just different. It's not a game, Nikka."

"That's what the nunchaku are for," Nikka says, smiling a little. She fidgets for a while, looking away, then starts to braid her twist out into four large plaits. "Listen . . . I've left you alone for too long. I'm sorry. I'm really sorry." I'm mesmerized by how quickly her fingers move through her hair. "I messed up. So I'm in this now. And the sooner you accept that, the sooner we'll figure this out." I can't process the apology, much less accept it right now. She starts on the last braid. "You know I can help, Harriet. You know I've got skills. I've got jokes. I've got mace." She smiles again, and I have to laugh.

"You look like you're six years old with your hair like that."

She tosses her head and poses. "Still cute, though. I forgot my bonnet; do you have one I can use?" She starts walking toward the dresser drawer before I even point her to it.

"I know Luke is being all head in the sand," she continues, rummaging through my things. "But you and I both know that was not the end." She takes a step back as I come over, grab my black bonnet with the constellations on it, and thrust it at her with one hand, closing my drawer with the other. "We started something together, and . . . Tunde's a part of it. I don't know how or why, but we're going to get to the bottom of this together."

"He was *my* brother," I mutter.

"And you know what Auntie says: I'm your sister." Nikka touches my arm gently, and it burns. She doesn't move away when I flinch. "Remember the matching pleated skirts? Remember? I'm sorry, cuz. I've been hurting too, OK? I'm sorry. I'm here, and I'm sorry." She looks away. "And that's not an excuse . . . it's an . . . explanation."

Was she sorry for the time she told me we'd been switched at birth, and she was Tunde's real sister? Or for just being the person he'd obviously wanted for a real sister? Or, even worse, being the one who should have been? I don't know what she's sorry for, and I don't want to ask and open doors that I'm not ready to walk through.

"What did you mean before, about Luke not knowing the stories?" I ask instead.

"Huh?" She starts painting a coat of fuchsia polish over her already pink nails.

"You said he didn't get it, because he doesn't know the stories."

"Oh, yeah, you know, remember how him and Tunde would make fun of us when we told them we were trying to tesser?"

After I'd read *A Wrinkle in Time*, I even tried to come up with a formula for tessering. "How did you know about that?"

"Are you serious? We had the club, remember? Well, secret society. Just the two of us. And only two meetings. But we had notebooks and everything. You really don't remember?" She opens the bag of chocolate-covered gummy bears. "I was always so jealous, especially when you guys fought."

"What?"

"You and Tunde. The bickering. It was like a TV sitcom. I wanted that so bad. You'd fight, then you'd be playing together ten minutes later like nothing happened."

"That's . . . *not* how it was," I say.

"I saw it with my own eyes," answers Nikka, handing me the bag and taking out a small bottle of turquoise nail polish. "I remember. I remember it all."

A week after The Funeral, I'd opened the front door just to get away from the loudness of my parents' silence and the screaming in my own ears, and Nikka had been there, sitting on the stoop, just waiting. She'd handed me a bottle of water.

"Gotta stay hydrated," was all she'd said. And we'd sat there until the moon was aggressive in the sky. Before she'd left, she'd squeezed my hand hard, as though she were passing something to me, through me, and it wasn't until I was eating lunch the next day that I'd realized I'd slept through the night for the first time in two weeks.

I forgot all about that. I look at Nikka now, admiring her own nails.

"I've been waiting for this," I say softly, and she leans in to hear. "Waiting for God to pull the rug out from under me."

"Uh, excuse me, I don't think that's how God works," she says, returning to making tiny turquoise dots at the tip of each nail.

"Hello, Noah's Ark?" I say. "Everybody's just scared and trying to make sure they make it onto the boat. Remember in Sunday School? Ms. Teresa just hugged me when I asked why God didn't just help the people do the right thing. I woulda thought Noah was out of his mind too, building a giant boat when it had never rained."

"I mean, I never understood that either, but I'm no genius, so . . ." Nikka shrugs. "There's a lot in there I don't get. I do get the God-loves-you-no-matter-what parts. *That* I can get behind."

"Typical. You pick and choose what works for you. That's definitely not how He works."

"I would say She, but *your* God is definitely a guy," she replies. She waits a beat, but I don't laugh. "I mean, you act like God's got a trapdoor on the ready, you don't know when or where to expect it, but it's coming, just because, and whoosh! You fall through. What I remember is the rainbow and the cotton-ball sheep we made. Remember?"

"No," I answer. "Must be nice." Nikka, who was proposed to three times in kindergarten and who always got extra sweets from the aunties, would obviously believe in the shiny, happy God. "Whatever. I'm not trying to get into some spiritual discussion with you. Talk to Charisse and your other friends about it." I pause. "I dare you."

"Why would I talk to them about this?" Nikka mutters back. "It's not the kind of conversation we have."

I let the silence settle between us.

"But you brought it up—"

"*Stop*, Nikka. If you want to come with me, you stop when I say stop."

"So I'm going?" She jumps up and hugs me, smudging the polish on her right hand.

"Yeah," I say. "You can come. Only because you're bringing stuff. But it's still my . . . quest or whatever. You follow my lead. And stop eating the supplies." I put the gummy bears back in her bag. I notice that she's got a lot of tissue packs in there. Does she know how much I cry?

"You have always been so bossy," Nikka says, calmly taking the gummy bears back out. "But yay! Dynamic Duo time! And we may as well eat these now, they're like more perishable. Oh, and I swiped this—" she pulls out a large wrench, "from my mom's toolkit. You got a bat? I couldn't find ours."

I laugh again, then I go to my closet. "Yeah," I answer. "I do."

I'm here, and I'm sorry.

After we shower and promise Momma that we won't eat in the bedroom, Nikka jams in beside me on the bed and we try to open the Doritos bag as quietly as possible.

"We're going to have to brush our teeth again," I say. "Between this and the gummy bears we're going to have serious yuck mouth."

"So what? Anyway, as long as you brush before you see Luke again, you're good. Ooooh, wait, maybe Teletubbies before *Octonauts*? The episode with the little girl and the moko jumbies? You know which one."

"What are we, three? And what does my breath have to do with Luke?" I ask. My face feels hot. "Also—listen, what did you mean when you said—"

Nikka smiles at me big and I trail off and look away. Damn! She wins again. Even though she's just down the block, Nikka has lived a world away from me since we were nine, and no longer invited to the same birthday parties. But . . . I can't shrug off her *I saw him too.*

I know I can probably pump her for Luke Info like *doeshehaveagirlfriend* and *doyouthinkhelikesme* and she'd probably explode with joy. I can't give her that.

Not yet.

That "yet" surprises and scares me, but I tuck it away for now—something to think about when I can think about other things. She's given me something tonight, though. I'm not sure what it is, or if I really want it, but it's here, nunchaku, nail polish and all. We don't talk much more, but we watch two Teletubbies episodes and I let her paint my nails purple.

COME ON IN, THE WATER'S FINE

"Harriet!" Momma's voice breaks into my dreamless sleep. I shoot up. It's 7:30 in the morning, Nikka is nowhere to be seen, and Schrödinger is looking at me with contempt. How could I oversleep like that?

Oh, yeah.

I shower quickly and efficiently and race downstairs.

"Your cousin left—she had a test this morning, but she said to text her so that you can meet for lunch," says Momma, putting sliced papaya and a smoothie on the table. "And when you see her, please remind her that the Peace Fountain does not actually contain water, so unless it's magic, it won't cause you to get wet."

Oops. I am torn between enjoying the fact that Nikka's been caught in a lie and squirming because I was a part of that lie and have no idea what to say if Momma starts asking questions again.

"Um, OK," I answer, and avoid her eyes by taking out my phone and fiddling with it. I slurp up half of the smoothie and grab the Tupperware dish of papaya. "I'll eat on the way—thanks, Momma," I say. I have so many questions, but I'm going to have to answer them myself. "Thanks, Momma," I say again, trying to tell her everything with those two words. "See you later."

When I get to the door, I turn back to look at her. She's finishing my smoothie and pouring a cup of tea from the ebony porcelain pot. A well-worn paperback is spread facedown on the table; I can't see the title. Momma's still in her nightclothes, which means she hasn't taken her morning walk yet, which is odd. I guess she overslept too. That key is still around her neck. I walk back over to her.

"Are you . . . OK?" I ask.

"Of course," says Momma. She holds my right hand in both of hers, looks down, and frowns. "Wait," she mutters, and reaches into a drawer for a mini tub of Vaseline. I'd slathered on lotion quickly; I guess I'd missed some spots, and we don't do ashy, even when there are other things to worry about. She rubs some Vaseline over and into my hands, and for a second, I think she's going to rub it into my face the way she used to after swim class when I was little. It was like she was always trying to make sure I'd never be ashy again, even though we both knew that the constant presence of chlorine in my life made that impossible. I'd thought I was being punished until I saw a woman doing it to her twins on the subway one day, and they'd all been smiling. Momma pauses, then just pats my hands again and puts the Vaseline away.

"Go on to school, you'll be late."

"Yes, Momma," I say.

Fully moisturized, I go straight to the pool.

"Hey, Miss Harriet," calls out a voice; it's the grandmother of one of my unofficial pool students from two years ago. I remember them well. It had taken the little girl three weeks to stick a toe into the water, and I'd held her hand the whole time. Now I wonder if she knew something I didn't. Her grandmother had crocheted me a poncho that Nikka promptly took and made fashionable. I clench my fists. I sincerely hope that whatever is going on in that water doesn't try to mess with one of my kids.

I don't know why I'm here now. Can I be here without Nikka and Luke? But I think, despite what I told Nikka, if I can fix this myself, I will. Can I finally be the hero of my own story? Do they have to know everything?

I wave to the grandmother and walk past her and the other old ladies climbing the stairs, on their way to raise the roof in Golden Soles Dance class. Nikka and I had watched them once, giggling at the lone man in the class moving a beat behind everyone else. He didn't seem to care.

I slip through the door to the pool. There are no CAUTION signs, no signs at all now. I spot my lifeguard. I close my eyes for a second, take a deep breath, and look right in his face. Nothing happens. He sees me and walks over, and I use every muscle in my body to keep from backing up.

"Hey," he says. "No school today?" He continues without waiting for an answer. "The pool is closing for a while. Repairs. We're draining it tomorrow." He drums his magazine against his thigh. "Got to find some temp work in the meantime."

"I just want to hang out and do a few laps before school. I don't have a first period class, and swimming helps gets me a good start on the day. Like breakfast. But I didn't eat right before. Also, I'm . . . trying out for the swim team." *Too much exposition, Adu.*

He shrugs, and I have a terror-filled moment of wondering if his bored lifeguard skin will fall away and reveal . . . I don't want to think about it. Nothing happens and he winks.

"Whatever, I won't say anything, you're practically family," he smiles. "Want anything from the vending machine?" I shake my head and start stripping down to my suit.

"Cool. See you in a minute," he says, leaving. The heavy frosted glass door closes behind him, softly but surely. I realize that he may be the worst lifeguard ever. After all this is over, I should probably report him.

I walk all the way back to the wall. The lion's head stares at me, his face impassive, the water once again streaming from his mouth. The only way I'm going to get myself into that water is if I get a running start.

I run, my feet hitting hard on the warm concrete; I really, really want to squeeze my eyes shut, but I don't. It's only a few yards, but it feels like miles until I take a giant flying leap, and jump in.

Underwater, the pool itself seems undeniably alive. The water moves against me, and I have to use my strongest strokes to get to the part of the wall where I'd seen the door. The concrete is warm to the touch; I rub my palms along the wall slowly, coming up for air more often than usual because the water seems to be also pushing down on my head.

But still: nothing. Do I hear laughter? Or whispers? Did somebody call my name? Twenty laps, back and forth. No door, no Tunde, no explanations, no nothing. Maybe now, I need Nikka and Luke to make the magic—whatever kind of magic it is—happen.

I'll never tell a soul, not even my own, but there's a part of me that doesn't mind if that's true. That's tired of being alone almost as much as it needs to protect itself.

Thirty minutes later, I climb out of the pool and sit on the rough concrete in the empty room. My lifeguard friend still hasn't returned, and it occurs to me that after almost a year of lifeless chitchat, I don't know his name.

15

I'm sure that I've missed first *and* second period by now, but I also know that I'm still an "untouchable" because they don't know how to handle the *Tragic New Girl,* so they won't call home until I've been absent for at least three months.

I stand, keeping my eyes on the water, and even though I know that I didn't find anything—that there's no door, and the lifeguard is a total failure and he's getting Cheez Doodles and Mountain Dew from the vending machine, and that the most likely explanation is that I'm out of my mind because we knew that already . . . even though I stopped believing in Impossible Things after all of my prayers didn't work—I see the water moving more than it should, as though a ship was sailing through its waters. I remember the heat of the doorknob and Nikka's eyes when she said she saw him too . . .

That story, the one with the little girl who sold palm oil, pops into my head again. The goblin keeps telling the good girl, Taiwo, to save herself, but she is so determined to help her momma, she refuses, and keeps saying, "I will not turn back," and following. Or maybe it's because she is scared of what would happen if she comes back empty-handed? Either way, she keeps going. Both sisters do. I just need to figure out how to be the one who doesn't get eaten by lions.

By the time I get to school, it's just after 10:00 a.m.—my lunch period—and the aroma of morning meatballs assaults my nostrils as soon as I slip into the building behind a just-ending gym class. I go straight to the library without even stopping at my locker just in case Nikka's hovering and has questions.

When I get there, Ms. Valentine hands me a book like she's been waiting to do it for years. It's *The Mole People*. I mumble my thanks and take it with me to my table. I don't open it, and I tell myself that it's because I already have *The Works* in my bag, but I don't take that out either. I just sit.

"I knew I'd find you here," says the voice of Alisia behind me.

I almost hug her.

"OK," I say instead, because I am apparently committed to being awkward.

She slides into the seat right next to me, unfazed. "You didn't text me," she says. She nods at the book on the table. "Becoming a believer?" She leans so close that I can tell she had the meatball sub on today's lunch room menu. I'm both horrified and impressed by the idea that she'd actually eat that stuff. "Wouldn't you love to just check it out for yourself?"

I can't speak, and my head hurts because I don't know what's going on or who to trust, and also because I'm hungry. I take my sandwich out of my bag. She's looking at me, waiting for . . . something.

"Do you swim?" I blurt out. *What?*

She nods vigorously like my question didn't come from out of nowhere.

"I love the water," she says.

"I sort of work at this pool, well, really I just swim there a lot, and I used to teach little kids . . ." I'm babbling, and I take a deep breath. "Anyway. My parents' store is right around the corner from this old pool, and usually I go to work, then I swim. If you want to ever come there." *And maybe meet invisible sea monsters and dead brothers. Playdate!*

"That would be awesome," she says, "to go there together this time. We have so much to—" Alisia stops as Ms. Valentine calls out the five-minute end-of-period warning. She pushes the *Mole People* towards me. "You're checking it out, right?" she asks. "Sometimes a story is so different the second time around . . ." She lowers her voice. "The people underground, they are living their second lives, you know?"

I don't know. "What do you mean? I mean, maybe people sneak into the tunnels for a kick every now and then, but . . . you really think there's a whole city of people right underneath us now?"

"Well, at least they *used* to be people," she murmurs, smiling. "I figure living down there changes you, right? They probably become all ghostlike, like a scary movie?"

I look away, because there's something in her eyes that I can't read and it's like we're at the edge of something and all we have to do is link hands and close our eyes and

JUMP—

I used to think the word *downhearted* was funny if you took it literally, but the prospect of a friendship with Alisia really does make my heart rise and swell. The phrase "misery loves company" has a whole new meaning. Alisia and I don't have a history of princess and witch, pretend you don't know me, or stolen brothers. Alisia just might know who I really am, and still not care.

"Do you want to meet up later?" I whisper, still looking away. "They're draining the pool soon, for repairs, so I have to go back before it's too late. I mean, because it's my favorite pool. We can go together."

There's no answer, and I brace myself, turning back with a disclaimer ready. "I mean, not—"

She's gone.

I don't see Alisia for the rest of the day, even though she's in two of my classes. I linger at my locker after last period, until club meetings and practices start. I have a whole nonchalant *Maybe you misunderstood* speech ready.

"So, what's the plan?" Nikka chirps from behind me, smelling of peppermint and berries. "What happened to you this morning?" When I don't answer, she sucks her teeth. "OK, back to attitude, got it. Anyway, I've got my suit, and a flashlight that's supposed to be waterproof." I glance at her without speaking as we leave the school building and walk out into the cool, crisp autumn air. Now Nikka looks like a puppy, hopeful and a little scared, and if I wasn't more scared and less hopeful, I'd wonder at her attitude more.

Alisia spoke about going to the pool as though it would be a reunion. She talked about second lives and true stories. Nikka has awards she doesn't even realize she's won, and friends who work hard for her approval. Who thinks we're going on an adventure, and who will take the lead and wear the crown because that's how the story goes.

16

Nikka and I head home together before I even realize that's what we're doing. I'm not surprised when Luke is waiting for us on the stoop.

"Hurry up, we got to get to the store," he says. "Auntie's already there, I came to walk you over."

Nikka pushes past us both to put her things in my room. Luke and I just look at each other until she returns, still holding one of the backpacks.

"What's that for?" Luke asks.

"And where do you think you're even going?" I ask, even though I know.

"With you guys, of course," she says. "Luke, we can fill you in on the way to the store, but Imma need you to keep an open mind."

Luke and I sigh at the same time, and then we leave.

The store is unexpectedly busy. Momma's on the phone; Nikka rushes over to help her at the register. I watch Luke pack reusable canvas for a woman with long, red curly hair, who keeps rocking her double stroller and cooing at the twins inside; they look unimpressed.

"Oh," says Luke, looking at the label she hands him, "you said you wanted to send this UPS."

"I do," says the woman, rocking the stroller harder as though the babies had started fussing.

"Well, uh, this is a Priority Mail label," says Luke, flashing one of his I'm-cool-so-you-are-too looks.

"OK, so can't you just tell the guy that it's UPS when he comes?" she snaps back, rolling her eyes.

Luke glances at me, and I smile, but don't say anything.

"Well, um, it's like, the wrong thing," mumbles Luke. "And I may not be here when the UPS guy comes or we could be very busy, and I might not get to have that conversation," he finishes.

"You're like, totally wasting my time," she says angrily. Luke's grin disappears, and he looks back at me.

Oh, come on. "Here you go," I say, handing the woman the right form and a pen. "You can go right over there, fill this out, and as soon as you do that, your package will be on its way." She eyes me but takes the label and then goes to fill it out. Me and the twins smile sweetly at Luke.

"It takes a special way with people," I say, and Nikka giggles behind me.

The four of us work through the crowd quickly and efficiently, communicating without talking much, and the air feels warm and friendly—and it's like I've shed the old itchy me and stepped into a person who makes people happy. I hope that no one says anything so it can stay this way forever.

"So, where were you this morning?" Nikka sidles up to me as I'm pretending to organize the shelves.

I shrug, but don't move away. She has that hopeful look again. For the first time, I wonder if Nikka talks to me because she misses my brother. Because I help her remember.

She folds her arms. "Fine."

I glance over at Luke, who is taking the broom from Momma. I lower my voice to a whisper and Nikka leans in.

"I went back to the pool."

"Duh," says Nikka. "So what happened?"

"Nothing," I say flatly, and stare right into her eyes, daring her to laugh or pull down the curtain of camaraderie. "There was nothing there. It was like . . . like it hadn't ever happened. Except . . ." My throat closes, and I wait for the Voice to fill my head.

"Except you know it did," says Nikka, touching my shoulder gently. Now her nails are painted bright blue. When did she have time to do that?

"Your nails look good," I say. "That was fast. I don't know how you have time to spend on that stuff." It comes out dismissive, which is not what I meant. I close my eyes; the room is cold now, the spell is broken, and it's my fault.

"Oh, please," Nikka says, holding out her hands. "They're fake. All I have to do is stick them on and pull them off. I did it at lunch." She takes off the pinky nail and offers it to me. "Want one?"

I have to laugh. I stick it on my right pinky. We smile for a moment, and then Nikka looks serious and pulls a tightly folded piece of paper out of her jeans pocket.

"OK, well, while you weren't in the library, I was. And so was that Alisia girl, who acted like she didn't know me. I'm not feeling her at all, cuz, just so you know. Anyway, I did some more research. There's a whole system of tunnels under those buildings at the university. Students have been mapping it out for years. I think the place where—where it happened, is right here." She opens the paper, which is covered in scribbly lines that crisscross and zigzag, and points to a crude blue X on the paper.

"Where is this from?" I ask. "Your *Book of Magic Spells* from second grade?"

"So anyway, we just go back to this spot, and I—"

"Hold up, why are you talking like some kind of expedition leader? Give me that." I snatch her map, and she lets out a sigh. "Wait, I don't get this map. These places on here aren't even in the building. And that spot is definitely not where the pool is."

She lowers her voice. "That's where I think the magic comes in. See, there's this empty space between the X and the pool . . . and this note says this square is a trapdoor. I think it leads to like, another layer, that's where we want to go."

"Another layer, Nikka? Seriously?" Luke whispers furiously over my shoulder, making us both jump. "Can you chill with this? Auntie is right here."

I look more closely at the photocopied square that's marked "trapdoor." I think I can see a faint design and push my face closer to the page. "It's the same design that was on the door I saw him . . . go through," I say in a low voice.

"So . . . let's go back," she whispers. "You and me, OK? I promise I won't talk about your chest, and you promise not to treat me like a living LOL doll. Let's put both of our twisted heads together and work this out." She raises her voice to tattletale level. "Tonight."

Momma is moving toward us, so I speak quickly and quietly. "OK, OK, whatever. Tonight. You come up with the excuse, though. You're a better liar."

Momma moves past us to lock the door and I realize that it's closing time. She turns to me and Nikka. "I've brought you all dinner." When we just look at her, she walks back behind the counter, gesturing for us to follow. I push Nikka ahead of me. Luke stands by the door, twirling the broom in his hands like he's going to dance with it, so I wave him over too.

"Here," she says, reaching past Nikka and handing me our old picnic basket. "Set up."

I stand there staring the wicker basket that we used to take to Central Park on Sunday afternoons, filled with "white people food" as Tunde would say, snickering as we munched on pickles, sandwiches stacked with salami, ham, prosciutto, provolone, and sundried tomatoes, and sipped citrusy Italian sodas. I haven't seen this basket in a long time. Nikka, her eyes wide, nudges me, and we silently pull out the blue adire tablecloth that we used to use to play "Ocean Bandits." Luke grabs the plates and sets them down too hard. I fight the urge to pinch him, mostly because I'm pinching myself.

Momma goes into the office and returns with the slow cooker, and the room is instantly filled with the spicy warmth of pepper soup. She sets it gently on the cloth, then makes another trip, coming back with steaming eba. Momma learned how to make Nigerian food like she was going to be tested on it, watching endless videos online and taking cooking lessons from Uncle Jidé, who joked loudly one

Christmas that he'd maybe married the wrong sister. Nobody laughed. Momma always gave Nikka covered plates of Nigerian food to take home, with an extra sweet smile, murmuring softly about how she could teach Nikka since her sister couldn't.

Momma lowers herself to the floor slowly, shaking off Luke's silly gentlemanly arm, and then looks up at all of us standing there.

"Why are you standing there with your mouths open and empty?" she asks, laughing. Yes, laughing! Momma is laughing, and it hurts so good that I want to cry. "Let's eat!"

Glancing at each other, we sit. "I'll say grace," Momma says, bowing her head. Luke and Nikka bow theirs, but I keep looking at this strange new Momma, wondering if she's also from those waters, and if I'll be allowed to keep her.

In the dark of the moon, in flying snow, in the dead of winter,
war spreading, families dying, the world in danger,
I walk the rocky hillside, sowing clover.

Momma finishes softly. That's it. Not the usual grace, and not a prayer I've ever heard before. I look up to find that she's looking at me, and suddenly I wonder if she knows I've been going to Confession—if somehow my Momma has been the one on the other side of that little window every time.

"Um, I never heard that one before," I say. "Is it from the Prayer Book?"

She shakes her head, and just says again, "Let's eat."

So, with the light outside fading, and on the floor of the shop, ignoring the passersby who peer through the window, we do.

17

The pepper soup is delicious, and even Luke, whose Senegalese palate has been softened by the flavors of Provence, sops up every drop of fiery sauce in his third bowl with balls of eba. I eat fast and without pausing, ignoring Nikka's frown. I expect Momma to say something, but she doesn't, so I keep going and going.

The food kept coming and she ate it. Even the meat that she had given up a year ago—she bit into a fat salmon-colored hunk of ham and swallowed after only two chews.

She could feel people trying not to look at her. She could hear their murmuring, the low nervous laughs that accompanied uncomfortable empty chitchat. Once in a while, she felt a hand on her shoulder, but she never looked up. She just kept eating, balancing the Styrofoam plate on her knees.

Uncle Border stood in front of her, too close to ignore. Still she didn't look up. Uncle Border moved closer, and she imagined wisps of smoke beginning to rise up from the spot at the top of her head where his eyes fell. Standoff. She always lost these things with family members. She looked up.

"Let's go outside." Uncle Border's voice was low and dry. Harriet stood up, placing her plate at the edge of the bureau next to her chair, idly noting that it would probably fall off in a few minutes.

On the front steps of the church, they sat. Uncle Border slowly shredded a napkin into pieces and cleared his throat a few times. Harriet stared straight ahead. She was hungry.

"Your brother," started Uncle Border.

Harriet zipped herself up tightly.

"Your brother . . . Tunde . . . he loved you very much," he mumbled. Harriet said nothing. The sky was gray and heavy, and Harriet wondered if it would fall on them and kill them all—where would they be buried?—or if it would just rain already, hard and fast, the way she wished she could cry. She could feel Uncle Border trying to make eye contact. She looked up at him and then quickly looked away, at the napkin bits in the flowerbed.

"Tunde always loved you, Harriet. Your brother loved you."

Harriet stood up and ran. She started slowly, then picked up the pace, slipping a little in her stiff, shiny funeral heels.

I didn't always love him, *she thought.* I didn't always love him.

That girl is a liar, I think now, as I wipe my hands. I *did* love my brother, and I have a chance to prove it now. I stop eating, and look up to find Momma staring at me, hard but not angry, like she's trying to memorize me.

I stand up. "Momma, thank you for dinner."

"Auntie," Nikka begins in her honeyest voice, "you go home, we'll clean up. Don't worry about anything. We've got everything under control."

Momma's eyes roll so hard that I can't help but laugh. She looks back at me and smiles. "What does a mother do if she doesn't worry?" she says lightly.

"Worry about nothing, pray about everything," I mutter, thinking of the plaque that used to hang over the kitchen stove. I wonder what happened to it.

Momma nods. "Yes, you remember. But we're not always so good at that, are we? Even when we know what's right, we can't help but do wrong."

I can't lift my eyes to see if she's looking at me now.

And all of a sudden I remember.

Many Rivers to Cross.

"Momma, that song—" I blurt out.

"Who wants story time?" she asks, just as abruptly.

What?!

She smiles at me, and I'm mortified. I know I brought up the bedtime stories the other day. But *now*? Oh, Momma. What does it mean when you get what you need, when you don't want it?

I can't even bring myself to look at Luke, who—

"A story sounds great," he says. "My grandfather used to tell us stories after dinner. About Yumboes, these underground spirits of the dead. Used to scare me so bad . . ." He stops.

I look at Nikka, whose eyes are wide.

"Oh, come on," says Luke quickly, "Auntie, listen. They think—"

"What's the story, Auntie?" Nikka interrupts loudly, and I shove Luke hard.

Momma doesn't seem to notice our activity; she just nods.

"This story is about a little girl who sold palm oil." Momma's voice is low and sweet; she's almost singing now, the way she used to when I didn't want it to be bedtime.

"One day when the little girl, who was called Kehinde, had made palm oil, she took it to the market to sell. She stayed in the market selling her palm oil until it was quite dark. And when it was dark, a goblin came to her to buy palm oil and paid her with some cowry shells. Kehinde took the cowries, even though she knew that those goblins never meant good. She liked to give second chances. When Kehinde counted the cowries, she found that there was one short, and she asked the goblin for the cowry that was wanting.

"The goblin said that he had no more cowries, and Kehinde began to cry, sobbing, 'My mother needs every cowry I earn. I cannot let her down.'

"The goblin walked away, and Kehinde walked after him.

"'Go away,' said the goblin, 'Turn back, for no one can enter the country where I live.'

"'No,' said Kehinde; 'Wherever you go I will follow, until you pay me my cowry. I won't let my mother down.'

"So Kehinde followed, followed, a long, long way, till they came to the country where the people stand on their heads in their mortars and pound yams with their heads.

"Then they went on again a long way, and they came to a river of filth. And the goblin sang:—

Oh! young palm-oil seller,
You must now turn back.

"And Kehinde sang:—

Save I get my cowry,
I'll not leave your track.

"No Momma," I say. "She says '*I shall not turn back.*'"
"Rude," says Nikka. "Don't interrupt. Sorry, Auntie."
"Don't—"
Momma silences us both with a look. Then she goes on.
"Then the goblin sang again:—

Oh! young palm-oil seller,
Soon will lead this track,
To the bloody river,
Then you must turn back.

"And she was scared, but she replied:—

I shall not turn back.

I nod, and Nikka rolls her eyes.
"And he:—

See yon gloomy forest?

"And she:—

I shall not turn back.

"And he:—

See yon craggy mountain?

"And she:—

I shall not turn back.
Save I get my cowry
I'll not leave your track.

"Then they walked on again, a long, long way; and at last they arrived at the land of dead people.

"Kehinde trembled, but she said 'I am afraid, it's true. But I love my family and I will let love keep me going until you pay me my cowry. No more, no less, just what I am owed.'

"The goblin gave Kehinde some palm nuts, with which to make palm oil, and said to her: 'Eat the palm oil and give me the stringy pulp.'

"But when the palm oil was made, Kehinde gave it to the goblin, and ate the stringy pulp herself.

"'I don't need palm oil. Just what I am owed. No more, no less.'"

"And the goblin said, 'Very well.'

"By-and-by the goblin gave a banana to Kehinde, and said: 'Eat this banana, and give me the skin.' But Kehinde peeled the banana and gave it to the goblin and ate the skin herself.

" 'I love bananas but will wait for my cowry. No more, no less.'

"Then the goblin said to Kehinde: 'Go and pick three calabash. Do not pick the calabash which cry, *"Pick me, pick me, pick me,"* but pick those that say nothing, and then return to your home. When you are halfway back break one calabash, break another when you are at the house door, and the third when you are inside the house. You will get your cowry then.'

"And Kehinde said, 'Very well.'

"She picked the calabash she was told and started on the long road home. When she was halfway home she broke one calabash, and behold, many lovely creatures appeared and followed her.

"When she was at the house door, Kehinde broke the second calabash, and behold, more creatures appeared and followed her in.

"Then, when she had entered the house, Kehinde broke the last calabash, and at once the house was filled to overflowing with cowries, which poured out of the doors and windows. And the girl's mother hugged her long and tight."

I mean, I guess that's nice, but she only got hugged because she brought back riches. What would have happened if she'd come home short?

Momma goes on. "The little girl had a sister, and her name was—"

Here I interrupt her again. "Her name was Taiwo. If one was Kehinde," I muttered, "then the other is Taiwo."

Ever since I was a kid, Momma has told me stories of twins, and Yoruba twins were almost always called Taiwo and Kehinde. We didn't have twins in our family, but I think she and Auntie Marguerite liked to pretend that Nikka and I were their version.

Yeah, right.

But Taiwo was usually the firstborn. "But you're out of order—" I start.

"And her name was Taiwo," continued Momma, as though I'd said nothing. "Taiwo saw all that Kehinde had brought back, she shared in it, and she listened very carefully to the story that Kehinde told of her adventure with the goblin. The family rejoiced, but Taiwo held something hard and small in her heart. She went to sleep with that hard, small thing, and tended it so it grew large during the night. The next morning, when Kehinde offered her more of the treasures, Taiwo refused them. She decided that she would get more, for herself. So she snuck out ahead, made up her own palm oil, and she snuck off to the market to sell it."

The stories were always the same. Greedy girl gets her comeuppance. Good girl finds a man or whatever. Momma is mixing up the story a little, but . . . it's still like being tucked in. I'll save it.

"Taiwo went to the market. The goblin came, bought palm oil from her, and paid her with cowries. He gave the proper number of cowries, but that dishonest girl hid one and pretended that he had not given her enough. 'Thief!' she screamed.

"'What am I to do?' said the goblin. 'I have no more cowries.'

"'Oh,' said Taiwo, 'I will follow you to your house, and then you can pay me what you owe me, plus compensation for my troubles.'

"And the goblin said: 'Very well."

"Then the two walked together, and presently the goblin began singing, as he had done the first time. He sang:—

Oh young palm-oil seller,
You must now turn back.

And Taiwo sang:—

Pay me what you owe me, plus more for my troubles.

And the goblin sang:—

You must leave this track.

And Taiwo:—

I shall not turn back."

The rhythm of Momma's story is making me sleepy. I don't want to, but I shut my eyes.

Momma continues:

"Then the goblin said: 'Very well. Come along.' And they walked on till they reached the *land of dead people."*

This time, I feel extra weight on those words. She draws them out slowly, and her voice breaks on "dead." I open my eyes, but she is looking away, toward the door.

"The goblin gave Taiwo some palm nuts and told her to make palm oil. He said: 'When the palm oil is made, eat it yourself, and bring me the stringy pulp.' And Taiwo ate the palm oil and brought the stringy pulp to the goblin.

"'This is the least I deserve,' she said, eating the palm oil.

"And the goblin said: 'Very well.'

"Then the goblin gave a banana to Taiwo and told her to peel it. He said: 'Eat the banana yourself and bring me the skin.' And she ate the banana and carried the skin to the goblin.

"'I should have two bananas for what you have put me through,' she said.

"Then the goblin said: 'Go and pick three calabash. Do not pick those which cry, *"Pick me, pick me, pick me,"* but pick those which say nothing.'

"Taiwo went. She saw the calabash which said nothing and she left them alone. She ran to the others which cried, '*Pick me, pick me, pick me.*' They were glittery and beautiful and she picked three of them.

"Then the goblin said to her, 'When you are halfway home break one calabash, when you are at the door, break another; and break the third when you are inside the house.'

"Halfway home Taiwo broke one calabash, and behold, numbers of lions and leopards, and hyenas, and snakes, appeared. They ran after her, and harassed her, and bit her till she reached the door of the house.

"Then she broke the second calabash, and behold, more ferocious animals came upon her and bit her and tore her at the door. The door was shut, and Taiwo pulled and cursed, but she couldn't open it. And there, upon the threshold, the wild beasts killed Taiwo."

Luke breaks the silence. "Uh . . . that was scarier than the Yumboes."

"It's so sad, her mom was right inside and didn't even know she was being eaten alive," says Nikka. "Can you imagine?"

"Why did you tell us that story, Momma?" I ask. What does she know? What does she want me to do?

"You mentioned it the other day," she says. "I was just telling you what you want to hear."

The candles have burned low; the shop is swathed in murky gray and brown shadows, and it looks and feels like home.

"I'm going home," Momma says, slowly rising to her feet. "I'll go home and worry and I will remind myself to pray and I'll do both because I can't help it." She walks right up to me and hugs me, then Nikka, then Luke. She comes back to me, and slowly takes that key from around her neck and places it around mine. It's very warm.

"Momma?" I ask.

"Maybe you're right," she says. "We should do some organizing in that supply closet. It's not too late. You all can start, as long as you stay together. At all times."

"Auntie—" starts Nikka, then she swallows. "Um, that sounds like a good idea."

I am frozen, remembering the hug, remembering the story. I touch the key.

"Uh, what?" says Luke, looking from me to Momma. Nikka shushes him.

Momma touches my cheek so gently, it's only because I see her do it that I know she's made physical contact.

"Momma!" I cry, as she turns away, and I don't care that my voice breaks, I don't care that I don't know what's happening, what will be, or even who I am anymore. My Momma is crying.

And leaving.

The bells on the door sound hollow as she closes it, and the ringing seems to stay in my ears for a long, long time.

I should have gone after her.

That's what I think as I stand there, still frozen, staring at the door. I should have gone after her, I should have said something else, like *I love you I'm sorry Momma please I'm scared*—there were so many things I could have said, but I'm just standing here with this heavy key burning my collarbone, and once again I've missed an opportunity. I listen for the Voice, but there's only the ringing of the doorbells still lingering in my ears.

Nikka has been rummaging around behind the counter. Now she takes a step toward me and that breaks the spell. She hands me a backpack.

"What's that?" asks Luke, raising his eyebrows as I put it on. I bite back the obvious "It's a backpack" and don't answer. Whatever's inside is substantial; it feels like I've got a sleeping toddler on my back. She has one on herself, and after a minute, points Luke toward the counter. He huffs and puffs, then goes and gets the one she's packed for him too.

"Nikka . . ." I start. But as she grabs my hand and seems to shine at me, the warning I want to give just sticks in my throat. So I just nod, as though someone else is controlling my body.

She points to my uniform. "Are you going to keep that on?"

"Why? Does one of your social media influencers have tips on what to wear when walking into a nightmare?" I'm trying to sound light, but it's only after I say those words that it hits me full on. I turn away in case anything shows on my face.

Nikka zips her jacket all the way up as though she's about to head into a blizzard. "No, rebel without a pause. I was thinking that you might get cold. Or hot. Or something. Bring a jacket just in case." She pushes past me to the door that opens to the storage room stairway, then turns back and grins. "Of course it won't be as cute as mine."

I grab my orange hoodie that stays balled up in a corner and put it on without a word.

"Don't think I'm not coming with," she says, the smug smile leaving her face.

"I'm the one with the key, Nikka," I retort. "I need to open the door." Now it's her turn to keep quiet. I wonder if my heartbeat is hurting their ears like it is mine. I slide the key into the lock.

"Wait a second," says Luke, who's been standing there like a spooked statue. "Going where? No one's going anywhere without me. In fact, I—"

Nikka grabs my hand, and I open the door. A rush of cool air almost shoves me back, but I lean forward, and the two of us step into blackness.

INTO THE WARDROBE

The stairway is gone. There is no storage room in front of me. I've just walked through a door into the tiny, dusty room that's been there for years, except the light switch is not to my left where it's supposed to be, and there is a flight of stairs a few feet ahead that looks endless. Nikka is clinging to me like a scented baby koala and as I try to shake her off without tumbling down to who knows what, I hear a heavy rustle close by. Very close. I squeeze my eyes shut for a second, and try not to think about the news report of the giant mutant rat that some guy pitchforked a while back.

I stumble a bit as the steps finally end and my feet hit the ground. We continue to move downward, and even tiptoeing raises clouds of grit and dust. I hold out my arms to brace myself as the incline gets steeper and the darkness thicker.

"Why is it so dark?" Nikka whispers.

"We're *underground*," I say, as though everything's crystal clear, but I don't say any more, because I don't want to think about how creepy and unreal and *I-don't-even-know-what's-going-on* all of this is. I'm not sure if the goose bumps rising on my arms are from fear or the increasing chill in the air—either way, I pull my hood over my head. This place smells like living garbage, and I do my best to keep from gagging, mostly because Nikka is hacking and coughing behind me like a lung-cancer patient smoking a few last packs.

A scream is so close to the edge of my throat that I—

"AAAAAAAAAHHH!" screams Nikka, and we both tumble forward. I grab at the darkness around me, and realize that the walls are very close. I brace myself so that we don't fall any further as Nikka falls into me, coughing and scratching with her stupid nails. We lay there for a moment, catching our breath. My eyes are still not used to the heavy, dusty darkness, but we're alone as far as I can see, which is not very far.

Suddenly, running footsteps approach from behind us, and I scramble up into the fighting stance that Tunde taught me when I was ten and needed to use it mainly to defend myself from him.

Luke. He's hoarse and breathless. "What the—" he starts, tripping over Nikka and falling hard, drumming up a new cloud of dust.

I relax as they untangle themselves, coughing again, and sitting up. "Smooth," I say to Luke. "Very smooth."

"Why did you scream?" he retorts, rubbing his ankle. I look at Nikka. She shudders.

"Something . . . furry. I felt something furry . . ." she mumbles. As Luke and I continue to glare, she adds, "It took me by surprise, OK? Sorry." She stands, wiping her hands on her now filthy jeans.

"Sorry," she adds. "I just . . . you know, we're underground, and there are always giant rats in books, and . . ." She trails off, shuddering. "Have you seen any oversized cockroaches? Oh wait, I bet the fur was coats!" She looks at me. "Remember? The coats! Oh, wait, I hope they're faux, though. Real fur would be not cool. I mean, except for cave people or whatever, they needed them . . ." With all of her nunchaku and this-is-just-like-a-fairytale talk, she's clearly more rattled than she's letting on.

"Huh?" says Luke, who's sounding dazed enough for me to wonder if he hit his head when he fell.

I reach out and grab Nikka's arm so that she can leave Narnia and join us in the real world. "Never mind," I say quickly, moving toward the sound of Luke's voice. "Cave people, Nikka? Come on. Luke, are you OK? Did you hit your head? You look a little spaced."

"Of course I'm OK," he snaps. Nikka snaps on a flashlight and now I can see Luke struggling to stand. "And yeah, maybe I am a little spaced," the sarcasm clinging to his voice like the slime on the walls. "I'm having a conversation about giant cockroaches and faux fur coats. After I just fell through the . . ." He winces as he tries to regain his balance, then leans against the wall. "I just need to catch my breath."

"Luke, why don't you just wait—" says Nikka in her soothing toddler voice.

"Leave it alone!" he growls. "I'm here."

"A little late," murmurs Nikka, just like Momma.

He stares at her like she's just slapped him.

Nikka turns to me. "I'm sorry I screamed. So. Moving on. Forward march?"

Let's assess. I am scrambling around underground with a tiny backpack cutting into my armpits. The boy that I once tried to cast a literal love spell on when I was nine suddenly has this urgent need to babysit me after disappearing for eight months. My cousin somehow still manages to look cute after falling down the rabbit hole into a potential nightmare. And I'm down here because I think my brother—no Harriet, say it: my *dead brother*—might still be . . . what? Alive? Undead?

I say a Hail Mary—I've memorized it over the last few months—and add a quick prayer that Momma will forgive me for doing something so Catholic since the Hail Mary is so mother-oriented, after all. I remember a Sunday dinner when

Momma had made party jollof and Auntie Cynthia brought her spicy fried chicken that I'd waited all week for. Auntie Clara came in saying that she had joined St. Francis in East Harlem, and Brother Samuel told us that he'd spoken in tongues one sweaty Sunday afternoon in his daylong Pentecostal service and then found one hundred dollars on the street which was sure validation that it was the only Way. I got sent to my room after only one drumstick for asking Momma how she knew our church was the one that Jesus was in.

The cold air is relentless. I can't stop shaking. But I nod.

"You guys know as much as I do at this point—"

oh yeah?

It's back. Of course. I resist the urge to put my hands over my ears and keep talking. "But what I know now is that I have to go in here and figure out what all this has to do with . . . Tunde." I straighten up as much as possible. "Just come on if you're coming."

All three of us hear what sounds like a scream at this point. It echoes and dares us to join in.

"So far, so bad," murmurs Luke.

"It was one of the peacocks," I say. "From the cathedral."

"And we can hear them all the way down here?" he shoots back. "Wherever we are? Come *on*, Harriet."

Nikka's voice is hesitant. "There could be people down here, like that book that girl was going on about." When I don't answer, she continues, "In the library? When Alisia wouldn't shut up?"

I turn away from them to take a few steps. And then a few more. I don't know what I'll do if I'm left alone with the Voice, and worst of all, myself. Another step. *I shall not turn my back.*

Now *I'm* getting it wrong.

I want to burst into tears when I hear them moving along behind me. Without turning around, I whisper, "Thank you for coming with me."

OK, so Nikka's whole "magic is real" attitude must be catching, because I keep expecting the bottom to drop out, sending us into a spectacular freefall—something like hurtling through the space-time continuum and landing smack on top of my brother—but after what feels like hours of this agonizingly slow crouch-crawl, coughing and sneezing in clouds of dust that only seem to get thicker with each step, I'm feeling less like I'm on a quest and more like a trapped mine worker.

We are inching along and we stop at every sound, so we're going slowly; still, the ground slopes downward.

"Remember—" starts Nikka.

"Yes-s-s," I hiss. "We all watched it together. *Journey to the Center of the Earth.* You guys broke my 3-D glasses.

You can't do this every minute, Nikka. Every moment is not some magical memory straight out of a book or an old movie. It's already getting old."

"Uh, excuse me, *you* broke your glasses," says Luke. "You sat down in a huff right on top of them. I don't even remember why you were mad."

"Because she was awake," says Nikka. "And you and Tunde finished the popcorn. Then he almost choked and she had to Heimlich him and totally saved his life and—"

"Are we really talking about this right now? Because—wait, shhh, what was that?" I stop. "Did you hear that?"

"I was on *your* side," hisses Nikka.

"Wait," pants Luke, who's been bringing up the rear the whole time. He leans against the wall again, sending a bunch of somethings scurrying. Nikka shudders. His breath is coming in short, sharp bursts, and Nikka glances at me.

"Let's take a break, um, get our bearings," says Luke. "The backpacks, Nikka. What's in the backpacks?"

Good question. I glance at Nikka, who looks smug, and answers, "Just supplies . . . you know, things I thought we'd need for a . . . quest."

She is so annoying. "Thanks," I mutter, grabbing one.

I dig around in the dark and pull out three small water pouches and a bag of throat drops from one of the smaller front compartments. There are a bunch of tightly wrapped packets; I'll look through them later. Right now, those "candy medicines" as we used to call them seem like gold, and I pass them around first, then the water pouches. For about a minute it feels kind of regular, but as we're crouching in the darkness, I hear something in between wind and wailing, like the Zombie Castle at Playland, and I'm not laughing.

It's water. It's talking to me—no, *shrieking* at me—as we continue on in the dark. It's trying to tell me something, but I don't understand. All I can do is be very afraid and follow its sound.

We creep forward slowly, and the incline gets steeper.

"Ssh!" whispers Luke, even though no one has spoken for a while.

"What?" Nikka snaps.

I hear something dripping slowly, and far-off screams, and . . . footsteps? Multiple footsteps, moving quickly from behind us.

I know who it is before I see the three boys, now wearing retro 8 Ball jackets over their hoodies, casually running and smiling like we have no chance of escape.

"Don't turn around," I say to Nikka and Luke, and of course they both do; Luke raises up a little higher and I realize that we can stand upright now. *"Run!!!"*

We are running and falling and scrambling downhill, and the sound of rushing water is getting louder. I don't need to turn around to know that they're gaining on us; I can feel the back of my neck prickle. Nikka is still gripping my hand, and Luke is limping, so I grab his hand too and pull them both as we go further and further down until the ground . . . stops. I look down, but I can't see anything but blackness. I hear the rushing water below and don't know if there are rocks or waves or giant cockroaches, or . . .

"Hey," calls one of the Boys, lazily, like he just wants to chat. Their jeans and Timbs are so normal. Their hoodies cover almost their entire faces, but I can see that all three are smiling, and their teeth glisten like jewels. The air is even colder, and I can't imagine what that water must feel like. I pull Nikka and Luke toward me and whisper, "On the count of three . . ."

"One," starts Nikka.

I turn back around. "JUMP!" I scream, and I squeeze their hands tightly as I leap into the void, pulling them down with me.

19

We hit the water with a huge splash and it takes my breath away; I was right to aim for feet first, I don't know what the drop would have done to any other body part. I'm still going down, and I've lost my grip on Nikka and Luke, but I see them to my left and swim over to grab them both again. I'm not sure if the Boys have jumped in after us, but I'm taking no chances, so I flip and start swimming straight down. The water is getting darker and thicker and colder, like icy oil, and it's hard to push down, but they're here because of me and I don't let go. We're going deeper and deeper . . . and it's OK. I've never been a marathon breath-holder underwater; Tunde used to beat me at that too, but for some reason I am OK. I turn my head to look—Nikka is right with me, looking like a mermaid in a picture book, her curls fanning out behind her. Luke's eyes are wide and angry.

The water is churning, getting even blacker, colder, wilder. How long have we been under? How are our lungs not bursting? How would we make it back to the surface? Suddenly, Nikka's hand slips out of mine; she's opening and closing her mouth and gagging—I grab her hand again and try to smile. The freezing water hurts my teeth. I wiggle my right leg, and she gets it right away—we used to play Dolphin every summer at Candlewood Lake. She grabs my leg, and I wave to Luke, who is steady, but slowing behind us. And not far behind him, those three awful Boys, moving closer effortlessly, smiling as they gain on him. They look longer and pointier, and less . . . human, somehow, their bared teeth sharper, their eyes cold. I don't want to scare Luke. Whatever kind of weird water this is, I assume the rules of "you make it worse if you panic" still apply. I tuck my head and push back to him and stick out my leg to grab just as one of the Boys reaches for him. I pause for a second to kick hard, using Nikka to get two of the Boys in the head, and dip back down. The sound of the water is like someone screaming directly into my ears. I can see the bottom now, I think, and I don't know what's next.

Just keep swimming, just keep swimming.

Out of nowhere I remember how Tunde and I used to sing that little fish movie mantra to each other. I reach out and touch the bottom, and it's not the smooth concrete I expect, but soft and slightly fuzzy, like a throw or blanket that you'd fight over on a chilly night. I look left and right for a way of escape, then I realize that the Boys are gone. I resist the urge to shake Nikka and Luke free right away, turning all the way around to see where the Boys might have gone. Nikka is touching the floor too, and after making a face, she starts to scrape away at the black fuzz with her perfect nails, gesturing for us to join her. Luke does, then so do I. After a few frantic seconds, we are rewarded with what looks like a trapdoor, and since there's nothing else to do we pry it open and drop down through.

This time we hit the ground with a thud, and Luke groans loudly. As we sit up. Luke is muttering and rubbing his ankle; I edge closer to him.

"I think you did more than just twist this," I say. "Why didn't you say something before? I thought you were just out of shape."

He gives me a thin smile. "Out of shape? Yeah, right? You need to take a closer look at these guns." He makes a muscle, but winces when he tries to sit up straight.

"Just lean on me," I say.

"I can manage—" he mutters.

"So, either you lean on me, or you wait here," I continue, and he clamps his mouth shut as Nikka and I get him propped up against me.

"Do you think Auntie knew?" Nikka whispers after a few moments. "About . . . this?"

If Momma knew something, did she know everything?

She couldn't. She wouldn't have been able to hug me like that if she did.

"Maybe she knows something," I start, "and maybe, just maybe, you're a little right."

20

Now that it's dry, I can see that we're in some sort of hallway or tunnel. Dusty gray stones are embedded into the walls, like homemade bricks. Phrases like "BOB DIAMOND WUZ HERE," "T-Rex luvs Melinda," and random profanity are scratched into the stones, and more than once I see "NM to the Infinite Power" in a dull red ink. At first, I try not to breathe in the dusty air that smells like dirty laundry and moldy bread; Nikka silently hands us blue face masks, and she doesn't even blink an I-told-you-so.

There's just enough room for us to move through single file, so I have to pretty much carry/drag Luke on my back, which means we move at a snail's pace. His talking doesn't help.

"You don't have to carry me, I'm fine," he mutters, shifting and squirming and making things that much harder. I tell him so.

"Can you just *stop*," I say. Something scurries past our feet and it takes everything in me not to jump.

"The more you all try to make yourself believe in ghosts and juju and—look, we fell. Faulty construction, old building . . . you realize that we're just in an old subway tunnel, that's all. Probably rats and roaches and—"

"Shut up!" whispers Nikka. And this time he does. We move along in silence. I can hear my own breathing, and something else. Something familiar.

Water. Rushing water. Again.

We come up on the bank of what looks like a river, but it smells chlorinated, like pool water. Whatever it is, it's rushing past hard and fast, the water slamming against large, jagged rocks dotted throughout. Across the wide expanse of water I see a rough stone wall, with something square and gold breaking up the damp gray rock. The key burns my collarbone. I lean forward as much as I can without falling in, and it looks like a square manhole. I think I can make out a keyhole at its center.

"We have to get across," I say. I can handle this. Slow, steady front crawl, I can pull Luke, maybe dog paddle if I get tired. But I won't. *I shall not turn back.*

"What we have to do is figure out how to get back into the store," snaps Luke.

"Maybe Auntie," says Nikka, "maybe we should ask her—"

"You really want to worry her more?" I ask.

"I mean, you heard what she said, she's already worried," replies Nikka. She yanks at her hair and then her sleeves, as though she's trying pull herself apart.

I put a hand on her shoulder. "So we should make it worse. Got it. Would you do that to *your* mother, Nikka?"

"I was just asking!" she cuts back, shaking me off. "Stop trying to make me prove myself to you! I've earned my right to be here."

"Why don't you stop talking about this like it's some sort of reality-show competition?" I say. "Dynamic Duo, right? I knew I shouldn't have trusted you for a second."

"If anyone can't be trusted, it's you!" she screams suddenly. "You really think it's fun and games, babysitting you every day?"

The words hit me like a punch to the jaw.

She didn't mean any of it. The let-me-paint-your-nails and *Cuzzly Bears* and *Remember Whens.*

I didn't realize how much I'd believed her until I feel how much it hurts right now.

But, of course, it's what you deserve.

We stand there like we're in the most intense game of Red Light, Green Light ever. The dripping water sounds heavy, like it's full of more than just molecules of hydrogen and oxygen.

Stalling, Harriet? Not sure you can do this alone? Because you played yourself for a second didn't you? Make no mistake: This is All. On. You.

I turn away from them both. "I'm not going to keep arguing," I say.

"Why not?" asks Luke, his voice rough and scratchy. "Arguing is what you do. 'She has a late birthday,' 'She can't help it.'" He's breathing hard now, almost gasping, like he's been running a marathon at a sprint. Or like he's trying not to cry. "You *can* help it—you just don't *want to*. You *choose* to be this awful."

I draw in a deep breath and I don't turn around to face them, because now I'm just barely holding in the tears, and even in this darkness, I don't want them to see that.

"Was that part of T's instructions too?" I can feel him flinch. "I *told* you both to let me do this alone." I turn back toward the water, but my feet won't move forward. "I'm going. Now." It's so dark. I want to take a step, but I'm frozen. If I could just *see* better . . .

"Then I hope you're going to pull a boat out of that backpack next, because even you can't swim this," says Luke.

I shall not turn back.

"She doesn't have to swim," a voice calls. "Shows how much you know."

I look to the left, where fog rolls and pushes forward. When I squint, I can just make out a person's shape moving toward us in the shadows. I think it's a person; the voice was harsh and hollow, meant for consequences. My heart is pounding. "I can't see you," I say loudly, like I'm running things. "Can we help you with something?"

Laughter. "I knew you had it in you," the voice says, now warmer, and I realize that it sounds familiar. "I'm never wrong about these things. Yes, you can help me as a matter of fact. You can help all of us. But first," the fog retreats as if on command, and the shadow moves forward, dragging something large behind it. "I can help you."

It's Alisia, and she's pulling a boat.

I want to hug her, but I know I'm wet and slimy and gross—I look down at my clothes. I'm not. Not at all. I look as though I haven't been underground at all, and I'm bone dry. I glance at Luke and Nikka, who look like an illustration of "drowned rats." Nikka pulls clumps of the black fuzzy stuff from her hair.

"Oh look," she mutters. "The calvary."

"You mean 'cavalry,'" I whisper.

"No, I don't," she snaps back. Then her eyes soften a little. "Listen, I didn't—"

"You did," I say. "And it's done."

No take backs, cuz.

"Who—" starts Luke, just as Nikka says "Fancy meeting you here" to Alisia in the sweet-nasty voice she uses in the presence of a threat.

"What's up, Alisia," I say, all casual, like meeting up in an underground cave is perfectly normal. She smiles at me and I grin, in the middle of this madness, because I sense an ally, someone who might help me beat back all the ugly feelings coursing through me right now. Nikka's not even trying to hide her sneer. I trust my gut, and her obvious disdain is the clincher.

Alisia's boat is made out of some kind of metal, and has graffiti all over it—the kind I've seen in old pictures of New York City with fat bubble letters spraypainted in bright neon colors. I can make out the words "Tomb Runner" along the side.

"Sweet ride," says Luke, walking up to Alisia like he's in charge. "Who are you, what are you doing here, and what the—"

"She's Alisia, from school," says Nikka, and I can hear the eyeroll dripping from her words. "She's Not Like Other Girls."

"Ignore them," I say. "I guess you know this place. What's on the other side of that . . . door thingy?"

Alisia shrugs. "This is the first time I'm seeing that. Nor surprised, though. He told us something would happen when you arrived."

He? I want to say Tunde's name out loud, but it sticks in my throat. *I knew it.* This is what I've been waiting for. This is what has been waiting for me. If this were a book or a movie, I'd say something witty and nonchalant about how I was born ready or every moment of my life has prepared me for this one, but I just nod, and step forward like I'm about to enter the Hunger Games. Maybe I am.

"Hold up," barks Luke loudly.

"Back off, Luke," I warn, without turning around. "This is something I have to do." I take a deep breath. "Alisia, my gut tells me I need to get to whatever's on the other side of that door." I hold up the key around my neck. "Can you get us across?"

She nods. "I can definitely get you across. That's why I'm here. But those two," she shrugs, "I don't know. I don't think they're allowed." She leans in and whispers, "You would not *believe* what's in store for *you*. It's beautiful."

For me. Just me. For once. I turn around to Nikka and Luke. "*Now* will you go? I won't be alone."

"You're kidding, right?" says Luke. "You have to do a thing we don't understand, in a place we never knew existed, for a reason we don't know . . . because your 'gut' is telling you to? Oh yeah, of course, we'll just leave you to it so you can hurl yourself into—" he waves his arm at the churning black waves.

"That wouldn't be any different from normal," I mutter. And I see the flash of hurt and understanding in his eyes, and I'm glad. "This doesn't have anything to do with you. Whatever obligation you think you have, I applaud you or absolve you or whatever. Congrats. It's been real." And nice. For just a little while, when I was stupid and I let myself believe: It really was nice.

Nikka slides up next to me and whispers in my ear. "You don't think it's a little . . . convenient, her showing up down here like this? Allegedly to 'help'?" she says. "I know you don't want me to say it, but witches in stories—"

"*Convenient* is not a word I'd use in these bananas circumstances, Nikka," I cut in, without turning toward her. "You're just pissed off because she's on my side. Maybe she's a *good* witch, ever thought of that? She's never been anything but nice to me."

"She doesn't even *know* you!"

Exactly.

Out of the corner of my eye, I see Luke inching toward us, like he's a soldier about to launch a surprise attack. Nikka notices too; she shakes her head slightly, and he stops. She goes on, expertly pulling her hair into a high ponytail. "Cuz, I'm not leaving you down here. So talk to your little friend, do whatever you gotta do, because I'm not going. Look at Luke. He's not either. I'm not gonna tell you again. Well, I will if I have to, but—"

"OK, OK, shut up," I say. Now she's holding my arm. "You really stay trying to ruin things for me, don't you?" She literally tosses her head like she's queen of the swampy underground or wherever we are. I shake myself free and go over to Alisia.

"We don't have a lot of time," she says. "Believe it or not, this is what the calm waters look like. There have been so many storms lately, it gets kind of . . . volatile down here. It's not a place to stay, and I've already made my choice. I've got to get back before—"

"Back where?" asks Nikka, walking over and getting all up in Alisia's face like she's about to dance-battle her. "Can you get us back aboveground? We got here through the—through a door, um . . ."

Alisia just looks at her.

I want to shake my cousin, but . . . "Can you?" I ask after a minute. "Get us back . . . home? I mean, at some point?"

Alisia smiles directly at me. "Anytime you want. We all go back and forth and the university has no clue. If *you* want to go back now, I can show you the way. Or . . . I can take you through that door. It's your call."

I look back at Nikka and Luke, who are standing with their arms folded, like bouncers at a club. I sigh.

"I get that they're annoying, believe me I do, but . . . they got it in their heads that they're protecting me or something, even though—"

"You don't even have to tell me the stories. I know you've been through it." She walks over to Nikka and Luke. "But you two should leave now, before it's too late."

"If you're trying to scare us, it's working," mutters Luke.

"But we're still not leaving," says Nikka.

Alisia looks back at me, and I shrug. "They don't get it, or me," I say. "I think you understand."

After a moment, Alisia's face breaks open into a grin that makes me shiver. "Well, there's more where that came from," she answers. "So you can just hop in and we leave them, or . . ."

Arrgh! I want so bad to exist in a time when they aren't a part of my story but . . . I realize, even now, I can't. "Let them come," I say, trying to put ice in my voice. "We can ditch them later." I wonder what she meant by *more*?

Alisia shrugs and shifts impatiently. The waves are crashing closer to us.

"Yes," says Luke, holding his hands up like he's been captured. "Let's go."

We push the boat to the edge, and Alisia helps me into the middle, like I'm royalty, and nods the other two in. Inside, I realize that it's mostly a converted subway car, but the roof is gone, and there is something like skis along the bottom. "This is so cool," I say.

"We have a lot of future engineers," says Alisia. I want to ask *who's we*, but we need to get going. Alisia's appearance makes me even more sure that I'm on the right track—that I'm *on my way*. "Make yourself useful," Alisia says to Nikka, shoving a long pole into her hands. "Push off, then row. Do you know how to row? Or should he do it?"

Nikka doesn't answer, just grabs the pole, and promptly falls backward, almost tipping the whole boat over.

"Watch it!" yells Luke, who already looks queasy. If I look at him too long, I might puke myself. Some heroes. I wait for Nikka to hand the pole to Luke, but to my surprise, she settles in and pushes off.

"Buckle up," says Alisia, winking at me. "It's about to be a bumpy ride!"

I don't like amusement parks because I am rarely amused. "Amused" is for people who don't have to work hard to control their temper, and who only eat one slice of pizza and never the last one.

But now I remember that once I laughed until my nose ran and my stomach hurt, at an amusement park. Once upon a time I'd gone on a wild ride.

YOU MUST BE THIS TALL

When they were all little but old enough to know better, they'd snuck onto the Wildwater Rapids! ride once. Harriet had run past the "You Must Be This Tall To Ride This Ride" sign, behind the other three, toward the bored operator who didn't even look up, just took their tickets and kept trying to sweet talk the girls in line behind them. In the little log-shaped plastic boat, Tunde had buckled in next to Harriet despite her whispered "Noooooo! Get off!" and locked his arm around her shoulders in an angry hug. She'd tried to shake him off, but he only gripped harder. They'd both screamed the whole way. As recycled water slammed her entire face and body, she couldn't even scream. When it was over, Tunde had immediately pushed the safety bar up and jumped out without a backward glance. They were all quiet for the rest of the afternoon, even when Momma and Auntie Marguerite took out the foil-wrapped snacks from home instead of buying the five-dollar packets of stale popcorn and blue cotton candy they usually begged for. Then at our apartment, Tunde had done the boxer shorts dance thing and they'd both laughed and laughed, holding their stomachs, the tears streaming down their faces until they weren't sure they were laughing anymore.

This is ten times worse than the *Wildwater Rapids!* Luke is clearly trying not to puke and Nikka's hair is whipping around and getting in her mouth and her eyes are bugging out of her head. The black water is hitting us everywhere on our bodies, and I can't see or hear anything, all I can do is grip the sides. Alisia has pulled up another pole from the floor of the boat, and I don't know how she and Nikka are keeping us semi-upright, but I mutter random churchy words over and over like a nun in a horror movie.

We slam into the concrete on the other side and Alisia quickly jumps out and ties the boat around a metal post. I jump out too, spitting water and I don't even want to know what else out of my mouth and running to the gold square.

"Can you wait?" calls Nikka. "I just like, *saved* us. I need a moment."

Her teeth are chattering and she's shaking with cold; I'm somehow still dry and warm, so I just slow-clap. "Kudos.

You should look into a rowing scholarship just in case you don't get enough pageant scholarships."

You choose to be this awful.

Alisia laughs. "And you're welcome for the help, in case you didn't notice," she adds. Nikka says nothing, and Alisia looks at me as if to say, *See?*

Luke almost falls climbing out, and I go over. "Come on, just lean on me." He waves me away. "You being stubborn is going to slow us down."

"We *should* slow down," he says, pointing at the manhole cover. "You're about to put your key in that lock. What kind of door is that even supposed to be?"

"I don't know, maybe the kind in a world where we can breathe underwater and maybe see ghosts?" snaps Nikka. "We said we'd follow her lead, so . . ." She tries to shrug, but she's shivering too much. Luke opens his mouth then closes it.

They are so close that they are literally breathing down my neck. I match their rhythm, closing my eyes for a quick second before I put the key into the lock—and turn.

21

The door twists open from the center, like a puzzle, and I step through the opening first, into . . . a party?

Thousands of string lights hang from the ceiling of a large stone room, and giant torches stand on glittery columns in the corners. A horde of kids who look about my age are dancing, and laughing, and talking, and singing like it's normal to be partying a gazillion feet underground. There are streamers, banners, disco balls, and even tinsel, like a holiday homecoming prom ball all in one. A real live DJ wearing a silver helmet and giant red sunglasses leans over a deck on one end of the room, who nods at me right before he yells out, "Oi! The princess has arrived!" in what might be the worst British accent I've ever heard.

But everyone stops and cheers. I look around for the princess until Alisia nudges me. "Wave," she says. "You can say something later."

"Wait, *I'm* the . . . princess?"

"Of course you are," she laughs. "Wave!"

I look around, half expecting Nikka and Luke to yell "PSYCHE!" or worse, Tunde to jump out from behind a column and scream "BOO!" or dump a bucket of pig blood in my face like that movie *Carrie* he told me to watch with him, when he found my first box of pads in the bathroom. Five minutes in, I wanted to run out of the room, but I sat there while he watched me, disappointed that I wasn't reacting.

Nothing happens. Slowly, I lift my arm and end up doing something between a Black power fist and a pageant wave. They cheer again.

I have no idea what's going on.

Some of them are dressed in formal clothes, like prom dresses and tuxedos; I see some droopy corsages here and there. But others are wearing jeans and T-shirts with work boots like mine, and there's a good amount of cosplay going on. I see leather jackets dripping with chains, tutus, camo gear, tracksuits—it's like everything goes and nobody cares. Two different Neos from *The Matrix* salute me, and I smile back automatically. There are a lot of elf ears.

"Oh great, NerdCon," says Luke. "Are we in Middle Earth or whatever?"

As the DJ says something about *taking it way back with a Roni Size banger* and turns up the music again, I look down at my own soggy self; there's sludge from our boat ride all over my boots, but otherwise I'm still not in as bad a shape as I should be. And Luke and Nikka look like they dove into an oil spill.

"Let's go get cleaned up," Alisia whispers to me. "She'll be back!" she yells to the crowd.

"What about the minions?" a girl shouts, making a face like she smells something bad.

"We'll take care of them," says a deep voice from . . . somewhere.

Everyone except me, Nikka, and Luke laughs again, and I'm hustled over to another door before I can say anything else. I hear a scuffle behind me and turn to see the Three Boys (how did they beat us here?) pulling Nikka and Luke through another door.

"Wait—" I say, pulling away from the two girls gently but firmly leading me away. "What are they doing to them? Luke's already hurt, and Nikka must be wiped out, even if she's talking strong, that's how she is. Those guys were following us, and—"

Alisia jumps in. "Don't worry, those three are with us. I hope they didn't frighten you? They play too much sometimes." She flashes a tight-lipped smile.

"Why were they chasing us, then?" I ask. "It didn't seem like playing."

"Were they chasing you?" she asks lightly. "Maybe there was a reason it felt that way . . . ?" She trails off, leaving a question in her voice that I'd rather not answer. Yeah, maybe it felt that way because there are too many things that I don't want catching up to me.

"So, they'll be OK?" I whisper to Alisia. "That's fam, I mean. I know they're . . . I didn't want to bring them with me, but . . ."

"Don't worry," she answers again. Her eyes flash, then she smiles. "They'll be taken care of. What you need now is a warm bath, a change of clothes, and a celebration! You're doing something monumental. Enjoy it."

I have so many questions. But it's warm and dry and there's music and people cheering and smiling at me, at me, and I belong here and they know who I am but they're cheering and Nikka and Luke are always fine because that's how their story goes and I just want to be the princess for a minute, so I nod and say,

"OK."

She takes me into a dark tunnel so narrow that I have to crouch the whole way. Briefly, I remember my fifth-grade reader response project on The House of Dies Drear; I'd written an overlong play that mostly consisted of long walks through dark passageways and ill-timed jump scares that never paid off.

Then the darkness ends abruptly, and the lights are so bright that I'm sweating. More graffiti lines the walls, the bright neon colors giving the illusion of more light than there actually is. We come to a warped wooden door, and I gasp when she pushes it open.

It's a bedroom—no, a *bedchamber*, like the rich people have on old-timey TV shows. Flashlights hang from the ceiling, and a huge, cushiony purple canopy bed commands the room. Three rats sit quietly next to the bed, reminding me that I am indeed underground in New York City. Except, they're wearing red velvet vests and little bell-cap hats like they work in a fancy hotel. Still, they are rats.

"How is all this even down here?" I ask Alisia, looking around. Is that an actual Keith Haring mural? Tunde had done a whole research paper on eighties street art, and he paid me two dollars an hour to pick up library books for him "since you love the library so much." These walls are bold and bright and defiant, like the photos of old subway cars that he'd included in his paper. There's the word SAMO— wasn't that Basquiat?! "You didn't say the Mole People were living like *this!*" I turn to Alisia, who's smiling.

The rats are still and staring, and I point to them. "Are they real?" Then one of them *smiles too,* and its teeth gleam like crystals.

Alisia keeps smiling, but doesn't answer, which seems to be the thing around here. I feel stupid for asking questions. After the pause has gone from awkward to unsettling, she murmurs, "Your clothes are over there," and points to the bed that I just want to fall into. "Through that door is the bath, it's all prepared." She actually says "the bawth," and I want to laugh but I don't dare. She hands me an orange whistle, and a fluffy purple robe. "Use the whistle when you're done, and I'll be back." She leaves before I can embarrass myself with more questions, and closes the door with such finality that I'm not surprised when I try it a moment later and it doesn't budge. I walk slowly past the rats, who follow me with their beady eyes. I hear the thick *drip drip* of water, but I don't see it anywhere.

The bath is deliciously warm and smells like cinnamon. Actual rose petals float on top of the water, and they seem to part on their own when I get in and submerge myself like I'm in a romance novel. There are no windows or any other doors in here, so I keep my eyes on the entryway I've just come through. The rats haven't followed me, and I don't realize until I let it out that I've been holding my breath. Multicolored Christmas tree lights line the ceiling, and I feel like I've been given a gift and for now I'm going to act like I deserve it. I still myself and listen for the Voice, but nothing comes. No warning. No taunts. No instructions. Maybe this is exactly where I'm supposed to be and what I'm meant to do.

Another rat has silently lined up next to the others, and the quartet just sits and stares into space as I tiptoe back into the bedroom, tighten the robe's belt, and pull the hood over my head. I don't know why I'm tiptoeing, and I keep trying not to look at them. I try to disguise my shudder, because they really aren't bothering me, and they can't help being gross. Nikka must be freaking out right now, rats really send her, but I also know the gorgeousness of the room is probably making up for it. Is hers all purple too? Or maybe Barbie princess pink. She's probably still soaking in her tub. My cousin believes in spa days like our aunties believe in the Resurrection. I turn my attention to the clothes laid out for me on the bed and gasp. I'm almost afraid to get closer, in case it all vanishes like some sort of cruel illusion, but slowly I reach out and touch a confection of a dress that is truly fit for royalty. And it's . . . for me?

If they only knew.

The bodice is so soft and light, I pull it on; it feels like a hug, like nothing and everything all at once. The full skirt glows and glimmers and I look closely—it's made out of thousands of tiny buzzing bugs that look like fireflies. I step into it carefully, and the buzzing gets louder, as though they're happy.

I don't know what's happening, but it's something to do with Tunde, and that's enough. But there's also a warm feeling in my center that's whispering it's something to do with me too—maybe with me getting saved in a way that's better than anything I ever heard in the two or three times I actually listened in church. Better than what I deserve, at least. So I twist my hair up into a bun and a few minutes later I'm blowing the orange whistle. I slip my feet into a pair of pearly sandals but check to make sure my boots and back-pack are still around. I may need to switch back to hated step-sister mode fast. I put on the backpack, with the boots inside, then slip a satiny cape over my shoulders so that it doesn't show. Then I make the sign of the cross, blow the whistle again, and wait.

22

Alisia is the one who brings me back to the party. She actually calls it "The Prom," but she makes air quotes every time she says it so I'm not sure how to react. I settle for small, quick smiles.

"OK, seriously, what is this place?" I ask her, trying to look like I expect to wear poufy princess dresses and sparkly shoes on a regular basis. It's already clear that questions are not a thing around here, and I'm not trying to antagonize my first friend in years, but now, out of the warm bath haze, I need some information. "Also, you look nice." Alisia is wearing a long navy satiny dress; it looks a little like lingerie, and like what Nikka would call "a cuteness."

"We call it 'The Underground.' And thanks." She glances at me. "I forgot about that one."

"Who's we? And is it like a club or something?" I've heard of clubs that are in old churches or warehouses. I notice that "I forgot about that one" isn't exactly returning the compliment. But she saved us—she's here to help. "Why . . . how . . . it's as though you all knew I was coming." Whoever "you all" is. "Do you know—" I stop. *Do you know my dead brother? Is he down here?*

When she grabs my hand and squeezes it, I think about our shared giggles in the library, and the tightly folded note. If I can see Tunde, undo what I've done . . . and have a friend . . . I keep my mouth shut. I can figure this out. "So . . . where exactly are we? I'm a little . . . thrown off now."

"Yeah, I got you. Of course you are. It's not every day that you travel through spacetime. But you look good anyway."

I try to make my "thanks" as casual as hers. *Spacetime?!*

Was Nikka more right than wrong? I almost laugh. "Are you saying we like . . ." I lower my voice even though we're alone in this dark, damp tunnel. "Uh, *tessered* or something?" I wait for her to laugh, but she just turns and keeps walking ahead of me down another (or is it the same?) dank hall, and I have to scuttle along behind her in these stupid shoes to keep up. We're back at the ballroom before I can get more non-answers.

Now I take a good look around this serious ballroom-looking place and notice a long banquet table to my right, and a giant chair—a throne, really—at one end, decorated

with twinkling string lights. Two of the Three Boys, now smiling and looking like they train puppies and kittens all day
long, hold out their arms to escort me to it. I look at Alisia,
who nods, and since I know I stuck my Swiss Army Knife in
the hard bra part of my dress, I link my arms through theirs.
The Third Boy pulls out the throne just like a Boricua knight
or something; he helps me gather my skirts and settle into
the chair like he wasn't literally chasing me in some kind of
murderous rage a little while ago.

"The Princess has arrived! Let's get this party
started!" says the same deep voice from earlier. I twist
around to see, but I can't figure out who's talking.

In a flash there are kids putting platters and three-
tiered trays and a carousel filled with bodega delights—piles
of chips in snack bags, all kinds of nuts, chewy candy. Alisia
slides into the seat next to me as I uncover a platter of fried
chicken.

"KFC," she whispers. "Not many left in the city anymore; Popeye's and those chicken sandwiches got everybody brainwashed. This was a big get—only for Prom, Night
Man said."

"So this *is* a prom," I say. "Who's Night Man?" She's
holding up the platter in front of me like it's holding dia-
monds, and I take two drumsticks, not caring if that's what
princesses do. I'm hungry, and this is not the time to tell her
that the only fried chicken I eat is made by my momma or
Mr. Charles Gabriel on 145th Street. "I just . . . how . . .
why?"

Alisia focuses on piling her plate with food. "So, Night Man will give you the whole story, it's not my place. But the short version is that most of us are in high school, and all of us are miserable there. We were made for more and better, and *they* don't realize that." She smiles as she draws out that "they."

As she speaks, I look around at the other kids in the room. Even though their clothing and hair is giving them some kind of Cinderella's ball bliss, I can see the evil stepsiblings in their lives behind their eyes.

Speaking of . . . with a jolt I realize that I've forgotten that Nikka and Luke are down here with me, wherever *here* is. I crane my neck to find them in the cavernous room.

"I told you, they're fine," Alisia says, seeming to read my mind. Which could be a thing down here. "And by the way, it just shows what a good person you are, thinking of them, when I can tell they've never been that concerned about you."

"I know that's right," I say without thinking. I feel a little pang, and quickly bite into my drumstick and sip my glass of . . . sparkling apple cider? Nikka and I used to pretend it was champagne. "But, um, still, they're OK, right? Luke was kind of hurt, and Nikka did pretty much get us here, so . . ."

"How much of your life have you spent worrying about them and people like them: what they do, what they think of you, what they say about you? They are fine. You trust me, right? And now is the time to celebrate—you have found your people, if you haven't figured that out by now. We're so happy to have you here." She looks straight into my eyes. "And you're here because you have something to do, Harriet."

I am trying to look ready and worthy, so I fight to keep my smile inside. Another sign!

"Why didn't you wear the tiara thing?" asks Alisia. "That was supposed to be the cherry on top."

"What tiara thing?" I ask.

"There was a crown or tiara or whatever you want to call it, in the room with your dress. Oh well, doesn't matter." Her smile looks like it hurts, and her eyes become small slits. "We all know who you are."

The DJ starts some deep house music, and now that I'm getting a good look, it's painfully clear that nondancing nerds in the real world are still nondancing nerds in whatever this strange subterranean place is. They most definitely do not magically catch the beat through some wizarding or whatever. Most are jumping and jerking around; a few can dance, but there's a lot of clapping on the one and three happening, Black people included. There are a lot of glasses, cosplay-inspired partywear, braces . . . all the hallmarks of sincere and full-fledged dorkdom, and not in an ironic way. And there's an interesting mix, like on the DIVERSITY POWERS THE FUTURE! posters on the college office wall at school. In fact, from the looks of things, down here the white kids are the tokens.

"Beautiful, right?" murmurs Alisia, watching me look around as she tears into a bag of Utz. "We built something down here that they only pay lip service to up above."

"Is this like a . . . youth center or something? Are you a volunteer?" But Alisia just smiles again, this time like we're co-conspirators, and offers me some salt-and-vinegar chips.

The music changes to Beyoncé and a roar goes up because everyone loves Beyoncé, even the geeks. I let Alisia pull me onto the dance floor, stuffing a mini bag of gummy bears and two granola bars into my dress pockets.

Tunde used to tell me about the school dances he went to, and he'd make them sound like a war zone, because I guess they were for people like him. Jockeying for position in the high school hierarchy. Claiming more than your space. Making other people shrink.

For the first time, I think: *How exhausting it must be to be cool.*

I wonder if the attempts to teach me chess, to pretend not to know the difference between knitting and crochet, to cheat at UNO so we'd have to start the game all over again . . . were those Tunde's moments of rest?

I get separated from Alisia and bump into a couple; when they turn around, my apology dies in my throat. They're smiling, but there's something else behind their eyes that is a little . . . *freaky*, Nikka would say. My confusion must show, because they glance at each other and then one of them murmurs, "Je m'excuse," and they move away quickly.

I twirl like a girl in a movie, holding up my lightning bug skirts and dancing "like nobody's watching"—except they all are, and they're clapping and cheering and I keep dancing, but I'm also looking around for the smirks and eye-rolling, but it's not there. They're chanting *"Go, Princess, Go!"* without a trace of irony or sarcasm. A girl gives me a hug and then twirls with me, gesturing to the kids around us to do the same. The smallest of them clasp the edges of my skirt and holds it up like the "parachutes" we used to have in preschool music. They move in a slow circle, helping me to twirl a little slower, no longer cheering and clapping, but with the tear-filled eyes of a group of miniature mothers. It reminds me: A few days before my first day of school this year, Momma did my goddess braids herself. It was as though we had an unspoken agreement not to turn on a movie, and I didn't look at my phone. She just worked and worked on my hair, and I'd matched my breathing to hers, until I'd fallen asleep.

I tell myself that the goose pimples that have raised up on my arms are because it's cold down here, and I remind myself that if anything goes wrong, I've got the nunchaku.

And friends, a small and new voice whispers from a far-off place inside me. *Friends*.

I'm almost grateful when I stumble and am forced to stop, as kids keep whirling and smiling around me. *Tunde*. I am here for a reason, and I'm not about to let a pretty dress and some junk food get in my way. I just have to make Alisia talk, or find this Night Man, or . . . I stop dancing abruptly and push my way back to the table, which has already been cleared. My food is gone, and so is Alisia. I scan the smooth stone walls for a door, but I can't even figure out where we'd entered from anymore. The party rages on around me, a little wilder now, a little more intense. The mood shifts, even though nothing seems to have changed. I drop into my seat, realizing that I have no idea where I am, what is happening, or what I need to do next. I'm not on some quest. I'm still just me, alone and ashamed, wearing a dress that belongs on Nikka—

OK, really, where are they anyway? Maybe they figured out how to get out of here on their own. I can't blame them. I told them to leave like a hundred times . . . I stand and scan the room again just in case I missed Nikka shaking her booty in the middle of a circle of admirers or holding court in a corner. There! I see Luke, sitting and holding his head in his hands, and Nikka is next to him, looking around the room for . . . me? We lock eyes and she half-smiles and shrugs. I start walking toward them; they're still wearing the wet, dirty clothes they had on before, and Luke might be . . . crying?

23

They look like my insides, and without thinking I laugh; there's a sudden sour, metallic taste in my mouth. "Uh, why didn't you guys clean up? At least a shower?" I try not to make a face. "You smell nasty." I lower my voice. "I'm trying to make a good impression, so since you forced your way down here, you need to get it together. Still trying to mess things up for me, right? Even . . . underground."

Luke lifts his head. "Just talking out the side of your neck because you think—" He stops and looks at Nikka. "Forget it. Yeah, you're right. We need to *get it together.*" He throws a mean glance at my outfit. "Oh, but one thing, Harriet? You look ridiculous."

I don't want it to hurt, but it does, and I don't have a response.

Nikka stands, slowly. "No, she doesn't, you just need a nap, Luke." She starts to reach for me with a greasy hand, and instinctively, I recoil. "Oops, sorry. Cuz, you look beautiful, but um, we didn't get an opportunity to take a shower or anything like that. They took us to some metal closet and we've been in there up until now, with some uh, rat friends." She takes in my dress, my hair, the cape. "You clearly got the deluxe package."

I scan the room for Alisia, or even the Boys. "I mean, maybe they still thought you were going to . . . hurt me or something?" I say, trying to make myself believe my words even as I remember that flash in Alisia's eyes when she'd said they'd be *taken care of.* "There must be some big misunderstanding happening. Let me find Alisia—" This is not how I want the story to go.

"There's no misunderstanding," said Luke. "These freaks were getting off on pushing us around like the nerds getting revenge in some stupid movie. And we definitely don't need you to get your little friend Alisia."

"Freaks?" I spit back, shoving down my own thoughts from just a few moments earlier. "You just have to bring that whole attitude everywhere, don't you? And OK, by your logic, you *are* the 'popular kids' and if my movie night memory serves me right, you're getting exactly what you deserve." I don't remember who found the sketchy link to a blurry copy of an old movie called *Massacre at Central High,* but the four of us had watched it one Saturday afternoon, huddled around Tunde's laptop. A week later, when he'd had to get the computer serviced because of the malware that he'd downloaded too, I whispered "movie magic" and side-stepped his swat. We were both laughing, though. I think.

"You're really defending a bunch of creepy bridge troll psychos you don't know?" Luke pats the stone bench he's on and tries to hide his wince. "You feel sorry for them because you don't know them, you have some fantasy that—"

Nikka gets between us, holding up her hands, and I notice that they're rubbed raw. "Can we not do this right now, or like, ever? We did *not* just go through it to . . . bicker. What's our next move, Princess?"

Is she being sarcastic? I can't read her tone, and there's no time to try. The dance floor is slowly emptying, and people are whispering, some staring at us. Now I notice a damp, unpleasant odor of sweat; it could be because it's pumpkin time at the ball, it could be me. Either way, my spidey-sense is telling me that Prom Night is about to end. Smiles are fading and a new and icy brightness fills some of the partiers' eyes. Maybe this Cinderella vibe could get a little more *Carrie.*

"Very funny," I say. "Anyway, I need to find out what it meant when I—when we saw him." My brother's name is stuck in my throat and I have to push it out. "When we saw Tunde in the pool."

Nikka nods, encouraging and businesslike, like she's taking my order at McDonald's.

Luke groans.

"I mean, the odds are that he's a spirit, right?" Nikka says. "Maybe he's here because . . . you need him."

How much does Nikka know? "You mean, *he* needs my help, like you said before." She doesn't answer.

"Look, you miss him, and I get it," says Luke, his voice breaking. "You think I don't miss my best friend? My brother? But this isn't it."

Luke had been there that day, in the cafeteria. He'd been sitting at the table, and I heard that he lunged across the table full of biodegradable lunch trays and chocolate milk cartons to try to push Tunde out of the way of the shot. He's never said anything to me about those moments, about how as usual, he did the heroic thing. I never asked.

It's not that I don't know them, I want to say. *It's that they don't really know me.*

Carefully, I sit down next to them and we watch in silence as the slow jams start. I hear a gargling rumble and look at Nikka. "Was that you? Or a train?"

"It was my stomach; I'm starving," says Luke. "We also didn't get anything to eat, if you're wondering."

I point. "There's food everywhere! Just grab something. No wonder you're hangry."

Nikka takes a breath. "Cuz, they told us we're not allowed. And . . . we don't want to make them mad."

I stare at her. "Stop playing. Come on, Nikka. We're not in an actual fairy tale. They're not ogres. I'm sure—" What was I sure of, exactly?

"Ask her how her hands got like that," says Luke. "'Grab something.' Yeah, right."

I look straight into Nikka's eyes, who tries and fails to smile. "I shouldn't have been trying to eat Entenmann's anyway," she says quietly.

Suddenly, the lights go out completely. A group of kids push a giant stage on wheels to the center of the floor, knocking aside a few partygoers who don't move out of the way quickly enough. We all crowd to the edges of the ballroom; I think I see Luke in a scuffle out of the corner of my eye, but the three of us are shoved apart and everyone around me starts cheering and waving their hands in the air like they care very much, until the DJ gets on the mic and says, "It's time." Immediate silence. I look around and all the kids except for me, Luke, and Nikka are absolutely still. The girl next to me, who looks like a sort of South Asian Harley Quinn, puts one hand on my arm and her other to her lips. I see someone kick Luke, and I start to cry out—but Harley Quinn claps a hand over my mouth. A spotlight shines on the empty stage.

"I had a dream," says that deep, dry, disembodied voice. "I had a dream that this valley would be exalted, that these tunnels would—" The voice abruptly stops and descends into screeches of laughter. No one else in the room joins in. The room seems to have gotten colder, but the faces around me, and the sudden appearance of the Three, unsmiling, right beside me, make me afraid to even tremble.

"Let me stop playing," continues the voice, deep and smooth, almost oily now. "Party people, what a wonderful thing you have done. Once again, you have achieved the impossible. Once again, the underestimated and overlooked have demonstrated that a truly beautiful world can be: a place where power resides in the hands that deserve it." The voice pauses, and then APPLAUSE signs light up the walls and everyone starts cheering again. Well, almost everyone. I notice that Harley Quinn next to me is only slow-clapping; when she notices me looking, she starts cheering loudly.

"Enough!" says the voice, and I am reminded of the supervillain in a bad school play. The APPLAUSE lights go out. It cackles again. "I love this part. I won't keep you much longer. I just wanted to congratulate you. And thank you. You have allowed me to build a world that could never be 'up there' (a few boos rumble through the crowd; then the lights flash, and everyone's quiet again). I have shown you the infinite possibilities. And there's more! There's always more. You have been told you can't have everything you want. That you have to choose. But now you know what I've seen. You can have it all. You can *be* it all. I am working to share the power of the universe with all of you, and again, I thank you for the opportunity to serve you."

This can't be serious. It really is like one of those dumb movies we used to watch on Tunde's laptop on a Saturday afternoon. I try again to catch Nikka's eye, or Luke's, just to anchor myself in something real, because I'm not sure if I'm about to burst into laughter, or tears, or even throw up. But I don't see them at all anymore; Harley Quinn smiles at me, and I cry out before I can stop myself: her eyes are clear and dead, like she has no pupils. Her smile falters, and she blinks; no, her eyes are brown, like mine. A trick of light. My head hurts. The voice continues, but my head is pounding, and I don't hear the words, because it sounds like it's saying the same thing, over and over. Whatever it's saying, everyone's eating it up. They are mesmerized. I close my eyes.

Suddenly the voice yells, "THIS ONE'S FOR YOU!" and sirens blare and the DJ starts playing house music again with the bass turned all the way up and just when I think my head is going to split in two, I feel the heat of the lights going back up.

The applause lights are out, but there is thunderous applause anyway, and whistles, and cheering. Harley Quinn tries to link her arm through mine but one of the Three slips over to her, whispering something, then whisks her away by her elbow.

I start to push my way through the crowd and notice as I walk through that actually not everyone is cheering. A few kids are talking closely with each other, and some turn to stare at me. I see the pupilless eyes again and can feel my body tremble uncontrollably. A fever. I must be sick. She'll be so self-satisfied and smug about it, but I'm going to have to ask Nikka if she has something in in her backpack that can help.

The strobe lights come back, and I shield my eyes, stumbling into people as I walk. They say, "Excuse me, Princess," every time.

Nikka and Luke are back huddled together on the stone bench, so still that for a second I think they've been turned to stone themselves. The kids standing around them remind me of crows; I suppose it's because they're all dressed in black, but there's a hunger in their eyes that's even more unsettling than the flashes of nothing I've just seen. They part, smoothly and almost like it's been choreographed, when I get close. Luke's head hangs down; Nikka's face is red and splotchy, and I try not to be glad about the fact that she may have been crying.

"What was *that*?" I ask over the music. My voice catches, my throat scratchy and dry. I swallow a few times and fish out a throat drop. "It was like something out of *The Wiz*, right?" If we talk about it, if we laugh together about an old movie . . .

They stare back at me. And for a second, though I know it's these stupid lights, but for a second they don't have pupils either. Then the DJ yells out, "You know y'all *love* the slow jams!" His British accent is gone.

"Did you leave your backpacks in your rooms? They're not that heavy," I say. I reach into my pockets and pull out the granola bars I'd just stashed. I toss my backpack to them and move my hammer into my dress pockets. So much for Nikka being so well-prepared. She really thought this was going to be some sort of semi-literary adventure.

Then I think of her holding my hand in hers, painting my nails.

I kick off the pearly sandals. "Hold onto that bag," I say to Nikka, still trying to find Alisia in the crowded room.

"Yup," she says, slowly standing up and sounding bent but not quite broken. "You got your nunchaku, though. And your hammer? But you should keep your bag, more food is in here—"

"Keep it, they've been giving me all kinds of food," I say. "And every snack you can think of. They even had those racist chocolate babies we used to buy on the Lower East Side when we were little."

Luke's snort makes me smile. It's better than the stony stare. Nikka pulls two protein bars out of the bag, tosses them to him, and he tears them both open with his teeth.

I close my eyes. "So . . . I don't have a plan . . . What do you think, Nikka? Any ideas?"

"Not you asking me for help!" She starts to clap, then winces. "Ouch! OK, so . . . I'm guessing that voice means there's somebody bigger than all these people, someone *in charge*, who runs this—"

"Stank Geek Community Center," says Luke, raising his voice to be heard above Khalid asking if we can just talk.

Nikka ignores him. "And I'm guessing you'll get to make a request, maybe even three. So ask for what you want: to see Tunde. Then . . . I don't know." A couple who seem to be dancing to a song only they can hear bump into her, hard. When they glare, Nikka says "Sorry" without a trace of sarcasm.

"Or maybe just how to get the hell out of here," adds Luke, biting into his second granola bar. "And maybe ask them how we get the upgrade you got. Or just some wet wipes and a drink of water . . . if it's not too much trouble."

I put a hand on his shoulder as gently as possible. "I'm sorry. I don't know what's going on, but you didn't ask for it, exactly, and I'm sorry."

He smiles. "Yo, did you just *apologize*? Nik, did you hear that?"

Once, when I was ten, the four of us were in a contest to see who said sorry first, and I didn't even know it. I still won.

"Very funny," I say. "I'm trying to be nice here, don't make me regret it. How's your leg?"

"It's fine," he says, looking away. "And I did ask for it, remember? I said I wanted to be here for you. I just wasn't expecting it to be like . . . you having to carry me and stuff, before."

As a couple of anime-looking girls walk by us and blatantly point and laugh at Nikka, she narrows her eyes.

"And while you're getting next to the power source, we can get a better idea of this place. If your girl Alisia drops the attitude, maybe she'll talk."

I can't point out again that maybe Alisia's attitude has a lot to do with Nikka's, so I just mutter something about a misunderstanding again. My stomach can't help but fall when I see all Three Boys approaching again. One of them grabs my elbow, not hard, but like he wants me to be afraid, so I slowly shake myself loose. I wonder where Harley Quinn is. "Can I help you?" I ask. Once again, his smile makes me shiver. He inclines his head as though I'm supposed to just leave with them.

"What's your name?" I ask. "I'm Harriet, but my friends call me H. You can call me Harriet." That gets a low chuckle from Luke, and all Three glance at him like he's roadkill.

"Nice to meet you," responds one of the other Boys. "It's time for you to get what you came for. It's time to meet Night Man."

"Yes!!!" whispers Nikka, sounding like her mom when she gets Bingo on Saturday afternoons at church.

"So I didn't exactly come here for that—wait, isn't that a comic?" I remember the "NM" slogans on the tunnel walls. "Um, but if that will get some questions answered, cool," I add, pulling myself up straight. "And just one thing— my friends here, they need to get clean and comfortable." *They called me Princess.* "Um, immediately. Can someone take them to my room?" Their stares are making me put more question into my words than I want.

"My . . . chambers, I mean. Perhaps baths can be drawn for my—for them." Now everyone, including Luke, looks like they're about to laugh at my poor imitation of a princess from the kind of book I never read anyway. I glare at Luke and Nikka. *I'm trying to help you out, idiots!* Nikka winces and looks down, while Luke rolls his eyes and looks like even that hurts. I've got the upper hand and they're still trying to pretend they don't know me.

I turn back to the Boys. "Hey, it sounds like there were some mix-ups earlier." I sound like an ass. "We're not trying to invade your secret hideaway or whatever. Just take them to the room I was in so they can wash up. And give them some food. Got it? That's, that's an order." What am I even saying?

The one Boy who's been quiet so far steps forward. "I'm sure we can clear this up. I apologize for any confusion. Why don't you go with Greg, *Your Majesty,* and I'll take Nikka and Luke to your *bedchamber.*" The oily sneer in his voice is almost, but not quite, disguised. I ignore it; Nikka and Luke look like they're about to collapse.

As I hesitate, Nikka pulls Luke up slowly. "Go, cuz, we're good. We're fine. I'm sure that uh . . ."

"Mark," says the smooth talker.

"Mark will take good care of us." She looks straight into his eyes, turning on all her charm. For once, I'm glad.

They'll be fine. She'll do her thing and work her magic, and they'll be fine.

"After you," says Greg to me, with an exaggerated bow. I see Alisia behind him, and the sneer on her face almost stops me in my tracks. She catches my eye and smiles quickly, then looks back at Greg.

"Wait," I say. I sit and switch out of the Cinderella shoes into my boots. I'm not really a princess, hidden or otherwise. I give the backpack to Nikka.

"Talk to him nice," she says in a low voice. "Please."

I pretend I don't hear, take a deep breath, and think about who or what the hell someone who calls himself Night Man is going to be.

MIND THE GAP

Greg guides me toward the top of a flight of stairs. I peer down, but the fluorescent light is blinding. As I hesitate, I hear a muffled loudspeaker announcement coming from the brightness below. "Please stand clear of the closing doors."

"Wait, is this a subway station? I didn't know trains ran this far down! I thought all the abandoned stations were . . . well, abandoned . . ." I'm babbling and I fight to pull my mouth closed and take discreet deep breaths.

"After you," Greg says again, with the faux courtesy of someone who's pulled a lot of pranks. I lift my head and start down the stairs into the light. At the bottom, I turn, but he's gone. I'm on what looks like a subway platform. At least, I think it does. There's a heavy mist around me; it's moving with a purpose and feels almost playful. I can hear activity—a high, sad voice singing an acoustic version of Lizzo's "Good As Hell," and a group yelling the familiar subway dance call "It's Showtime!" in the distance. I smell a churro cart somewhere nearby. Then I hear the unmistakable rumbling of an approaching train.

It's gorgeous—silver and covered in more 80s-style graffiti. The squeal of it slowing on the tracks is loud and painful, and I want to cover my ears, but I can't move. It stops, and through the mist, I see the doors open. No one exits.

"*Bing bong!*"

"Please stand clear of the closing doors."

Move, Harriet!

My legs are filled with lead; I want to move forward, but I'm motionless and trembling as the mist teases and swirls around me.

"Showtime!" call out the dancers again. They sound closer, and the music from their speakers is beginning to clash with the singer, whose voice has strayed a bit—she's no longer on pitch.

"*How you doin'?*" she rasps.

"*Bing bong!*" It's louder.

"Please stand clear of the closing doors!" Urgent.

I use all of my strength to lift my legs, and as one foot lifts, I see there are wads and wads of . . . gum? on the bottom of my combat boots, sticky and bright pink. I recognize the scent—I thought Nikka was the only person in the world who bought bespoke gum, Hubba Bubba only, from Economy Candy. I look around, but she's not here. It's just me, and . . . whatever these people are. I—

"*BING BONG!*"

It's so loud it hurts, and I wince as I pull and pull until it feels like I might leave my legs behind. Finally, I come unstuck and run for the closing doors, falling into the pole inside the subway car as they slam shut behind me.

"We are being held in the station," says a high, sing-song voice.

As I slowly get up, I look around for a seat.

There's no one else in the car. It's completely empty. As we pull out of the station, the singer, the dancers, the churro lady, and a whole chorus of people on the platform press closer to the windows of my subway car. Most are smiling, but it's not friendly, and a few are laughing so hard that they're gasping for breath. I back away from the window and fall into a seat as we move out of the station, and I realize it's the Boys calling out as I leave.

"It's showwwwwtiiiiiiime!"

I don't know where I'm supposed to get off, but we're not stopping anyway. The train is going faster than any subway I've ever known.

This is your last stop

This is the last stop on this train

Last stop

It's not coming through the loudspeaker.

It's coming from inside the house.

Oh hey. You're back, Voicey. Long time no—

GET OUT OF THE TRAIN NOW!!

Something pushes me up and I stumble forward, grabbing the pole for balance. The train doors are open, but now they are rimmed with sharp spikes—teeth maybe? I don't know, but they are closing fast.

I leap out of the train onto . . . grass? The doors shut behind me, then they open and shut a few times the way they do when someone is trying to hold the door open. But no conductor comes on to the loudspeaker to yell about not delaying the train. They just clamp shut with a heavy final CHOMP and I hear chewing sounds as the train wheezes out again.

This station, or whatever it is, reminds me of the day the four of us—me, Tunde, Luke, and Nikka—got caught in Central Park in a thunderstorm and ran out onto Fifth Avenue to the closest shelter, which turned out to be the Guggenheim.

"Taking advantage of pay-what-you-wish, huh?" murmurs the woman at the admissions desk. "Do you get many chances to come here?"

I look her in the eye and offer to pay full price.

"What my good sis means is that I'll be paying for all of us," says Tunde, plunking a quarter on the desk and shaking himself out vigorously.

I open my mouth to protest and Luke pulls me aside. "This once? Let it go?" The admissions woman smirks.

We all walk to the elevator, shoes squeaking, without speaking. No one gets in with the four stone-faced Black teenagers, so we have it all to ourselves.

"Like you think you're proving something when you're not, cuz," says Nikka, sighing. "What would've been the point of giving them all that money? When we didn't have to?"

"She thought we couldn't pay, that we were there because it was the free night or whatever!" I answer. "They always think we don't belong!"

"They're always gonna think what they think," says Tunde in that calm 'I'm older and wiser' voice that makes me want to stomp my feet like a toddler. "Whether we pay twenty-five dollars or twenty-five cents. So why not pay twenty-five cents and keep it moving?"

"But she—"

"Is not who you should be concerned about," interrupts Nikka. "Seriously, can we just pick a floor before they think we took over the elevator?"

I jab a random floor, and stare at the wall.

Luke whispers, "I'll get you a Mister Softee with the difference," and Nikka and Tunde stifle laughs.

When the elevator doors open, we're in another world. "Flying Carpet: MTA Reimagined" is the exhibit, and we forget to fight for the next forty-five minutes as we explore a weird transit wonderland.

We don't leave until the museum closes, and Luke buys me a double twist cone with rainbow sprinkles. No one else gets ice cream, and I feel a little silly, but we sit on a bench just inside the park until I finish. The ice cream is delicious. It's just drizzling, but Tunde holds his umbrella over the rest of us, his face turned up toward the evening sky.

The station floor is actually fake grass, like a soft astroturf. I assume that the wildlife noises I hear are artificial, or at least I hope they are, because I'm not ready to wrestle a chimp. No sign of Night Man or any human. Large coleus-looking plants are growing everywhere, their bright green and brick leaves reaching out toward me, and I try not to touch them as I step forward. A beautiful black cat darts across the floor in front of me, followed a few seconds later by the biggest rat I've ever seen. I shudder, but neither pays attention to me. I hold my breath and wait in case anything else is going to come out of the shadows, but it's just me again. I walk through vine-covered turnstiles toward a sign marked THIS WAY TO FUNKYTOWN. A double-ended arrow is below the words. I look both ways; one hallway is inky black, so dark and opaque that I can't tell how far it goes. The other is blindingly bright, light with an almost painful intensity. But if I squint, I can see a few steps ahead of me.

I choose the light.

I only have to walk a couple of minutes before some old school hip-hop beats start pulsing. And then:

"You made it!" says that deep voice I'd heard earlier.

I don't know what I'm expecting. A shiny suit like a vintage hip-hop video?

A monster?

A dungeon?

It's even brighter in here than it was in the tunnels, and I have to shield my eyes a little. It feels like the ghost of a nightclub around me: plush but faded cushioned benches haunt the corners, a row of chandeliers with a few missing lights hang precariously from the ceiling.

I shall not turn back.

"What's good?" I say, trying to see past the bright light. I still can't see him. I look around for somewhere to sit and settle for a large slab of rock that could be a table, a chair, or a bed.

"Is that a patented Princess Harriet hello?" There's both warning and welcome in his voice.

"It's the hello you get when I'm in a situation like this," I say. "You know my name; I'm assuming yours isn't actually Night Man. So . . . who are you? What are you? What's all this? Was all that . . . Wizard of Oz stuff you?" I fold my arms deliberately like I have the right to make demands and try to look around.

"Harriet isn't your real name either," he says smoothly. "You've always believed you were meant for something more, and you're right. You're here, where you can choose, like I did."

I stall because I don't know what else to do. "So your name is like Ezra or Hubert or something like that?" I ask. He was right about my name: Momma had told me that I'd almost been called Folasadé, after her favorite beautiful and reclusive singer, "but then the nuns happened," and, as Nikka was quick to point out, "you *look* like a Harriet."

Night Man finally steps forward, and the bright lights go dim. Except for his skin color, which seems to be an unnerving beige-y gray, he looks like a nerd in mid-makeover mode—someone who would get a "he'd be so cute if . . ." from Nikka and her friends: facial hair that could be deliberately sparse or just a struggle beard, his skin smooth and opaque. He could be twenty, or he could be fifteen, like me. He's wearing a black Adidas track suit, a cape, and Doc Martens, with a Burger King cardboard crown perched on his head, and something about his blank expression makes me unsure if the crown is ironic or not. He smiles a smile that expects one back.

"I'm Night Man," he says simply. This guy doesn't quite fit with the Most Likely To Be Ignored At Best vibe of everyone else down here. That's probably why he's in charge. "How was the Prom? Did you get enough to eat? What did you think of my DJ?" He stands there as though he doesn't need to be held up by the ground beneath him. He talks with his hands; they move quickly, giving the impression that he has a lot more than two as they wave around.

I shrug. "I mean, they snatched it all away before I even got to the Hostess tray, but yeah, thanks for the grub. And, um, I'm not really the clubbing type, but the DJ was good." I squint as steam wafts up from the stone floors, winding its way around me like tentacles. "How do I—we— get out of here?"

"You want to leave?" He sounds genuinely surprised. "That's funny. I thought you wanted to . . . escape."

I stare at him for a long minute. Then, I make a choice. "You know about my brother, don't you? I don't know how or why, but you know." Maybe Alisia told him. I'm sure she heard the whispers at school. Maybe she wants to help me. Maybe she knows and hasn't turned her back on me. Maybe I can turn my back on me and leave the loser behind.

He nods. "That's why you're here. Alisia thought you could use some help with your search."

"Is Tunde . . . here?" I forget to act cool and lunge forward; silently a trio of rats move toward me, but he holds up his hand. My words echo, like a special effect, and I half expect balls of fire and puffs of smoke next. But all that happens is that Night Man bends down and takes out a case underneath his chair, opens it up, and hands me a flashlight.

"Uh, thanks," I say. "I have one of these. A few, in fact; my cousin is extremely well-prepared. Speaking of—" He holds up a hand, and again, we're suspended in time, listening to the ever-present *drip drip*.

After five long minutes, he nods, indicating that I can go on speaking.

"Uh, so OK." I realize it's easier, for some reason, to talk to this weird boy-man who seems to know nothing and everything about me. "This is going to sound stupid or wacky or like I'm on many drugs, but if you know that my brother died then you know that it's impossible for him to also be here. But . . . I think he is. I saw him . . . in the pool. My cousin saw him too." I'm holding onto that. I stop, and my hands are on my hips before I even realize it. "Nikka and Luke . . . are you in charge of what's going on with them? Because it doesn't sound like you're giving them Marriott vibes at all, and I keep asking—"

"Do you?" he asks, expressionless. "Do you really keep asking?"

"Well, I—"

"I think you only asked twice, but then I'm not a numbers geek. Philosophy's my thing. Maybe three, but I don't think so. And you've been here for a while already, so proportionally . . . you don't seem that worried?" He shrugs. "I don't know, maybe I'm counting wrong. Anyway, you were saying, you were *so concerned about your friends.*" There's no mistaking the derision now, and I decide I'm not saying anything until I get some answers. I sit back down on my slab and fold my arms.

After a minute or two, he laughs. "You and Alisia bonded for a reason. You're here for a reason. A once-in-a-lifetime chance to change your life. It's what you've been waiting for, right? You're one of us, Harriet. Welcome home."

A memory of that rose petal bath washes over me. I'm not afraid of Night Man, because *I know him.* He may look like he's got swag to spare on the surface, but I can see the hurt behind his eyes.

I'm the one they were calling Princess, and I'm going to make myself at home.

I'm here for a reason, and it's to help my brother.

I *am* good at numbers. How many times do you get a once-in-a-lifetime opportunity?

(And I have a hammer in my pocket.)

"OK," I say. "Honey, I'm home. What's next?"

"Hold up," Night Man says. "This is a lot for you to take in. And you don't even know the whole story. Should I show you around?" He bows slightly and smiles widely, less ringmaster and more friendly uncle. I can't tell how old he is; he could be my age or twice that.

Momma always says it's a good idea to really know where you are before you try to go anywhere else.

"Yeah," I say. "And can you . . . explain what exactly is going on down here while you're at it? What *is* this place? What was that party or whatever? Who the—who, um, are *you*?

"Walk with me," he replies, and starts walking out of this blinding light into a pitch-black passageway without looking to see if I'm following. I look back toward the door I came in.

"What about Nikka and Luke? I need to know they'll be OK out there," I call, with more authority than I feel. "Your friends—"

"They'll be fine," he says, stopping, but I can sense tension in his voice. "They'll get what they deserve."

That doesn't sound reassuring.

I keep pushing. "If you're in charge here, wherever here is, then can you let *your* people know to leave *my* people *alone*? For real."

He turns round and we hold each other's eyes for a long moment, then he snaps. The largest, most vile rat I've seen lumbers forward. Night Man scribbles something down on a piece of paper and hands it to the rat, who, without a glance at me, takes it in his—*hands?*—and leaves the room. It's all very Gregor the Overlander, and I can't help but think that Nikka would get a kick out of this.

"OK, I've sent a message to make sure that your so-called friends are not harmed in any way. And given food," he adds, as I open my mouth. Then he starts walking again, and I follow.

The dark of this tunnel is warm and close, like a bear hug. "It doesn't smell in here like it did in the other rooms," I say.

"Oh, you noticed that? Most people don't, but I shouldn't be surprised. You notice things, right? I wouldn't have brought you here if you weren't special."

"So . . . explanations?"

"You're right, I wasn't always called Night Man," he laughs. "But I like to think of it as my real name. You know: The secret identity is actually the true identity."

"I'm not a big comics person," I say as we walk. Tunde, Luke, and Nikka could spend hours discussing the intricacies of Marvel. It got on my nerves. "A lot of randomness that's disguised as deep. Not my thing."

He just tilts his head, then points forward, into a deeper darkness. "It's easier if I just show you—at least it will definitely be more fun."

It's been a long time since I've had fun.

"What exactly does that mean?" I ask. "Why exactly should I trust you again? And you still didn't tell me your name."

"I think there's something here that you need. Why don't you tell me why you think you're here? You don't really believe it was *random*, do you?"

I'm tired of believing. Of thinking. Of guessing and second-guessing. I just want to get out of my head for a while, and not be sorry for who I am and what I've done. Just for a little while.

"And that," he says, smiling widely, "is 'exactly' why you're here."

Did I say all that out loud?

"Come on," he continues. "You've dreamed about this—this is the princess moment you've been waiting for, and you're really going to waste it? The Prom, the crew, the pretty dress? But it doesn't have to be for just a little while, you see."

With a jolt, I remember my first attempt at trick-or-treating, with Nikka, of course. Auntie Marguerite had convinced Momma that we wouldn't all burn to a crisp for dressing up and eating candy for one night, so even though Momma grumbled for a week about "Hell-O-Ween," she acquiesced. Even at six, I knew better than to push my luck by asking for a store-bought costume, and she'd begrudgingly helped me turn one of her old bathrobes into a Ruth costume, complete with a set of tracts that I was supposed to give out whenever I took a piece (ONE piece, only) of candy. I wore my rainboots just because, and Momma humphed but didn't say anything. I sang and stomped all the way over to Nikka's, but when she opened her apartment door and I saw her—royally glorious in a lavender party dress with a silver tutu underneath for extra pouf and sparkle, plus the rhinestone tiara that I recognized as the one Jimena from down the block had showed off for weeks before her quince—I told Momma that I wanted to go home right away. She handed me a fun-size Snickers on the way.

"OK," I say. "Show me."

"Next stop, fanriffic fun!" Night Man yells with a grin. "Wahooo!"

He puts out a hand and when I grab it, it's cold and dry. "How do you like your popcorn?" he asks.

"What—" and then the bottom drops out from under me.

24

Something is pulling me down through a vertical tunnel, so hard and fast that it takes my breath away, and I think it wants to. It's even colder, freezing even, but there's no water. Thousands of tiny blue icicles are like lights around me, but as I fall they close in and push against my skin and it hurts, bad, but I bite my lips shut to keep from screaming. The icy needles are poking at me everywhere, and I hug myself tight, trying to make my body small and I'm still falling, falling, and I can't breathe, I made a mistake, I am falling and fainting or maybe I'm dying, and this is so bad, I think I want to, but—

CRASH. I fall to a hard surface with a thud.

"BING BONG!" *This* voice sounds like Night Man, and it is. I can just make him out, waving me toward him to move, and I stumble toward him just as toothy subway doors crash down from the ceiling and up from the floor to crunch anything in the space that I'd been a second ago.

"We're here!" his merry voice rings out in the darkness. I don't realize that my eyes are squeezed shut again until I try to open them. I look up, taking big gulps of air—are we outside?—and my eyes try to adjust to this new, blue light. I can hear the faint sounds of New York City streets: honking horns, sirens, music from a passing car, one side of an angry cell phone conversation. It sounds like we're close to street level, which is impossible because at this point we must be multiple stories underground.

"Where . . ." I croak, still trying to catch my breath. Night Man reaches out a hand to help me up, but I ignore it and stand on my own, pretending that it doesn't hurt. I stumble a bit as I take in big gulps of the dank air and try to look around. I see . . . giant black leather recliners? A wall of mirrors? I turn slowly. Every wall has mirrors of different sizes, shapes. Some seem to be moving, others are almost opaque. I walk over to the one closest to me. My reflection stares back at me, wide-eyed and tight-lipped, as though I'm ready to fight me.

So what else is new.

"Have a seat," he says, bowing with the kind of exaggerated flourish that makes me wonder if I really just look six years old and more than a little ridiculous in my party dress outfit that had seemed so magical just a little while ago.

I refuse to ask any more questions. I step carefully over to the chair; it's directly in front of one of the biggest mirrors, big, red and cushy, like a loveseat meant for two. I sit primly, trying to take up all of the space with my skirts. Night Man laughs and settles in next to me. The blue lights go down, and I am *pushed* into a hole—

"What's it like, to be such a stupid dork?" Tunde says . . . to me.

There's another me in front of me. My brother and me are in front of me and looking like I can reach out and touch them.

Wait. What the—I whirl around to look at Night Man and there's no theater anymore. I'm just . . . sitting on nothing, suspended in the thick darkness. I can't see him, but I can feel he's there. And I can hear him . . . chuckling?

"No, Princess, it's not time travel," he murmurs. "Just watch. Don't speak, and don't dare move. Just watch."

"You tell me," Other Me says. "Or can you tell me how it feels to be so basic? Dating her dropped your IQ more points than you can afford."

I don't need to see this. I remember this. How could I forget this? But . . . something is different. I see me, but it's not me. Tunde looks . . . different. Something's off.

Other Me yawns. "I mean, is that the best you can do, call me stupid? And after the last year, do you really want to go there? I'd be surprised if you remember what the honor roll looks like, since the Curse of Katrina."

"You think I'm talking about grades, slug?" he sneers. "Of course you do, that's all you have."

Just like I did then, I feel his words like a slap, and Other Me says what I said that day, "It smells in here. Maybe that's why you got dumped. Your funk scared her away. Maybe she could smell you rotting from the inside."

"Shut UP!" he yells. "And get out."

I move from the doorway all the way into his room. "Ooh, struck a nerve, did I? Don't feel bad, I guess you can only get dumped when you've actually been dating in the first place."

"What do you even know about dating, Beast?" He throws a pillow at me. "You can't even make up a believable boyfriend from that nerd camp you went to. Even Momma doesn't believe that. And you think Luke doesn't know you sit around and write his name over and over like some kind of witchy spell?"

I don't even pause. "Everyone likes Luke better, that's why—" I dodge as he jumps off his bed to lunge at me, but he stops and laughs, a short, hollow, bitter laugh.

Or is that Night Man next to me? I don't understand what's happening.

"Why am I even bothering to get mad? My loser little sister thinks we have something in common now. Ha! You don't even exist on the same planet as the rest of us; imaginary friends are all you have left. Even Nikka would rather be on punishment than hang out with you anymore.

And my boy Luke, yeah, the only person he feels sorrier for than you is me, because I have to be related to you—"

"Shut UP, Tunde," *Other Me warns.*

"*Because I'm saddled with a mistake of a sister like you—"*

"I'm warning you," *Other Me mutters,* and it does sound like some kind of incantation and I'm leaning forward in my seat, trying to stop Other Me because I want to stop her from saying it, stop her from making that unspeakable magic again, even if this is some kind of dream replay torture or vision or cruel joke, but Night Man is holding me and covering my mouth as Tunde and Other Me keep going with this stupid, stupid, pointless fight. And something's off, something's not right, but I can't—

"*I wish you were dead!"*

I hear it, clear. The words flung out into the air. I want to catch them and stuff them down my throat but I can't and anyway SOMETHING'S OFF and—

Other Me is suddenly on the other side of Tunde's slammed door, ugly-crying. And I hear it again.

"*I wish you were dead."*

I didn't say it, though. I stare as Other Me wipes angry tears, just like I remember, but—

"*I wish you were dead," says Tunde again, from the other side of the door.*

I didn't say it.

He did.

He did?

What is going on?

Suddenly I'm falling again

down

down

down

and with a hard thud I hit my cushy seat.

I'm sobbing, here and now, and we're back in the room, and
Night Man is next to me, still chuckling while he passes over
a tub of popcorn, and says,

"I hope you like extra butter."

"What the hell was that?" I ask, grabbing him. For a second,
something mean and frightening lights up behind his eyes,
but then he gently moves my arms away.

"I hate when popcorn gets spilled," he says, slowly
brushing off his jacket. "But the rats will take care of it." He
turns back to me, smile returning. "Sorry I had to do it that
way. It's just easier for people to take when they just . . . get
hit with it."

I feel like I've been stabbed. "Did you drug me? Is
that what this is? Look, I'm not—"

"It's real life, another way," he says. "It's what you
wondered about in planetarium camp. It's what Neil
DeGrasse Tyson won't show you and Jet Li will—even if that
movie wasn't great. I mean, they tried, and mans could fight,

but the *science*." He shakes his head. "We still watch it once a month down here, just for laughs." He looks at me and sighs. "I thought you'd be a little quicker, Princess. Your wish is my command, so to speak. Parallel universes? Trading places? Those seven impossible things make the life you want . . . possible."

I sit back in my seat and close my eyes. When I open them again, Night Man is still there, we're still in the room. Two rats scurry in discreetly and quietly pick up the popcorn on the floor.

Somehow, this is real. I stand up and look under my seat, then up at the blank screen. "How did you do it? How did you know that I . . . how?"

"It's complicated," he says, yawning and stretching, then standing up. "But I wouldn't have invited you here if I thought you wouldn't get it. No one is allowed here unless they get it—unless, at least, they're useful in some other way. But the Underground is for those of us who've always known we are special. For us to live to our true potential."

"I don't know what you're talking about, and I don't care," I say, shaking my head. "I'm here because I saw my dead brother in the pool. Do you understand me? And now, here, after this godforsaken journey to the center of the earth, I just saw my *brother*. And me. I was watching *myself*. I saw us on that day . . . the day he . . ." I trail off.

"The day he got shot and died?" says Night Man lightly. He shrugs. "Yeah, you did. Such a tragedy. And you remembered, right? But . . . not? Some was a little different?"

I nod slowly. "It was . . . off. It was wrong." Now I'm begging, and I don't care. "Please tell me. This is too much. Just . . . please."

It seems to be the magic word, because Night Man smiles while he shakes his head softly. "It wasn't *wrong*. It was *possible*." He moves so close to me that I can feel his breath on my cheeks, but I don't move away. "You want to take back what you said? This is even better." His voice drops, and changes, and suddenly it's that other Voice, the one that's been taunting me for months. ***"You don't have to say it at all. You can make it all go away: the shame, the pain. Like it never happened. Like you never happened. You can be another You."***

And then I slide to the floor and start to cry.

NO FAIR (FOR REAL THIS TIME)

"We didn't have any time to prepare!" says Luke. He is doing pushups, his breathing raggedy, but he doesn't stop. We're in a classroom, just the three of us and a teacher, who is standing, arms folded, in front of an old-fashioned chalkboard. The wall clock has no hands, but it's ticking loudly.

"How do you prepare to split your heart in two?" says Nikka, who is trying to put my hair in an elaborate updo. I try to twist away from her, but her grip is surprisingly strong. *"Seriously,"* she says. *"How?"*

I know this one! *"You break it little by little, until it barely holds together. And then, all you're prepared to do is hurt someone else."* I clap, pleased with myself; this is probably extra credit. But Luke and Nikka just stare back at me, without smiling. And the teacher leaves the room.

25

I don't know how much time has passed. I could have been sleeping for hours, or just a few minutes. Did I pass out? My eyes have that swollen feeling, like I've been crying *(no! you don't get to cry!)* but when I reach up, my face is dry.

"Haven't seen a tantrum like that in a while," says Night Man. "You're lucky I keep things pristine down here," he goes on, with a note of disgust in his voice. "Because rolling around like that would normally be nasty in this city. The Greatest City in the World? I don't think so."

I don't like this! No fair! My inner monologue sounds like it's three years old, petulant and overtired. I stand, and it hurts more than I let on. "Leave me alone! I don't have time—" I stop, and Night Man nods.

"You don't really know how much time you actually have, do you?" he says. "What if I were to tell you, as much as you want? Or don't want?" He drapes an arm over my shoulder. "Walk with me, Princess. You're gonna love this."

"*I want to see my brother.* I want to know what all of this means, and why you know—or *think* you know—about me. And who you are."

"So walk with me. And . . . you can call me BenoiX. Ends with a capital 'X.' See? I'm giving you my name. I must really trust you."

I let him lead me out of the room into yet another tunnel, then we start down a long, narrow flight of stone stairs. As we pass, black-and-white portraits stare solemnly at me from the walls. After a bit, I realize that they're some sort of weird before and after shots. The facial expressions are the same in both before and after, only the clothes change, and the "After" photos are all dressed in this close-to-ridiculous formal party clothing like the outfit I'm wearing now. The eyes, there's something about the eyes . . . I stare at the last two photos, confused, until I realize with a start that it's Nikka and Luke up there too; their Befores must have been just taken, because they look exactly as I left them a few minutes ago. I swallow and turn away.

We keep going down. These walls are glossy, and the graffiti art on the walls is bright and varied, from flowers to skulls to goblins to yellow smiley faces, all of it tagged with BenoiX. There is a moss-like carpet beneath my feet, and the lower we go, the more I am able to breathe; I hear contradictory sounds of the outdoors, like car horns and sirens and chirping birds and crickets; I also hear distant rumblings of the subway, and none of this make sense this far below the ground, but I realize that I have no idea where I am at this point.

I should have brought Nikka's stupid compass.

My dress is so heavy, and the hammer keeps hitting my thigh. "Stop, I need to take these off, I say. While he stands there watching me, I slowly rip one of the skirt layers at my left hip and tie it into a makeshift purse/basket. I can feel the hammer under the cape, but I can't move it without letting him know it's there. I feel a little less off-kilter around this bootleg magic man knowing I have a few tricks up my own sleeve.

"Seems silly to ruin the dress," he says. "I could have held on to your little hammer. You're going to have a bruise."

You really thought you could hide something from the guy who just showed you . . . YOU?

We continue down the steepest flight of stairs ever, in the kind of loud silence that is excruciatingly awkward. He starts humming, and his voice is smooth and warm, even as it bounces off the walls and echoes.

"How far down are we, approximately? And how did you get down here anyway? Like, the first time?" I ask casually. *You're too intense,* Tunde used to always say. *It puts people off.*

He looks back at me and makes a decision. "Why not? I've got all the time in the world." I step slowly and carefully while he's going down these treacherous steps without looking. I wonder how long he's been down here. "I was a freshman here when I was fourteen," he starts.

"Oh, you really are literally an evil genius," I say, and the laugh dies in my throat under his blank stare.

"I had a lot of time to myself, hung out in the library enough for the librarians to feel sorry for me—they're good at that, I know you know—and that gave me . . . privileges. First, they looked the other way when I ate in Rare Books—nothing egregious, just baby carrots, raisin boxes, I'm not a Philistine, of course—then they just . . . forgot I was there. Started leaving before me at the end of the day."

"Come on," I blurt out. "I get it, you're the lonely, underappreciated hero who's smarter than everyone else. Your origin story. Now the name, the circus outfit . . . what did you do, discover a secret world of superhumanlike robots to do your bidding? This is sounding a little like a bad movie."

"Funny you should say that," he says, as we finally get to the bottom of the steps. "It's exactly like that." There is a door just inches in front of us; I have to stay on the next-to-last step just to fit in the tiny space with him. He puts a hand on the doorknob, and pauses, turning slowly to look at me. "All of your dreams are about to come true."

What about the nightmares? Those too?

This time the Voice sounds like it's right at my shoulder. I whip around, but of course there's nothing there. He opens the door, reaches into the thick-looking blackness, and pulls a rope toward him. He grabs a piece lightly in his hands and passes a length to me. "Hold this, and don't let go. I mean it. It's gonna hurt, and you're gonna want to, but Do. Not. Let. Go."

I take the rope. "But—"

"Did you ever wonder why people started saying 'Geronimo' when they did a rope swing? I mean, how did *he* get into it? People are so stupid. And racist, but what else is new?" He shrugs. "Anyway, I digress. Hold on, Princess. We don't want another tragic ending, right?" Then he yells "AHHHHHHHHHHHHHHH!" and leaps, pulling me along with him.

There are thousands, maybe millions of tiny threads on me, weaving in and around my entire body, simultaneously pulling and squeezing, prying my fingers off of the rope. I try to yell to BenoiX but the ropes snake their way up to my mouth. I'm gasping for air and there is none, only this thick, heavy . . . nothing, and it hurts and I want to let go and fall, just fall away and forget.

You can, you know. Just let go. Let go of your stupid ideas of rescue and redemption. Let go of people who are better off without you. Let go. Let someone else take over. Someone better. Let GO.

My hands are bleeding now, and the threads around my body are like hot wires. I grip the rope even tighter, letting the tears stream down my face. Night Man's cape is flowing behind him, in my face, and I can hear him laughing as we swing. Then we stop.

And we're at the bottom of the steps again. With the door right in front of us. Right where we started.

"What the—" I'm gasping for air, my entire body burning.

"I know, it looks the same, but . . . seriously, are you going to make me explain it?" He shakes his head. "Every time I think they're going to get it . . ." he mumbles. "I really had high hopes for you, Harriet, but I guess you can be forgiven. You have a lot of unnecessary baggage on your mind—and on your back, by the way. The backpack is cute but useless. Like your cousin, hee hee. No dragons to fight here with your nunchucks—excuse me, *nunchaku*—and bat."

I try to curse him out with my eyes, but even that hurts.

"It's the multiverse, silly!" BenoiX cries gaily, and even does a little dance. "It's string theory, infinite possibilities, another YOU. Do you really not get it? It's your real second chance! You're not a loser! You finally got picked. Congratulations, Harriet Adu, YOU'RE A WINNER!!!"

For the first time in my life, I faint.

When I wake up, we are still on the steps. BenoiX is sitting next to an enormous rat, eating a slice of cheese pizza. The rat has pepperoni, and is munching delicately, as though he's trying to buck expectations.

"Pepperoni or plain?" someone asks, and when I realize that I'm not sure which one of them is speaking, that I'm hearing the voice as if through a wall of water, I stand. All of this feels unreal and hazy, and not in a mystical way, but more like *The Wiz*. Then I remember that scene in the subway station when a man is selling toys that grow and turn into menacing monsters. That scared me sleepless for days. That kid Wiz from school pops into my head, whispering, "Ooooooh."

We are in a university lecture hall. I'm sitting in a chipped wooden seat with one of those folding tray desks that pen you in, *you will learn or else*. BenoiX stands down front, a slice of pizza in one hand. He's writing on an old-fashioned chalkboard, and as the chalk squeaks with every stroke, the rats cover their ears. I close my eyes, then open them again. Nothing changes.

"So this is . . ."

"The closest I would say is . . . a wormhole." He finishes his pizza and brushes his hand on his pants. He draws a spiral, punching the chalk at the center so hard that it breaks. "Well, technically, we went through something like a wormhole. Now we're in the Threshold. It's like a waiting room before you go into one of the Other Worlds. You know, a chance to catch your breath before you make a decision?"

"What decision?"

"To trade places, of course." When I continue to stare at him, he shakes his head, seemingly disappointed again. "I really thought you were smarter than this . . ." He looks at me with narrowed eyes. "Maybe I brought you too early? I know that your friend Luke is an MCU fan. He'd probably understand this on a very *basic* level."

Tunde and Luke were Black Panther and Spider-Man for three years straight on Halloween. They'd spent hours discussing Loki and Doctor Strange. They drew the line at on-screen Hawkeye, because even I knew he was corny, but they still debated his story. And when I'd tried to join in their garbled parallel universe conversations with actual astrophysics, they'd told me I *didn't get it*. Yeah, OK. Why would I actually watch a YouTube video about the "nine realms" when real doctors were working with ten possible dimensions? They never had an answer for that. But like everything else, there are *levels*, I've learned. There are regular-degular geeks like me, who eat in the library and do the extra credit, and the ones who are allowed to cosplay at age forty and act superior about imaginary things like infinity stones and magic rings.

"Are you saying that Marvel stuff is real?" I ask BenoiX now, unable to keep my voice from trembling. "Which one are *you*, then?" Tunde used to call me She-Hulk.

He walks to my seat and pats my arm like he feels sorry for me. "I know, it's a lot to take in, but do get those little gears of yours going. There's a lot to do. So: There are other versions of you in other versions of this world. It's all true. It just takes the, how do you say? Lonely, underappreciated, oversmart heroes—and heroines, of course—to figure out how to move through space and time." His accent has changed: It's less Bronx now and more movie British. I don't think either is real.

HARRIET'S 6TH GRADE SCIENCE PAPER

Grade: B-

The universe has not always been "the universe." Before the Big Bang, once upon a time, a long, long time ago, there was a ball of dust and stars and matter packed tight like the snow-balls I threw at my brother, haha. Anyway, the ball of dust exploded one day, and it spread out and cooled over time. And time is the thing. When we're looking at stars in the sky, we're time-traveling! How cool is that?!! We're looking at the past! We're looking back all the time.

Anyway, so that expanding wasn't just like a balloon blowing up. It's cosmic inflation and the universe expanded super fast!!! And then it slowed down, and a glob of matter became galaxies, stars, molecules—that's what we call 'space.'

But cosmic inflation didn't just happen in one part of the universe, although my dad says it's typical Western thinking to think that. It happened everywhere, everything, all at once, and stopped or kept going at different space-times. Universes keep forming in the bubbles and moving away from each other, in an ever-expanding universe. SO COOL, RIGHT?!!

The universe we live in goes on forever. But it's made of the same stuff, and the patterns that create the reality we know eventually repeat themselves, but really far away, where conditions of that part of the universe might be slightly differ-ent, just a tiny bit!!! They get You, only better, and YOU, only worse!!!

Grade: B- Please remember that research papers must cite sources. Watch run-on sentences and overuse of exclamation points.

"So . . . that's what you're all doing down here? Moving through space and time . . . just because?" I try to keep my voice light and dry, and it's not trembling anymore, but I have to keep my hands clasped so they don't shake.

"Well, no, not all of us. Not yet. The others, they aren't quite ready. They're afraid to . . . untether themselves from what you call 'the Real World.' But *I* do," he goes on. "And maybe . . . you, for now. Because that Marvel stuff, as you call it, is as real as you and me." He stretches. "And because you just might be as special as you've always imagined."

Suddenly my desk tray slides down hard, and I'm ejected from my seat to the floor. BenoiX's face is impassive as I stumble upright. "You missed out on some good pizza," he says softly. "I wouldn't let that happen again." It sounds like a threat. When I don't respond, he nods and says, "After you."

I step forward and squeeze my eyes shut and brace myself, but nothing happens, so after a minute I open them. The lecture hall is gone, and we are suspended in deep black air, like stars on a cool, clear night. Now I don't see just one other me: there are about fifty of me, distorted, short, giant, wavy . . . "Seriously?" I blurt out, spinning around, and spreading my arms. "A funhouse?" I'm weightless, like I'm back in the water. I do a slow roll, a Warrior Two pose (*see Nikka?*) *and* pretend to dive into the nothingness.

He shrugs. "I can't help myself sometimes, subtle can be boring. OK yes, welcome to my Hall of Mirrors, which was no easy feat to build down here, I'll have you know. The rats will tell you."

I bet they will. I stop moving and fold my arms and pretend not to notice all of the other mirror mes do the same thing—almost. One scratches her elbows; another hugs her own neck.

"You, only better, and you, only worse," he whispers. I shudder. "And upside down, sideways, any manner of monster in between. I mean, I could show you stories . . ." Now *he* shudders. "That DJ at the prom? He's a member of a trip-hop band called Vixinity in another universe. Wears glow-in-the-dark suspenders, a fake mustache, and calls everyone 'bruv.'" He shudders again. "I may go back and eliminate that one myself, on principle." He notices my frown and smiles again. "Transmogrify. Doesn't seem like a real word. More like something in a"—his voice shifts to a higher pitch—"scary movie?"

As I open my mouth to shut him up, BenoiX holds up a hand. "Aht! Let me finish. You have a choice to make. You can do what you've been dreaming of—or should I say nightmaring?—and get a do-over. Erase that moment you have been regretting for so, so long. Erase it all. Clean slate. Crisscross."

I force myself not to ask any questions, not even with my eyes. I'm not giving him anything—it's the only power I have, even if it's not real. We stand staring at each other; I hear faint sounds of water dripping, and the scurries of what I hope are just rats in the shadows.

His shoulders slump. "You're really not going to give me this, are you? Fine. Basically, as you've already seen, there are other realities where you didn't use the power of your words to kill your brother." I keep staring, and he sighs again. "It's more fun if I show you again."

"But—" I start, but it's too late. I'm wrapped in the threads again, and this time something is pushing me through all of these mirrors, and I can feel the glass shattering around my body, and I don't know how my body is staying together, and I—

"This one is fire," says Tunde, *looking very much alive and real. This Tunde is smiling, trying on hoodies in my room. "What do you think?"* Everything looks exactly the way I remember it.

Other Me is lounging on my bed—my Other Bed, I guess—with my battered copy of God and the Astronomers and an apple on my lap. "I mean it's a hoodie," Other Me says, and then I mouth the words along with her. *"But yeah, that one is good."* It had been my favorite, actually. With an image of Nina Simone across the front, scowling at the world. The first time Tunde had worn it, some oldhead at the

Morningside Park basketball court asked him if it belonged to his sister. Tunde didn't answer, dunked on the guy about two minutes later, and I'd cheered along with the *pick me!* girls who were waiting to talk to him like they always did.

"She reminds me of you," Other Tunde said. It was a crisp, early fall day, still warm enough for me to have my window cracked. A couple of half-hearted NYPD sirens sounded in the traffic on Columbus Avenue, and Schrödinger meowed back. "Nina Simone, I mean."

"Why? You're always talking about how I can't sing," I say. *"Even though you torture us all with your shower concerts."*

"Haha," he mutters, posing in the mirror again. "Did you take the last apple?" he asks.

"I took the last two."

Three . . . two . . . I don't realize that I'm whispering until BenoiX puts a warning finger to my lips.

Other Me throws the apple to Tunde, just like I did when this day really happened, and pulls another one out from under the book.

"Thanks," he says, and bites into it, holding it in his mouth as he maneuvers his way out of the hoodie. "Ta da!" he says, and I mouth along with him, "like magic."

"You are so extra," I mutter, but I'm not mad at it. It's one of those sibling moments that feels warm and sweet, like a cup of hot chocolate. "You could have just waited until you took the hoodie off."

He folds it carefully and tosses scowling Nina over to me; I catch it, one-handed. "Ta da that," I say. "What do you want me to do with this?"

"Keep it," he says. "I know you like it. And it seems like yours anyway. You must have put your juju on it while I was asleep."

"You serious?"

"Yeah," he says. "Happy half-birthday. See you later, I'm going to the park."

"It's not my—" Other Me looks at her phone. Six months to the day.

He's out of the room before I can say anything, and I hear him singing in the hallway, "I Wish I Knew How It Would Feel To Be Freeee!"

I sing with him, softly, and almost on key.

27

I'm pushed backward, firmly, but it doesn't hurt this time. As I stumble back into the cold gray space where BenoiX is standing, I reach forward involuntarily. "Wait—I want—can I go back?"

"You liked that one, huh?" says BenoiX softly, as if to himself. "No one else has made it this far." He sighs. "You get one more, that's the deal. You want to take a break first?"

I'll do anything. Just let me go back. "I don't need a break," I say. "How are you doing this? Can you teach me, please? You said it's not time travel, but that whole thing happened before, exactly like that, I remember every moment."

"I know it seems that way," he says, with the exaggerated patience preschool teachers use. "But it was another strand of the multiverse. That wasn't you *before*. That was another you *then*."

"What?"

"There were little differences, so infinitesimal (I love that word), you just didn't notice them. It takes a lot of practice. But I want you to have even a limited understanding, because you'll have to choose."

"What do I have to choose? If I can see my brother again, I choose that—" I'm talking too fast; my voice breaks, and I swallow and take a breath. "Can you just do that? Can I just keep . . . watching? Can you bring him back?"

"Is that all you want? To see him again? Are you sure?"

"Yes, I—" I stop, and he nods.

"No, it's not all. You want it to go away. You want to erase it, yes? *Eliminate it.* You don't want to be *you*. I know. That's the gift I'm offering. But first, one more. It's *only fair*." He sings that last part again.

"What—" But then the bottom drops out again, like a trap door, and I'm screaming.

Other Me yawns. "I mean, is that the best you can do, call me stupid? And after the last year, do you really want to go there? I'd be surprised if you remember what the honor roll looks like, since the Curse of Katrina."

Why are we back here? Why am I seeing this again? I try to say something, but I can't move. The air around me is viscous and thick; I don't feel BenoiX anywhere. I'm alone. Then it's like the scene is fast-forwarded.

I'm seeing Tunde's funeral. But it's not the funeral, exactly. Uncle Border's suit is blue this time, and Momma is talking to Auntie Francine, who wasn't even there because she couldn't get off from work at the hospital.

Fast forward. Or is it rewind? Back in the bedroom, back hearing "I wish you were dead!" but this time it's the real thing—or is it, because the pillow he throws at me is different, and my hair is in a braided bun?

"I wish I knew how it would feel to be freeeeee!" Is that real Nina Simone?

Then—the funeral again. Auntie Francine is not there, but the Mayor is, and Tunde is getting a posthumous award for his bravery and that didn't happen at all, but—

I don't understand.

There's a ride called the Centrifuge at Playland; I'd go on with Tunde even though I was afraid that it would tear my skin from my body. You whirl around in a cylinder, faster and faster, the force plasters you against the wall, and you laugh and try to peel your body parts away. But you can't. Until it stops. But this centrifuge I'm in is just going faster and faster, and I'm seeing the same scenes as I go around,

I wish you were dead/Tunde's funeral/I wish you were dead/ He's dead, he died, your fault

Like a nightmare carousel, but I can't use my hands to cover my eyes. *I don't understand.*

I hear Night Man's voice right next to my ear. "Don't you? Some things never change."

"What do you mean?" I force the words out even though the air is pushing against me.

"I mean what I say, and I say what I mean," he sing-songs. "Some things never change."

I use all of my strength to turn, and we stop moving. Suddenly, he's standing next to me, smiling a little.

"I'm *prettttty* sure he'll always die," BenoiX says, drawing out the word 'pretty' and waving and holding out his arms for a hug like a spider disguised as a kind uncle. "We can keep going, again and again, and you'll see little differences and new to you possibilities, but . . ." his voice hardens. "Your brother will always end up dead."

As soon as he says "dead" there is a roaring in my ears, like the pool lion has come to life and is coming to get me.

"Even our sometimes suspenders-wearing friend TurnT, who calls himself a DJ," he continues, as though he's reading school announcements, "doesn't know the magic of synth pop." He sighs again. "But I digress. Fortunately, my dear twenty-first-century wonder, you made it here. Because I can help you. At least, if you want me to. You choose. Everyone has a choice."

The roaring is louder, and I shout even though he seems unaffected. "What do you mean?"

He gestures again like I should come in for a hug, and I will my body still. He shrugs, and grins. The roaring stops. Maybe time as well, and my heart too.

"Crisscross," he whispers.

"What?"

"Even if he still dies . . . it doesn't have to be your fault."

28

The Rats trot ahead of us, and BenoiX waves to me that I should follow. I do, because I have no choice. Or, according to him, I do—but I don't understand it yet. Or he'll give it to me. I am trying to form real thoughts, real words, but it's like I hit myself in the head with my useless hammer; "it doesn't have to be your fault" just rattles around in my brain.

We are back in the movie room now, but instead of a screen, now there are mirrors here too, all filled with a thick blue-gray smoke; nothing is reflected. There's a giant man-hole cover in the center of the room, as big as the skating rink at Riverbank Park. A metal alligator (or crocodile, I never remember the difference) crouches in the middle of the circle, its pointed snout closed tightly; coppery teeth that gleam as though they'd been recently cleaned peek out through the sides. *Right,* I think wildly. *Alligators are the ones that live in the sewers.*

"Looks like a Tom Otterness piece, doesn't it?" says BenoiX. "Some of the kids down here are gifted artists, and that croc is one of my favorites."

Crocodile.

BenoiX points me to a recliner facing it, and I sink into a soft, pillowy seat. "Sit. Talk. Now," he says, with a new hardness in his voice.

"So you know the whole story, then," I say, looking down at my hands as he slowly circles the chair. "It was my fault. Once upon a time, I . . . wished my own brother out of existence. Then . . . he didn't exist. My parents lost their firstborn son. My cousin lost her brother-from-her-almost-mother, and Luke lost his best friend. All because of me. I'm a monster. I don't know how you know, or why, or what is happening, but . . ." I trail off. It's a relief, almost, not being alone in the knowing.

"You've never gotten to the penance part before," BenoiX says calmly. "You've been afraid, but you don't have to be. We're all monsters, Harriet," he adds lightly. "The difference is that down here, we accept it, we enjoy it. Don't worry about whether or not you can ever be forgiven. Know that you don't need to be. Welcome home." He points to the Rats standing silently in the shadows; they scurry forward and begin slowly opening the metal crocodile's jaw, gripping the spiky "teeth" and pulling. As they pull the jaws open, the hole gets wider and wider. I can hear a *tick, tick, tick* from the depths, and lean forward, but BenoiX puts a hand on my shoulder. The Rats struggle, sweating and cursing under their breath, which would almost be funny if they weren't also squeaking as their fingerpaws or whatever they are get scratched and cut by the spikes. Bit by bit, and the ticking gets louder and louder.

"The croc is ticking," BenoiX whispers. Then he laughs without a trace of cheer.

What did you mean about it not being my fault is what I want to ask, but once again what comes out of my mouth is different. "Oh, I get it, haha." I say. "A *Peter Pan* reference. Hilarious." I make an effort to roll my eyes and put my hands on my hips, so he doesn't see them shaking.

"You've got a Golden Ticket," he says, as though he's reading a script and not listening to me. "You are where you were always meant to be."

"Why?" I whisper. "Why am I here?"

"Because you know there's nothing—and no one— for you up there."

I'm so tired. I think of the soft princess bed upstairs and wonder if I'll get to sleep on it at some point. I look down at myself; the party dress is filthy and shredded, like it has no memory of what it used to be. There is sludge dripping from my hair, and something black and tarry stuck to my tights, and on my skin where the tights are ripped. *You look like a runaway slave* Tunde used to say whenever he saw me twisting my hair before bed. Until the time Momma heard him and made him write an essay about the Underground Railroad and why it was important to say *enslaved. Their situation was not their identity. You will not perpetuate the theft of their humanity.* He'd included her exact words in the essay, and she hadn't noticed. Or maybe she had, and liked it. "What did you mean, it doesn't have to be my fault?" I finally ask. "Can I . . . take it back?"

"You can never have said it. *Crisscross.*" He stops circling. "We do talk the same language, don't we?" When I frown, he sighs. "*Strangers on a Train!* Come on, you don't watch Hitchcock? We all do down here. He's one of my favorites. A master. Too obvious and basic for you?"

"He was kind of a woman-hater, so I'm not a big fan," I answer. "But *Rebecca* was almost as good as the book." A flash of anger lights behind his eyes, then just as fast, it's gone, and he begins walking around me again, and I know there's nothing there, but it feels like he's creating a barrier— like there's a boundary now, between me and him.

I've been exposed, and I'm alone. And I need his help. *Talk to him nice.*

"I . . . thank you for letting me see . . ." I shrug, because there aren't enough words to say how confused, sad, scared, and . . . hopeful? I am right now. "But why me?" I imitate him just a little, in a show of false bravado that I'm sure he can see right through. "To what do I owe these pleasures?"

"Oh. That. I told you, the others, they haven't fully committed yet. They're satisfied with . . . being in-between. With an endless Prom and someone else telling them what to do. With forgetting what came before, and living in . . . nothing after."

I can get behind the forgetting part. "What do you mean, nothing?"

"You can always," he pauses, "find out."

I wait, and he does too. "Do you think I'm not afraid?" I ask.

"I think you want it more than you fear it," he replies, without smiling. And as he speaks, a series of motivational posters appears on the wall behind him. LIFE IS WHAT HAPPENS WHEN YOU'RE BUSY MAKING OTHER PLANS. YOU HAVE TO LOOK THROUGH THE RAIN TO SEE THE RAINBOW. There's Neil DeGrasse Tyson smiling underneath LIVE LAUGH LOVE.

Then . . . Neil DeGrasse Tyson winks. And the words change to DO OR DIE.

"Speaking of fears . . ." BenoiX is smiling again, and picking a remote control. "Here's one of yours. Go on in, the water's fine!" As he presses a button I'm ejected from the seat toward the gaping crocodile mouth. I automatically twist myself into a dive just before I go into the hole and hit . . . water? It's so cold it burns. I tread water and look up at him waving to me from the edge.

"Time for laps," he says. "You've been slacking off lately, haven't you?"

"What—" The ticking is almost unbearably loud down here.

"You want my help, you work for it. 'The elephant does not limp when walking on thorns.' Ancient African proverb." He smirks.

"Very funny," I say. "That's about as ancient and African as . . ." *As Momma*, I think, and my heart hurts with missing her.

"Well, I thought it was good," he replies, sounding bored. "Anyway, we're starting with what you love. Start swimming."

The water is getting thicker. "Just . . . swim some laps?" I call out. I start a couple of strokes and try to ignore the ticking. "And then you'll tell me where my brother is?" I can't quite keep the begging out of my voice, and I hate myself for it. The water is *hot* now, so hot it burns. Again. Like before, but different. Like no matter what, it's going to burn. The ticking sounds like it's over my shoulder, and I turn to see three crocodiles, real ones, or whatever *real* means down here, moving toward me.

I start swimming.

"Do some laps, and they won't hurt you," says BenoiX. "Just keep swimming, just keep swimming."

Shut up! I want to scream, but I focus on the joyless, painful strokes. I make it to one end of the pool and touch the wall; my fingertips blister from its heat. The crocodiles are a few seconds behind me, and I avoid their eyes as I flip and head back in the other direction. *Now I understand the phrase "hot on their heels" . . .*

Back and forth. The water's getting hotter and hotter and the ticking is louder and closer, but I just keep going. *I will not turn back.* The water is pushing back at me, daring me to move forward with each stroke, and the crawl is excruciating.

I stop to tread water. "So are *you* supposed to be Peter Pan or something?" I wave an arm toward the crocodiles, who are moving slowly toward me as though— "This isn't how I remember the story."

BenoiX dangles a large stopwatch like he's my coach. "Tired?"

My situation is not my humanity.

I hated that stupid story anyway. I go into a backstroke without answering. It takes everything I have not to scream.

I flip over and move into a butterfly without looking up at him. I'm crying now, real ugly crying, snot and everything, but I'm in the water. It doesn't count. It doesn't count. It doesn't count. I let it become a mantra, and my stroke gets smoother.

It doesn't count. I don't think that means what you think it means.

I don't know whose Voice that is anymore.

"Tick tock," he says. "You want me to get to the point, don't you? You slow down when you think too much. You might run out of time."

Time to what? Is he reading my mind? I take the deepest breath I've ever taken and go back to my basic crawl. Back and forth. Back and forth. I've lost count of how many laps I've done. I don't rush, and I don't look back to see where the crocodiles are.

I can do this all day, I think as loud as I can. *Can you read* that?

"Talk to me nii-ce," he sings.

When this is over I will never swim laps again.

Finally, he lowers the stopwatch and offers his hand. I grab it, and he pulls me up swiftly. The ticking fades and I'm shivering. A Rat brings me a dirty blanket.

"Thank you," I whisper. I think it smiles.

"Do you know what you were swimming in? Disgusting." BenoiX says, wrinkling his nose. "Funny. You looked so comfortable in it."

I keep my mouth shut and wait.

"It's worse than just sewage," he goes on. "Think of it as all the despair and shame that you think you leave behind when you pop into that little college pool of yours. You think you feel free in that water, but you're just going back and forth. You don't leave anything behind."

We stare at each other. "Thank you for the opportunity to swim," I say finally. "I love that you have a pool down here. Makes me feel right at home."

Another flash of disappointment, then it's gone, and he laughs. "I knew you were special."

I close my eyes and wait.

"So anyway, I can see that you won't be satisfied with just . . . nothing. I know you don't buy into the Prom and all that. You're on a mission."

I will not turn back.

"So you can switch places with one of the other ones," BenoiX says. "And the multiverse means you just," he snaps his fingers. "Live in one of the other realities. You can enter at the moment before your . . . regret, and voila! Simple swap, crisscross, ding dong the witch is dead. C'est la vie. Or should I say, c'est la mort. C'est la même chose, certainement." He laughs that dry, hollow laugh again and I really start to wonder if he is human.

His French accent is impeccable.

"So," I begin, keeping my voice level. "I go through one of those mirrors to another . . . dimension? And you're saying I just . . . tell the other Me to come here? Then she has to, uh, live *this* life? Will she know what happened? Will Luke and Nikka—will Momma know?" Would she care?

He just smiles.

My momma is worrying about me, I think. You can't say she doesn't care. *Naa naa na naa naa!*

I didn't say anything.

I speak to stop the voices in my head. "Won't the Other Me seem . . . different? And how would I get her to swap?" It's not like I'm offering the Good Life.

"Oh, you're right," he says, rubbing his chin like the college professor in a movie full of white people. "Yes, that would get . . . sticky, wouldn't it?" He claps his hands together like he's just had a thought. "Well, fortunately, no problem! Hakuna matata! You wouldn't have to worry about all that!"

"Why?"

"Well, you'd have to kill the other one of course. OK, I'll forgive you this one, because I know you didn't see it, but . . . Jet Li? I told you, that movie was deep."

"I did see it," I whisper. It was a movie night special. When the pandemic hit New York City hard and Momma prayed so hard every time one of us set foot outside on the empty city streets that I tried not to go out, ever. She had turned the TV on during the first big fight scene, and she'd sat down, impressed with Jet Li's grace. "It's like a ballet!" I'd burst out laughing within five minutes of watching, but I kept watching. Tunde had come in from his daily run, with Luke and Nikka, ripped off his surgical mask, and shouted "Jet Li! Dope!" and demanded a pause until he found it on demand so we could all watch from the beginning and give it "the respect it deserves." Momma made hot pepper popcorn, and I broke out the actual sweater I'd been knitting for over a year (I never finished that thing), and we laughed hard, even Momma, like we were trying to laugh away some horrors we knew were coming. And they did come, even worse than any of us had expected. That's what I think of when I think of that movie. "Yeah, I saw it. So what?"

"So remember Yulaw is killing off his other selves to get stronger, to be, heh heh, the One? That's . . . basically what you can do. But you don't have to kill them all. Or should I say, you all. Just pick one. Any one you want. Like a card. Pick a card, any card."

This does sound just like one of those street card scams that no one ever wins. But I saw them—those Other Mes. I saw Tunde. If I just focus on that . . .

"Can we go to more of them?" I ask. "I want to see more. I want to see my brother."

"Why?" he asks. "You've seen what I can help you do, who I can help you be. You don't have to just see. Just make your choice and you can be. Forever."

"So can you just go over it again, give me the details and stuff? How did you set this all up, exactly?" I ask, after a pause. "Why are you down here? Why is everyone?" My whole body aches, but I know how to buy time with questions, even when sometimes I'm not sure if this is one of those times when I don't really want to find out. Whenever film crews or the NYPD would put up barriers on the sidewalk, telling us that we couldn't walk down our own streets, I'd ask why. Victor, the doorman of the building across the street, used to call me the One with the Questions. These days, he just averts his eyes when I come out of my building without Tunde. "How did all of these kids get down here? Do you all live here? What is Alisia's, um, role?" I'm afraid to ask out loud if she was just pretending to be my friend in order to bring me here. "Also, just . . . why? Why?" I repeat.

"Why, why not, you won't get caught," he sings back in a whisper. "I keep telling you. Consider yourself special. You hit the jackpot. Won the lottery without even going to the corner store." His voice hardens. "All you have to do is choose. Get it done. Now. No trials, tests, monomythical messy stuff that just makes the story longer." He taps his foot. "No, ahem, *fun and games*."

I shift in my seat, and I feel, rather than see, the team of Rats tense up and turn their eyes toward me. "I mean . . . I don't really understand . . . I don't want to kill anybody."

But you already did.

I hear it, clear and cold, like a bucket splash of ice water. I throw BenoiX a sharp glance, but his face is serene and still. Maybe he didn't say it. But it didn't sound like the Voice either.

"My jokes getting a little stale for you?" he asks, again in that low, pleasant voice, like we are meeting at the reception after a debate competition. Suddenly he reaches out and slaps a nearby Rat hard, so hard that it falls backward, and the violence of it shocks me so that my head snaps back as though he's touched me. The Rat hits the ground, and I rush over to where it lies, crumpled on the floor.

I try to avoid looking into its red eyes. "Are you OK?" I whisper. I whirl around on BenoiX, forgetting that I need him, that I hate rats. "What was that for?! Are you sick or something? What's wrong with you?"

The Rat pushes away from me, stands up, and starts chuckling, like this is all some hilarious misunderstanding. I stand there, open-mouthed, as it laughs louder, slapping its . . . knee, tears streaming down those beady eyes. What the—? BenoiX slaps it again and before I can move it holds up a foot and waves the other Rats into the laughing fit. Slowly, they join in. BenoiX moves away from us, and sits on his fat chair, which I realize now looks like some kind of over-stuffed plush purple throne. He looks at me, smirking.

Finally, the first Rat whispers, "Just laugh, Princess! Just laugh. If you want to help me, just laugh."

I look back at BenoiX, who gives me the tiniest of nods, and I force out a short, hoarse bark that could be interpreted as laughter. The Rats give me encouraging looks and laugh louder as BenoiX gets up again, giving each of them a short, sharp slap. Then he turns to me and holds up his hand—

If he tries to slap me I will take him out—I push away the thought before it can finish because I don't know what will happen if he hears it.

Then BenoiX throws back his head and laughs, and the Rats immediately go silent.

"That's why," BenoiX says, continuing the conversation as though nothing has happened. I've forgotten that I even asked a question.

I don't look at the Rats again. I don't know why they're being punished. Maybe they deserve it.

Maybe I'll spend eternity down here getting what I deserve, watching others hurt and not doing anything about it. Maybe that's my punishment, because I'm not enjoying *anything* about this.

"The rest of them up there, they get comfortable," he says. "They don't want more, the way you and I do. Fast food and parties are enough. They don't really want to change the world. And yes, sometimes Alisia is a . . . she invites guests down to join us, to become part of the community. She's been coming down here for almost as long as I have. But she still enjoys going back." He seems almost to be talking to himself now. "She says it's because she wants to share what we have with a select few, but sometimes I wonder . . ." He pats my shoulder. "Again I digress . . . though it doesn't matter. Time means whatever I want it to mean."

I let the silence settle as I pretend to take it all in. "I need to . . ." What do I need? Time to think. Time to remember why Nikka and Luke and Momma will be as OK without me as I think they'll be. Time to accept that what feels like a nightmare is all my dreams come true. . . . "I need to talk to my . . . to Nikka and Luke."

That's not what I meant to say.

And it's clearly not what BenoiX wants to hear. The air is suddenly cold and tight, like it could wrap itself around me, and his eyes flash for a moment, then he smiles. "Feels like making a deal with the devil? Of course. It's hard to let go. I forget what it's like. You should have come alone. Go back, and . . . confer. Remind yourself of *how much you mean to them*," he prods, "and hug and cry and do all those things people do. Then, Harriet, come back. Because you already know that you have to. It's not just about what you did to your brother." He pauses and holds my eyes. "You'll eventually remember that he did it to himself. It's about you knowing that you can be someone else . . . someone who doesn't feel shame, or regret, or loss. *Someone more than you are.*"

As he speaks, there's a whooshing sound in my ears, like there's a river in my head. It's too much. This is too much. I used to accuse Tunde of Jekyll/Hyde mood swings, but those had hurt only my feelings. BenoiX, for all of his promises and proclamations, threatens to hurt my soul.

"It's gotta hurt," he says softly, almost sweetly. "Those are the rules. But after a while, it won't. It's up to you how long that while is."

I turn around slowly, trying to act as though I know what to do and where to go next. "So, um . . ." I stand and make a futile attempt to smooth out my now tattered dress. I want to think that I look kind of badass, like a punk princess from the 1980s, but as I throw my head back I catch my reflection in a smoke-free ceiling mirror. I'm giving drowned zombie. My reflection sneers back at me.

"Also, of course your little fam has to leave then too," he says casually. "You really should have come alone," he adds again, almost mournfully. "It's just like the movies, they know too much now." He laughs. "The Rats will escort you back to the party, let you say your goodbyes." He's speaking in a bored voice, like he's sending me on a bodega errand. "Take some pizza with you."

"I'm not hungry," I say.

"They are," he answers, pointing to the Rats. "And since I won't be there, you'll want to offer them something to eat that's not yourself."

I hope they don't hear my intake of breath. I don't know if giant Rats can smell fear. By the way the one who steps forward bares its teeth, all signs point to yes.

"Wait—what do you mean they . . . Luke and Nikka . . . have to go? How do they get out of here?"

BenoiX doesn't answer me, just nods to the Rats, who turn and start walking down a long corridor, one that we didn't come through on the way in here, but this maze has me so turned round that . . .

"It's a labyrinth," says BenoiX. "Not a maze."

Did I—

"No, you didn't," he smiles again. "But it doesn't matter in here. I'm like Santa Claus. *'He knows when you are sleeping, he knows when you're awake! He knows if you've been bad or good—'* Oh wait, I guess that's not the same. Anyway, you get the drift. Better catch up, the Rats are impatient."

"One more thing—" I stop. "Luke and Nikka, what happens to them if I trade places? What happens to Momma?"

"Nothing," he says. "It'll be like you were never there, I expect. Or like you always were?"

"What does that even mean—"

"Do you really think they'll miss you?" And this time, it's BenoiX and the Voice in unison, like some horrible chorus.

I stand there, frozen, wishing for water so I can cry.

He grins. "Kidding, I'm kidding," he says, then his smile drops. "It won't be nothing. Like I said, it's gotta hurt. Let it be on your head!" He rubs his hands together. "And I can't wait."

"OK, yes, fine, let it be on my head, just me." I'm babbling and then I *am* crying. "Let them get out of here, I never meant, I didn't want —"

"Oh, yes you did. And you still do. Go. Now. Before you run out of time." He points down the dark corridor; the Rats have disappeared. "You'd better get going. There are Others down here who are not my business or my problem. You don't want to meet them. *'So be good for goodness' sake!'*"

I turn and run.

29

The Rats sound far ahead of me; I can't tell where they are, but I follow the patter of little feet that I hope belong to them. Other sounds surround me in the white-hot brightness of the tunnel—water dripping, low moans, an occasional scream. *OK. Great. Just keep swimming.* I shield my eyes with one hand and hold the other out in front of me as I walk; the tunnel seems to bend and curve more than I remember it did on the way into the Hall of Mirrors, but then again, I have no idea if I'm heading back the same way. I trip over something hard and cold and then pause for a moment to listen for my Rat guides. The silence that surrounds me is louder than anything I've ever heard.

"Over here," whispers a voice in front of me. "Follow the sound of my voice . . . that's it, slowly, slowly . . ."

I walk along until my outstretched hand touches something furry, and I swallow a scream. "Are you . . . one of my escorts?"

"Yes, and thank you for trying to help me earlier. Night Man was just making a point."

"Oh, it's you!" I say, louder, and my words echo. "I don't get—"

"Less talk, more walk," the Rat says urgently. "I don't want to meet the BRats any more than you do."

"What are—"

"*Shhhh!*"

The Rat leads me to a large, damp wooden door that's slightly ajar. It frowns and grabs my arm, pushing me through.

"Ow! Wait—you're not coming with me?"

"I'll be there. I have work to do first, and I don't want to make him—just go, please hurry." His eyes are sad as he gives me a gentle shove back into the ballroom.

Only a few kids remain at the party, which is looking as after-the-ball now as I am riches-to-rags mode Cinderella: It feels much bigger and colder, some kids are wearing custodian uniforms and wiping the tables, sweeping, and bagging decorations. One boy is on the floor scrubbing up glitter with a toothbrush, which seems like the definition of futile. The air smells faintly of lavender Fabuloso, and I try to hold my breath as I hold up what's left of my skirts and walk across the room. I pretend not to notice the stares and just focus on a point in the distance just over everyone's head. A trick I learned from my old principal.

Luke and Nikka are sitting exactly where I left them, as though it's only been moments. Has it? Or has it been hours? *Time means whatever I want it to mean.* Right now, I want to go back to the three of us sitting at Eton together, dipping dumplings in soy sauce and laughing about old movies. Will I spend my life wanting to go back? I close up the memory and walk forward.

"Welcome back," Nikka says flatly, without looking at me. Luke just nods.

"Not exactly the hero's welcome," I say. *If you only knew what I'd seen.*

"We're just . . . tired. What about you? What happened? Are you OK, cuz?" Nikka touches my arm lightly. She's the one who looks decidedly *not* OK. Any other day I'd clown her for being ashy, but now I'm scared.

"I'm fine," I mutter. "Are you? Listen, you have to get out of here. Now."

"No kidding," says Luke, rolling his eyes. "Glad you're ready to go. But I don't know if they're gonna just let us get up and go, you know?"

"What do you mean?"

Luke just looks at me, then gets up and takes two steps forward, and the Three Boys materialize out of nowhere to shove him down to the floor. They swagger away, laughing, as Nikka and I help Luke back up.

"*That's* what I mean," he grunts.

I look around for Alisia. "I'll handle this."

"Speaking like the Queen of the—" starts Luke.

"Of the *what?*" I ask. "Did you sit around making fun of people like you always do? It must have burned you from the inside to see people like me not even thinking about trying to impress you." *I'm talking to make them leave,* I tell myself. *I don't mean it.* This is my punishment, to have to make them think I don't care. He was right; it hurts.

"I was thinking bullies, actually," says Luke. "Queen of the Bullies. But even though you've got a fierce left hook and a mean mug for days, you're not a bully."

"These aren't *people like you*, Harriet" Nikka interjects, with an urgency in her voice. "You are *nothing* like them."

A matter of time, I hope. "Did you see where Alisia went?"

"I thought she was with you," says Nikka. "She followed you into the Lair or whatever that was. So, who is the Night Man guy? Is he old? I heard someone saying that he's the former college student who mapped out these tunnels in the first place, the one who got kicked out of school."

"I don't think so, but I'll tell you everything when we're out of this room," I say.

Well, sort of. I still have to figure out what exactly I'm going to tell them, because it definitely won't be the truth. I don't even think Confession is safe enough for the truth. *Let go and let God.* Yeah, OK.

"Wait, you're still not trying to *leave* leave?" asks Luke, agitated. "Like what will it take for you to understand how bananas this is? And it's more than just bananas, it's dangerous! I—"

I see Alisia push past the Boys and the party stragglers who have been watching us fuss at each other. "Amazing, right?" she calls with a wide smile. "How did it go?" She grabs both of my shoulders eagerly and turns me to face her fully.

Nikka makes a face. "Wow. Can you not be so rough? I guess I'm not gonna call it manhandling, but . . ."

Luke lets out a short laugh.

Alisia ignores them. Her eyes feel like they are burning through my skin. "It was . . . a lot," I answer carefully. I lower my voice. "You could have warned me." *How much does she see?*

"It's different for everyone," she says with a shrug. "It depends . . . on why you're here." Now there are questions in her eyes, but I look away. Of course, that's the moment my stomach decides to grumble. Loudly.

"I thought they gave you the royal feast, Hungry Hungry Hippo," said Luke, using the name he and Tunde had thought was so clever when I was in first grade and they were in third. "Your stomach sounds like the A train's approaching."

My hand reaches up to slap him before I even realize that I've moved. The *crack!* of my palm against his cheek echoes through the hall, and after long seconds of shocked silence, the clean-up kids clap.

Did I do thaaat?

"Steve Urkel? Now you're really playing in my face, aren't you?" I'm talking back to the Voice. Out loud. I feel Nikka's stare.

What? You and Tunde loved those old shows.

And we had. Even though we were in high school, the "no TV except for PBS and Black people rule" stood strong, and we didn't mind much because nineties TV was "a gold mine of Black sitcommery," as Tunde said.

"What the—" Luke rubs his cheek and staggers away from me. He's still unsteady on that leg; Nikka grabs him before he hits the floor.

"That's the way to do it," Alisia says, doing a little shimmy. "Let 'em know, Sis." She rubs her hands together. "But seriously, you didn't really get to eat. Night Man called you out quicker than he usually does, you missed most of the Prom. And I guess you've just done a lot of . . . traveling. I can set something up—"

I've forgotten all about the Rat who brought me back here; it steps forward and hands Alisia a note. "From Night Man," it says solemnly. It offers a deep bow in my direction, which doesn't register at first because I'm still looking at my hand.

"Nasty thing," Alisia mutters, snatching the note.

"Hey—" I start, but the Rat looks at me with pleading eyes.

Alisia reads the note for a long, long time, frowning.
Finally, she looks at me with a strange mixture of joy, fear,
and fury. "Oh, you a real one," she says softly.

"What?" I hold my hand out, but she slips the note
into her pocket.

"He says to reset the Prom. Start this party over
again. A do-over. Give you the royal treatment again, only
better." She shrugs off the question in my eyes. "It won't
matter to them," she whispers, turning with me toward the
stragglers. "They're all literally sleepwalking through what
they think is a life." She raises her voice. "He says it should be
'out of this world.'" She raises an eyebrow and whispers.
"And into another."

"Will you—" I start.

"I'll be there," she says. She jerks her head toward
Nikka and Luke. "But they won't. Greg! Mark! Theo!" she
calls, and the Three Boys jog over. "These two go in the
Hole."

As they grab Luke's arm, he winces.

"Stop!" I say. "What's the Hole? You're hurting them!"

"No they're not," Luke says quickly. "They wish."

"It's just a waiting room," says Alisia smoothly. "We'll
make plates for them. What do you want? A Cookout? We
can do a whole bonfire barbecue thing if you want."

Nikka gives Greg a hard knee to the crotch and he groans. "You were *hurting* me," she says sweetly, almost like she's flirting, except he's doubled over. I stifle a laugh.

"Just like you hurt your 'cuz' here, hmmm?" says Alisia. "All this time, making her think that *you* were the princess?"

"What do you mean?" Nikka's eyes are wide.

Alisia looks at me. "She doesn't even remember."

And I can see in Nikka's confused stare that she doesn't. That she forgot about all of those times, all of those "You be the jester. You be the dog. You be dead."

Your wish is my command, cuz. Would she miss me?

"Nothing about this is wild to you, Harriet?" asks Luke, his voice breaking. "A Cookout? Harriet, I don't know what you've just been through with that Night Man or whatever, but I know you've been through it." Nikka puts a hand on his arm, but he shakes her off. "I can *see* you've been shattered. Why did you smack me like that? That's not you. We are underground. Like under the subway or something. These kids are . . . something's not right. *You're* not right. And this witch is here talking about barbecues and bonfires? Snap out of it, please, so we can get out of here? *Please.* Whatever is going on with you, we can fix it." He stops, breathing hard, like he's just finished lifting weights. Nikka looks from him to me and back; then she squeezes his hand.

"Sadé! Sadé! Sadé!" Alisia walks over to the plat-form/stage to stand next to the DJ, leading a drawn-out chant of the singer's name. "Shaaaa-day! Shaaaa-day! Shaaaa-day!"

I wait for the DJ to slide into some dance mix of one of the singer's smooth tunes—but she's pointing right at *me*.

Nikka gasps. "When did you tell her your secret name?"

I didn't. It's another thing that she just ... knows. "You mean the one you told me I couldn't have?" I reply. *Remember? Do you remember that? Because I do. I remember it all. I didn't tell Alisia anything. But maybe she knows. But maybe you were wrong about me like you always are.* "Maybe you were wrong" is all I say.

I take a few steps away from Nikka and Luke; they are still wet, dirty, and smelling like they've literally been dragged through a sewer. But how is it that I'm wearing the prom dress ... but they still look like the Homecoming Royalty?

Because your cloak of shame is not that invisible.

But they're here, though. I look at my cousin and my brother's best friend.

Who have no idea of the troubles I've seen—

But they came with me anyway.

For some stupid reason, they just won't leave me alone.

For their own sake, I have to make them.

"Oh, you can fix me?" I say slowly. "You can't help it, can you? Always have to make me feel less. Always got jokes. Resting Witch Face. Hungry Hungry Hippo—"

"Are you serious right now? We've been doing that joke since we were kids! You always laughed. It's like how you used to call me 'Moldy Muppet Man' after—"

"Shut up, Luke," I say. I don't recognize my voice. *You choose to be this awful.*

Alisia hops down from the stage and positions herself in front of me. She pulls a whistle out and blows on it, letting out a long, slow call, almost like a whale song. It's beautiful. People start flowing back into the room; I recognize them from the party earlier, but something's different again, and I can't figure out what is. Their movements are languid and fluid, like a gorgeously choreographed dance. A few smile at me, but most look above my head, unfocused, at something I can't see. They're all wearing glow-in-the-dark white nightgowns and pajamas—what Nikka would call loungewear—and they look as though they've been awakened from a deep sleep. The maybe-British/maybe-not DJ strolls in, wearing what looks like a astronaut's white outfit. He gives me a salute, and there's a glimmer of light. I start; for a second I thought I could see through his hand. He strolls over to the turntable and then starts up the kind of pulsing, bass-heavy dubstep that you feel in your stomach. A few people drift out onto the dance floor.

Some kids who look younger and a little less at-home down here begin setting a table, and a group of Rats build the promised bonfire. Two girls bring me a clean long white dress and a new pair of boots.

One of them points to a curtain in the corner. "You can change over there, Princess. The Rats will stand guard."

The Boys step forward and Nikka and Luke tense up.

"Wait," I say quickly and firmly. "Before they go to the, um, Hole, I want to talk to them." They look at each other, then me. "We have unfinished business. After that, they're all yours."

"Whatever she says goes, y'all," calls out Alisia, waving the note from BenoiX. "Until it's time. Night Man's orders. They can chill in the Waiting Room for a while. And don't touch them. I mean it: not a scratch."

I can feel Luke's eyes on me as they're taken away, but I don't look at him.

One of my favorite songs is playing, and all of the kids who are still in the room start dancing. They form a cir-cle, and Alisia steps down from the DJ platform and yells "Brown Girl in the Ring!" They open the circle, and wave me to the center.

Luke's right—*this is WILD*—

This is what it would be like to be an Other Me.

I join the circle. The kids cheer and push me to the middle and dance around me. I stand there and paste on a smile and try to feel whatever this is that they're giving me. They dance, and I want to feel better, or worse, or something, Anything other than this frozen nothingness building around my heart. *But maybe that's what it takes*, I think. Maybe that's how the story ends.

30

You know when people start a sentence with "I'm not gonna lie, but . . ." or "I'm just being honest . . ." or "I'm not saying this to be mean, but . . ."—and they are totally about to be horrifically mean and lie to themselves about it, or lie to be mean, or just saying something just to say something? Well, that's not me, and I'm just being honest: being me, only better, is . . . pretty good.

I've just had real jerk chicken and rice and peas with fresh pineapple-laced sorrel to drink. "A little birdie told me you have a connection to my home country," Alisia said, sounding like an auntie, after she asked the DJ to play Koffee. "Don't say I never did anything for you!"

We talk about how we love climbing Dunn's River Falls even though it's a total tourist trap; how we feel like superheroes after the mineral baths; how we're worried about the manatees in Negril. I barely even need to get the words out before she agrees, or has done it too, or *was thinking the same exact thing!* We are playing a game of Mirrors, reflecting each other, but still . . . for some reason, my heart doesn't leap with new best-friend joy anymore. There's a tension that makes me choose each word with caution; there is something in the air around us that I don't want to disturb. A faraway memory of a frustrating Scrabble game with Nikka hangs at the corner of my mind. We'd argued over the spelling of the word "simpatico." Nikka had been right, there was no "y," and I'd swiped at the letters, destroying the progress we'd made.

I stroke the satiny silver lounge set I'm wearing now. After I was whisked over to the dressing room to clean up and change, I was led to a round table with Alisia and a few other kids who are clearly top tier down here. They ignore everyone but each other—and me. The other kids, who are cleaning and carrying platters of food in and out, have been watching us hungrily the whole time.

When the DJ plays one of Nikka's favorite songs, I feel a twinge of guilt, but it's so small that I can snuff it out immediately.

"So, what are you in for?" Alisia asks casually, but I stiffen. "Seriously. Let's talk."

I eat my jerk chicken wing, trying to buy some time. Also, it's really, really good. As Uncle Border would say, "They put their foot in this food!"

I look over at the dusty, crusty bare feet of one of the kids bringing over more platters.

Ugh, I hope not.

Oh, you really got jokes now, huh?

What, you're done trying to spook me? I blink. *You're making small talk with the voice in your head, Harriet. You'll be spooking yourself soon enough.*

I shake my head and focus on the food in front of me like a good Hungry Hungry Hippo. There's a bowl of roast corn in front of me, and a green coconut with the top cut off to my left, cheerful yellow straw perched inside.

"Hello? I said, what are you in for?" Alisia laughs. "Sorry, figure of speech. I mean, you like it here, right? And it seems like BenoiX has even better in store."

"So you guys just live down here? You're all runaways?" Alisia doesn't exactly look like a real-world outcast. She looks . . . happy and healthy, and like someone who is adored.

That's why you were so glad she liked you. You really think it's gonna rub off?

I push the Voice away. "I mean, some of these kids seem . . . like they were born here." And not in a good way, I realize. The kids who are cleaning up are increasingly wan and sickly-looking. But Alisia, she's glowing like she's lit from within.

As a girl walks by with a large silver tray under her arm, a flash of light bounces off and hits my eye, and a memory shoots through me so hard that I wince.

Shine on

Shine on

Shine on

"Film school with Tunde" was an occasional surprise event for the two of us, when he was bored and Luke was busy. During one of our last ones, he'd pulled up a blurry copy of an old movie from the eighties with a cute guy who loved old kung fu flicks and spent the whole movie trying to reach the level where he got the Glow.

"I cut this girl once," Alisia says calmly, jolting me back to the party. "That's what brought me down here. These kids at my old school, every day they had something to say to me, about me . . . every day. So I let them know that I could shut them up if I wanted to." She shrugs and picks up a plate of boiled plantain. "What is this? I specifically said fried sweet plantain, did I stutter?" I think she's joking when she places her hands on the table and stands slowly, but then I see the flames in her eyes that are way more than just a glow. "Who's in the kitchen?" she yells.

One of the younger kids runs out of the room.

"Um, what's the big deal?" I whisper.

"BenoiX is always very specific about meals and theme, and this was meant to be a treat for you," she answers, her face like thunder and like someone who "cut this girl once." She tosses the plate of boiled plantain like a Frisbee, and a Rat ducks out of the way.

"I mean, it's still good food," I murmur.

"That's not the point," she says curtly, as the runner returns with two more Rats, who look . . . different. Harder, maybe. Their red eyes remind me of the flames I saw in Alisia's. The middle school-looking kids have stopped working; they're staring and shaking, wide-eyed, at Alisia. And me.

"You know, I'm fine with plantains either way," I say. "Green, sweet, all good." I try to smile. "I mean, you're Jamaican, right? Don't you eat green bananas or whatever? Hey did you know in Nigeria, plantains are called dodo? But they say planTAYN, not PLAHNtin like you." I'm babbling. "People think I'm Nigerian. And by people, I mean my mom." I'm making things up now, blending facts with what feels close enough to the truth, like Momma when she'd tell a bedtime story that started with whatever had actually happened that day. "Like they did one of those ancestry tests, you know?" *I'm sorry, Momma. I know I'm changing the story, but I have a good reason.* "And Momma is like twelve percent Nigerian, which she always suspected, and then she started making dodo all the time, and it's cool, it's one of my favorites, however it's cooked—"

"Well, now we don't have any," snarls Alisia, as though she wasn't the one who just threw the plate across the room.

I start babbling again, "I mean, sometimes, my brother, we used to pretend we had a show, like Food Network? We'd flip it, like breakfast for dinner, or a bacon and peanut butter sandwich. I was always in charge of the bacon—we set off the smoke alarm so many times! Tunde would, he would sing while he cooked, he could really sing . . . I wanted to, but I don't have the voice—"

Yes, you do.

I stop. Alisia is staring at me with an expression that makes me think again of Nikka, Luke, and Tunde sitting on Ms. Taylor's stoop, making fun of people as they walked by. Laughing, and laughing, and laughing.

After a heavy minute, she smiles. "You're lucky the Princess is here," she calls loudly, and almost everyone in the room takes a collective breath of relief.

Princess. I'm starting to hate that word. Nikka had a baby doll . . .

The kids and (Good?) Rats start moving and bustling about again, carrying platters, murmuring nervously. Someone slides a plate of sweet plantains in front of me eventually, and in a flash I think of Momma, putting my dinner plate down softly every night, even when I'm in trouble, even when she's sucking her teeth and muttering under her breath. Gently, even though sometimes I forget to say thank you.

A very young girl pours more sorrel into my glass, and when I turn to her, she gives me a wide gap-toothed smile. *No!* She can't be—can she? She looks like my little friend. First the park, then the pool. *Now here?* No. Not here. She shouldn't be here. I don't want to see her in this place where I belong. She touches my hand, briefly, then slips away before I can even say thank you. She's pressed a piece of silver paper in my hand, a tightly folded gum wrapper, maybe. I close my fingers around it before Alisia can see. As I stare at her retreating back, I realize that I can . . . see through her? I look again at the kids cleaning in silence and realize that they're . . . not there, almost. It's as though they're fading away. I blink. Clearly, the candlelight has me spooked.

"So anyway," says Alisia, "the pain had a point. They were wrong, they had to pay the price. And it was . . . expensive, let's just say that." She shrugs. "The pain *is* the point. Some people . . . a lot of people didn't get it. But here? It hurts good. This is a place where you can enjoy who you really are. And I do enjoy it . . . so very very much."

We're both silent for a few minutes. I eat some more, and watch the kids on the dance floor. The DJ is now playing something that sounds like grime, and there's one girl dancing off to the side, wearing a flouncy red dress, jerking and flailing, her feet moving furiously fast, almost but not quite on beat. It's a scene straight out of a teen movie—all she needs is a circle of laughing kids around her—but no one else seems to be paying attention. Her red heels are incredibly high, and her speed, at least, is impressive. But when she turns, her eyes are just circles, blank, black yawning tunnels, and her mouth is open in a silent scream, this gaping red hole. I blink and she's not facing me anymore. Her feet are still going, though, and no one cares. The crowd swallows her up, and I look away. It was a trick of the light. This is not

Coraline. My eyes are still playing tricks on me. *I'm too tired.* I scan the crowd for the girl again, but I don't see her.

"Uh, when can I talk to BenoiX again?" I ask Alisia after she's finished eating. Her plate is smoothly slipped away almost as soon as she puts her fork down. "I have some questions." I try to smile. "After I see Nikka and Luke?"

"Oh, you got the *special* name," she replies, raising an eyebrow. "He must really like you." She smiles. "I knew he would! We all do. We love you, Harriet. We really do." She pats my arm with a *there there* motion that is not reassuring. Maybe because those flames are back in her eyes? Or is that also a trick of the light? "He'll let you know when it's time. You may as well enjoy this time right now. I'm going to request a merengue set next, it gets things going perfectly. You may have noticed Rose. She loves to dance. And dance. You can really see it in her eyes."

There is so much light, and so many tricks. My eyes and brain hurt. "You know what," I say, "I'm exhausted. This is . . . amazing, but I need to lay down for a while." I try to put a casual note in my voice. "Maybe I can hang out with Luke and Nikka in that waiting room?"

She laughs. "I don't think you want to go *there*." She claps, and two Evil Rats trot over. "Kill the DJ," she says, and I start, because I'm honestly not sure what she means by that. But the BRat just goes over to the booth and whispers in the DJ's ear, and the music stops. Everyone on the dance floor turns toward me and Alisia in unison.

"Uh, I didn't mean to—"

Alisia puts a finger to her lips. "Shhhhh . . . *it's Showtime!*"

Heavy red curtains drop from the ceiling, and a stage rises from the floor. The kids in the room applaud politely, and after a look from Alisia, I join them. Rats move to either side of the curtains, and pull,

SCENE 1

LUKE and NIKKA are suspended in the air, just under the lights. They appear to be attached to wires, like marionettes. They "swim" toward each other, laughing. Three crocodiles move back and forth on the stage below, but Nikka and Luke don't seem to see them.

I turn to Alisia. "What the—what is this? Get them down, please! This is freaking me out."

She smiles. "Freaks, you say?"

LUKE
She thinks this freakshow—this
(He gestures out toward the ballroom)
is real.

NIKKA

It is! But I know how the story goes.

(Nikka twirls.)

LUKE

Why did Auntie send us down here with her? There's no point—

NIKKA

To make sure she doesn't come back, silly. This is where she belongs.

(They both laugh again, rubbing their hands together like cartoon villains. Suddenly one of the wires holding Luke breaks.)

LUKE

(still laughing) Uh-oh.

(They look down and see the crocodiles and stop laughing abruptly.)

(Another wire breaks, just as one of Nikka's does. They're both crying now.)

"What's happening?" I whisper to Alisia. "This isn't funny, they could get hurt!"

I hear the *Pop!* of more wires breaking, and Luke and Nikka are both literally hanging by a thread. "Stop!" I yell, jumping up. "They're going to fall!"

"Isn't that what you want?" Alisia asks. "Isn't this what you've asked for?" She points to the stage. "Your wildest dreams come true!" She and the kids start clapping again, with gusto, and she stands as though she's giving Luke and Nikka a standing ovation. "What goes up," she sings, "must come down!"

(Luke's wires break completely. As he falls, he grabs Nikka, and is dangling from her leg.)

I race toward the stage and I'm holding out the skirts of this stupid dress to catch them, because what else can I do
This is not what I want
What I've ever wanted
And I know I can't save them
(again)
But I have to try
I take it back
    I hold out my dress like a preschool parachute and close my eyes as the last wire *pops*—
    And they fall like feathers, wafting onto the dress, and I gather them up—
    Pop! Alisia snaps her fingers.

They're gone.

"Where are they?" I yell, turning back to Alisia. "What did you do?"

Alisia sighs, and walks me back to my seat. "It's clear that you need a little encouragement, don't you?" she says. "All this we've laid out, everything BenoiX told you, and you still need more."

"Was that . . ."

"It wasn't real," she says. "It was hilarious, but it wasn't real. Don't worry, or do . . . they're just Waiting. BenoiX just wanted you to understand that we can remove them if you don't. I thought you'd want the pleasure, but if you don't . . ." She trails off, and shrugs as if to say *Your loss!*

The pain is the point. "Alisia, I'm confused, and I just want to talk. Like for real. Can we just talk, please? "

"Their time's running out," she continues, as though I haven't spoken. She points to the Evil Rats. "They can take you now to your room now. I'll have those two brought up. I'm sure BenoiX wants them to meet the BRats anyway."

"BRats?"

"Bad Rats, it's BenoiX's little joke. I like Good Rats and Hood Rats, but"—she rolls her eyes—"apparently that's inappropriate. Even though they're rats."

"It's B-Rat," says one of them sharply. "Like the b-boys and b-girls of the eighties."

"Yeah, OK," Alisia smirks. She turns back to me. "They're . . . not like the others. Not exactly part of our community, but . . . we help each other out from time to time. There are a lot of them when you go further down and further in, you'll see."

They bare their teeth at me.

"I don't think I need an escort this time, I can find my way back to my room. Right there?" I point to a door, then another. "No wait, it's that one. And then I make a couple of lefts . . . Uh, yeah, I can figure it out."

"Already settled in, huh?" Alisia says. "He was right. He's always right about who Belongs. You want to talk? A little advice. Stop trying to please—to belong where you don't. The princess thing is OK, but I can tell you know it's not the real thing. It's not what you really want."

Our eyes lock, and I nod slowly. She leans in and her voice drops to a whisper. "It's silly and wrong to fight who you are. When you stop doing that, your real life can begin."

"I . . . really need to lie down," is all I can muster. "After I talk to my —"

"That's fine, go ahead, the BRats will go get your . . . little friends and deliver them to your room. Safe and sound." She smiles without showing teeth, and I think again that she and Nikka look like they could be sisters. Or cousins, at least.

My father had a little book of Anansi stories that he'd saved for us from his own childhood. He'd read them to us so much by the time I was six that he'd make up new endings and lessons, but Anansi always prevailed. "He wasn't just a trickster," Daddy would say, "He was a rebel."

I stand, almost toppling my chair and murmuring thanks to everyone who has been buzzing around us like anxious worker bees. "It's time to boss up!" Nikka had said to me during our last little sleepover, standing on my bed and throwing her arm into the air. I'd thrown a pillow at her for sounding like a talk-show host that our mothers watch. Now I slowly lift my arm over my head, too much like I'm not sure of the answer and not enough like a confident superteen, pretending not to notice Alisia's quizzical frown. I am going to get Nikka and Luke back home.

I have to try.

My family needs me to save the day.

31

When I get back to my room, I can't tell what's changed, but somehow it feels more like a hotel. The bed sheets are even turned down, with three foil-wrapped chocolates on the pillow. Everything is still sparkling clean, maybe even brighter than before. There is a faint scent of lavender now, and the memories of damp tunnels and dark corridors are already fading. I push down the thought that even if the Waiting Room is just that (*you know it's not*), it's nothing like this.

I shudder, remembering how real that stage looked.

I can't figure out how to turn down the lights. I shower, and even though there's a freshly laundered and neatly folded pair of jeans and T-shirt on the bed, I put my old clothes back on. Then I lie back on the bed and close my eyes, wondering if I'll get in trouble for doing that in these most-outside-of-outside clothes.

Should I stay or should I go?

If I stay here, will I glow?

Was Alisia just putting me on? Did she actually . . . hurt someone? Does that mean that she'll understand what I did? Did that . . . performance . . . mean that she thinks I'm not sorry?

Sorrynotsorry

Now the *I have a friend* flutter feels like fear. I don't want to ask her for more details. I don't want to know how far she'll go. But I guess "I cut this girl" tells me all I need to know.

You're kindred spirits, remember?

I didn't mean it. Doesn't she know that I wish I could take it back?

You can. So what are you waiting for?

The door slams open and I sit up quickly. A BRat pushes Nikka and Luke inside.

"Ow," says Nikka as she stumbles. I wonder why she hasn't figured out that her drama queen routine doesn't work down here. The BRat closes the door and locks it from the outside.

"How . . . how was the waiting room?" I ask, because I don't know how to start. "Did you eat?"

"You sound like Auntie," says Nikka. "Every time she wants to apologize, she gives you a plate of food instead."

Luke laughs a short, dry bark. "That's the Black Mom Classic, across the Diaspora."

"Why would I be apologizing?" I turn away from them. "I told you not to come down here. But you *chose* to ignore me." No. I can't bear to leave them—leave us—like this. With this Me in their memories. "Look. There's a lot going on here that you're not going to understand. I have a decision to make. I'm not sure how much time we have but—"

"And *you* know what's going on?" Luke hisses. "You've got a handle on this . . . ?" he waves his hand, and stops. "What decision?"

I lower my voice and talk fast: "I need you to listen to me and get out of here. I'm pretty sure I can talk to the Rats about taking you at least part way. Let Momma know I'm coming, I just have to take care of something here first."

"I don't know what you're talking about, but if you think we're gonna just leave you here—"

I turn to Nikka. "OK, you like talking about how we're family, so I need you to be about it now and trust me. Go back. I don't want Momma to be alone, she's lost enough—"

"You're scaring me, cuz," says Nikka, moving toward me.

"You're scaring yourself," I say, louder than I mean to. "Can you not be overdramatic right now? Just let me win for once?"

Luke lets out a loud laugh. "Now that's hilarious. You got jokes, Harriet. You and your sensitive self. How many times did my boy Tunde tell us to let you win? You couldn't even handle checkers without flipping over the board." He laughs again, without a trace of joy.

Nikka glares at him. "Luke, we talked about this, I don't think—"

We both ignore her. "What are you talking about?" I walk up to Luke and look him in the eye.

"Oh come on, game nights? Every time we played hide-and-seek, tag, everything? I mean, I get that he was doing the big brother thing, and he made sure that we fell in line, but damn, hearing you talk about 'just this once' . . ." his voice breaks. "It just reminded me of him, that's all."

It is so cold. I turn away from them both and realize for the first time there's a large oval mirror hanging over the ridiculously frilly dresser. It makes me think of Snow White. Now I see the tiara, on the dresser under the mirror. It's shining like it's alive. I remember that haunted dancing girl at the Prom.

"I'm not sure what you mean, but it doesn't matter," I answer. "Nikka, do you understand what I'm telling you?"

"Remember how he would slow down in races, even if you were actually winning, just to make sure you won by a big margin?" asks Nikka slowly, like she's speaking in a dream. "Oh—and the block Olympics? Remember?" A ghost of a smile plays around her mouth. "He made us look so stupid, cheering and yelling and giving you a slow clap standing ovation when everyone knew he could beat us all without even trying. Everybody looking at us like we were bananas."

"You are now," I say shortly. "Because you've either lost your mind, or you're making up stories, and when I tell you this is not the time—"

"TICK.

"TOCK."

It's BenoiX's voice, quiet and loud at the same time.

"TICK.

"TOCK."

It's slow and deliberate and coming closer and I don't know what he's going to do to them . . .

"You've got to get out of here," I say to Nikka, as firmly as I can this time. "Both of you. You have to go. Nikka. Please."

She sits on the bed, like we're having another sleepover. Like we're going to do our nails and eat chips.

"TICK. TICK. TICK."

It's just loud now, excruciatingly loud, and I cover my ears just as the tiara breaks apart and disintegrates into a glimmering dust.

"Do you not hear that?!" I yell.

They glance at each other, then Nikka pats the space on the bed next to her. "Cuz. Come sit. We haven't talked about it," she says. "None of us have. Maybe it's time."

"TICK. TICK. TICK."

I turn back to the mirror, where my reflection is somber and ashy, but I keep staring, like the main character in a young adult novel. "Nikka there's nothing to talk about. Please, please, I am begging you, just go." I appeal to Luke: "Luke doesn't want to talk about anything. Right, Luke? He wants to get out of here. Right Luke?"

He doesn't answer, which is one.

"That's true, Luke doesn't want to talk about it," says Nikka quietly. "He wants to be angry at himself, beat his chest or something. That's *easier.*"

Luke stares at her. "Serious, Nik, what are you doing right now?"

She stands and stares back at him. "I mean, you were there, right? Right there, in the lunch room. I heard you threw yourself in front of—"

"Shut up." Luke's words are short and sharp, and his voice is unfamiliar. I look from him to Nikka and back again. Before, this would have been . . . interesting. "Shut up, Nikka. I'm not here for your little mind games." Now it's too late to enjoy.

"TICK. TICK."

"We don't have—" I start, but Nikka jumps up from the bed and gets in Luke's face, staring at him, like she's trying to will something out.

Luke looks down. "You don't understand," he mumbles. "People don't—" And then he breaks. "I—I was too slow," he whispers. "I should have pushed him, tackled that kid, something." He walks to the dresser and grips it hard, and for a minute I think he's going to pick it up and throw it across the room, but he stands next to me, in front of the mirror. His shaking shoulders that tell me he's crying.

The thing is, I don't see his reflection in the glass.

Nikka doesn't make a move toward him, just starts talking again, her voice calm and low. "He wanted to skip," she says. "We were going to meet up for breakfast, at Common Good." Then her voice breaks. "But I told him I had to go to school early because . . . because this girl was trying to pull up on Mikey Travers and even though I didn't really want him, I had to let her know . . ." She sits back down on the bed, wringing her hands like Lady Macbeth. "Can we just remember for a little while?" she asks, her voice cracking. "We don't have to cry or ask why or be blessed because we mourn . . . I just . . . want to remember. Can we do that?" She walks up to stand on the other side of me, and as I'm sandwiched between them for a second I

I can tell them about the possibilities

About do-overs

Maybe there's a way for us to start over together

No. You ruined that already. And someone has to pay.

They can't even let you have this.

The Voice shoots through my chest so hard and sharp that I stumble.

Ain't that a—

"Why do *you* think this is happening?" I blurt out. "And don't give me stories and fairy tales and three wishes. You saw him too. Why do you think he was there?"

The longest silence winds its way around the room, above and below and through me, closing in on every part of my body.

"I didn't," my cousin says softly.

"What?"

"I didn't see Tunde, or anything."

"What are you saying, Nikka?"

"She's saying what I've been saying all along," says Luke. "She didn't see him because he wasn't there. He's dead, and we . . . just have to live with that."

Live with that.

"Why would you do something like that?" I whisper. "Why would you lie?"

"Because I love you, cuzzee," she says in a whisper so soft I can barely hear it. "I'm on your side, good and bad, all of them. Because it hurts. But it doesn't only have to hurt. It's time," she continues, "It's time for us to—"

"Shut up! Shut up! Shut up!" I yell, but neither of them moves.

> *Lalalalalalala they can't hear you*
> *They don't need you*
> *They don't want you*
> *They don't*

TICK
TICK

> *They are going to die down here*
> *And it's your fault*
> *Your fault*
> *Again*

TICK TICK

I'm made up of flames.

Every single muscle and nerve is burning and the pain is so bad, but I can't move or scream but I *am* screaming—

"We don't have TIME, OK?! I messed up. *I* did this. I'm being punished, because I—

BOOM!

they can't hear me

Or maybe they don't want to

they came with me

"Many waters to cross . . ."

Momma? Momma, it hurts, it *hurts, it hurts so so bad* and I—

Something hard and ice-cold breaks over my head, and for a moment I think it *is* ice, but it's water, Luke's dumped a bucket of water over my head, like a gag on TV, but it hurts, it's not funny, it's not funny at all—

Am I a joke to you?

"Do you know who I am?" I croak.

The Princess.

The One with the Questions.

Little Sis.

Little One.

The One Whose Brother

Listen to me

LISTEN

Forgive me, fam, for I have sinned

—and then there is a *CRACK!* as the mirror breaks into
pieces
"The curse has come upon me
cried the Lady of Shalott"
Mrs. Barclay's reflection looks back at me from the mirror,
gesturing wildly. I stumble back—
The mirror pieces fly toward me, and
I put my arms up to shield my face and the floor opens up
under my feet and I'm falling into a black hole
Falling
"He's just waiting to pull the rug out from under you."
And I see Nikka and Luke peering down at me.
I'm falling.
Their faces are frozen in fear.
This is a black hole.
They are leaning further and further in to look at me . . .
don't they understand what a black hole will do to them,
what *I* will do to them?
Do you know who I am?
This is not who I am.
The thought hits me like a slap.
I don't want Bad Rats and Good Rats
(maybe no rats and hoodrats though)
I don't want to be the Princess
Until my skin is translucent
Until I am ashes and dust
like your brother

"Come on!" Nikka is yelling, still leaning in, leaning so far in, holding out her arm to me. "Grab my hand!"

I don't reach up.

I won't bring them with me this time.

"It's my fault," I say. "I killed Tunde."

Can you hear me now?

I killed Tunde. I don't recognize my own voice;

Or, I do, but it sounds like that other Voice

I killed Tunde.

I need to say it

"I killed Tunde!"

The expressions on their faces let me know that they heard this time.

I close my eyes, and let myself fall.

I hit the ground with a force that makes me feel every bone in my body.

"Time's up!" says BenoiX, smiling. "You told," he continues. "Good call."

"Shut up," I say, struggling to stand. I spit black, oily sludge.

"You gave them a chance. Sentimental."

"Isn't that what you told me to do?"

"Did I? Probably a test, I don't remember."

"Did I pass?"

He stops smiling. "I don't care."

I look around. I'm back in that first tunnel we fell into—like maybe I'm going to start this terrible trip all over again. Except Nikka and Luke aren't here.

"How will they get out? Will the Rats help them leave?" I see Nikka and Luke's faces again, frozen, looking down at me.

"Aww, does it sting? Did you think that maybe they'd forgive you? Hug it out and then you'd all go for bubble tea? Why . . . yes, I think you did, for a moment! That's hilarious!" He laughs, exaggerated, with thigh-slapping and everything, falling over, rolling on the ground.

I just stand there and watch. I feel like a sub. *I'll wait.*

He's gasping now. "You thought . . . you thought, they'd *understand!* They'd—HAHAHAHA—relate, because they feel guilty too! Hahahahahaha! I can't take it! I can't breathe!" He's doubled over, and I just keep waiting because I've learned my lesson.

You need to hurry if you want to leave

Something's going to jump out from behind a door; I can feel it. Alisia with a machete wouldn't surprise me at this point.

You think you can wait it out? Do you want to fade gently into the night?

"You could have been any one of those other Selves!" BenoiX is gasping for breath now: He sounds like he might literally die laughing. "But you chose None. Nothing! HAHAHAHAHAHAHA!"

Something's going to happen to me,

to every Me.

It's too late for gentle.

Because I have to pay.

I'll be attacked by rats

I think I can hear them

Something's going to happen

It's getting louder

I'm going to be ready—

"HAHAHAHA—"

Then a bed crashes down hard, right on top of him.

And Luke and Nikka are sitting on top of it, breathing hard.

And after they stop, I realize that the sound that I'd heard was their screaming.

The laughter has stopped too.

And as the dust clears, they look over the side, where Ben-oiX's legs are pointing out from under the bed.

　　　"Nice kicks," Luke says.

　　　(LAUGH TRACK)

V/O: Previously on *Hard-Hearted Harriet*

MONTAGE:

MOMMA (singing on stage, spotlight, dressed in gold iro buba and gele that keeps unwrapping and falling over her head) Many waters to cross . . . (she gestures toward HARRIET, at a solo table in the crowd) Come on, sing it with me!

LUKE AND NIKKA: (dancing down a yellow brick NYC street, singing "Brand New Day")

HARRIET: (gets a bucket of water dumped on her)

V/O: Tonight, on a Very Special Episode of *You're Breaking My Heart*

HARRIET: You don't understand! No one understands!

NIKKA: (looking serious) Cuz, this is Something Serious. (LUKE and NIKKA slowly turn toward each other)

LUKE: (doing pushups) Ninety-nine, one hundred (pause) one hundred and one, one hundred and two. (laugh track)

HARRIET: (sees LITTLE GIRL about to dive into the pool) We've got to stop her! We're almost out of time!

(Image of HARRIET, MOMMA, LUKE, NIKKA, LITTLE GIRL in group hug)

(Now Harriet is at the pool, in her yellow bathing suit, about to take a running dive into the dry pool. She jumps, and—freeze frame, mid-dive. *record scratch sound*)

HARRIET V/O:

Yep. That's me. You may be wondering how I got here. One day you're a regular teenager, just minding your business when the worst happens. (she's hit by bird droppings from overhead) (LAUGH TRACK) Nope, not that.

CUT TO: Tunde's funeral.

Yeah, that was pretty bad. But not even that.

CUT TO: Harriet yelling "I wish you were dead!" into a void.

Yeah, that part. (LAUGH TRACK) Now all I have to do is keep my cousin from finding out, because then all hell will break loose (she looks at camera) Literally. (LAUGH TRACK)

FLASHBACK TO HARRIET'S APARTMENT: MOMMA is in the kitchen, dressed in slightly out-of-date very formal Nigerian iro, buba, and gele, totally inappropriate for the kitchen. She's stirring things in a lot of bubbling pots. Fela Kuti's "Zombie" is playing, and MOMMA is dancing as she stirs. Doorbell rings. HARRIET, slouchy and pouty, and wearing her yellow bathing suit, stomps over to answer.

NIKKA
(Walks in, exaggerated catwalk style, very dressed up, Disney princess–style, tiara, high heels. Applause, cheers, like when a favorite character appears.)

(opens with her catchphrase) Hey, cuzzo! (more cheers)

HARRIET
What do you want, Nikka?

NIKKA
(breezes past HARRIET)

Oooh is that egusi soup I smell, Auntie? Nobody makes egusi like you! I just happened to arrive at just the right time!

HARRIET

(exaggerated sigh and eye-rolling)

You literally come at the same time every day because you know it's dinner time. (LAUGH TRACK)

NIKKA

(air-kisses HARRIET and goes over to hug MOMMA)

MOMMA

I'm so glad someone appreciates a home-cooked meal!

NIKKA

And a good folktale!

(Doorbell rings again. They all look at each other, then MOMMA goes back to stirring, harder.)

HARRIET

(slouchy and eye-rolling)

Did you invite anyone else, Nikka?

NIKKA

(shrugging, wide-eyed innocence)

Did I do that? (LAUGH TRACK)

HARRIET

(throws up her hands dramatically)

That's not even from this show! (She goes to answer the door, and opens to LUKE.)

LUKE

Did I hear African stew and folktales? Count me in! I've already worked up an appetite. (winks at HARRIET. Studio audience *wooooooooooooos*)

MOMMA

Kaasan, son! Oh wait—you're not my son, you're the other one. (LAUGH TRACK)

HARRIET

(stares at camera)

That's . . . not funny. (awkward pause) And why do you keep speaking Yoruba? We're *not Nigerian*! (LAUGH TRACK)

(CUT TO: HARRIET, LUKE, and NIKKA sitting at dinner table. Green and white tablecloth. Yoruba statues everywhere. More Fela music playing. Bowls of stew, eba, etc. MOMMA still stirring at the stove. LUKE and NIKKA are eating heartily, HARRIET is picking at her food.)

MOMMA:

Why aren't you eating? (starts singing under her breath)
You won't take her bowl! You won't take her bowwwl!

HARRIET

I'm not hungry. And you're getting the words wrong
again, Momma! That's song's not even that old—
nobody gets Beyoncé wrong!

MOMMA

I'm doing it on purpose—I don't want the
Beyhorde after me!

HARRIET AND NIKKA

Bey*HIVE*!!! (LAUGH TRACK)

MOMMA

(shrugs and eats)

Eat your food. E jeun!

HARRIET

I'm waiting for you to say
something about my outfit, Nikka.

NIKKA

Something. (LAUGH TRACK)

HARRIET

Come on, what do you think?

NIKKA

(shrugs)

You like it, I love it.

MOMMA

Eat.

NIKKA

(eating her soup and eba with a fork)

You've got to keep your strength up, cuzzo!
Auntie, this is delicious!

MOMMA

(music changes to praise and worship)

Praise the Lord! I have one daughter who cares!
Let me get my crown! (she praise dances at the stove,
pulls a church hat out of a large pot, then starts stirring)

HARRIET

She's not your daughter. (LAUGH TRACK.
MOMMA shrugs and goes back to stirring.)

LUKE

I've got enough strength for us all. (He drops to the floor for some one-handed pushups. LAUGH TRACK.)

HARRIET

(pushes back her chair in frustration)

This is ridiculous! You're all ridiculous! Why are you acting like nothing's going on? (voice breaks) I'm going . . . (dramatic pause) TO THE POOL! (She runs out of the room as dramatic music swells. MOMMA, LUKE, and NIKKA look at each other, and FADE OUT.)

SCENE: Harriet peeks into the pool, it's empty, eerie, spooky, etc. Scary music plays. She steps into the room.

HARRIET

(small voice)

Hello? Anyone here?

(scary music rises)

I'm just taking a quick dip, nothing to see here, just going— (she starts as though she hears something) Ahhh! What was that? (A solitary rat in a bathing cap runs by. Harriet relaxes.)

Oh, just a rat. (she freezes) Wait a minute, A RAT?!!! AHHHHH!

She turns to run out of the room and the LITTLE GIRL is in the doorway. She's dressed in the same bathing suit as Harriet.

LITTLE GIRL

Hi.

HARRIET

(jumps into her arms)

Ahhh! Rat! Help! Rat!

LUKE, NIKKA, and MOMMA, who is carrying a pot and spoon, run into the room.

LUKE

I heard screaming! I'm here to save the day!

(looks around) Did I miss it?

NIKKA

It's *evening*, Luke. The day's over. (LAUGH TRACK) What's up, cuzzo? (CHEERS/APPLAUSE)

HARRIET

(steps out of LITTLE GIRL'S arms)

Up? Nothing's up! What could be up? Everything's down!

Wayyy down.

LITTLE GIRL

Whew! That was like carrying a—

HARRIET

Watch it!

NIKKA

A lot of baggage, right? (she walks over and holds the LITTLE GIRL'S hand) No one can carry that much baggage.

HARRIET

Watch it!

MOMMA

(singing)

This

LITTLE GIRL

Come on in, the water's fine!

(she takes a running start and makes an expert dive into the pool, disappears from view)

HARRIET

Oh my—she can't swim! I have to save her! (she tries to start running, but she's not moving forward)

LUKE

Did somebody say "save"? (LAUGH TRACK)

NIKKA

Listen, cuzzo. You can't save her. You can't save anybody until you save yourself. (she shares a meaningful glance with LUKE)

HARRIET

(still running)

What are you talking about? Stop wasting time! She can't swim, she's going to drown! (she breaks free of the invisible force that was keeping her in place, and starts the dive that we opened the episode with, but LUKE jumps after her and grabs her back into a bear hug) *Oh now* you want to be romantic? Where were you when I needed a date to the Big School Dance? (LAUGH TRACK)

LUKE

In case you haven't noticed, my timing's always a little off.
(LAUGH TRACK)

NIKKA

(Seriously and gently, and bathed in a bright, soft light.
She snaps her fingers, and they are suddenly in
HARRIET's bedroom.)

No, cuzzo. Wait. You're already drowning, don't you see?
(she walks slowly over to HARRIET and LUKE,

and the three of them sit in a row on the bed)
We need to talk.

MOMMA

(spotlighted in a corner, softly singing as background)

"Many waters to cross . . ."

HARRIET

I don't want to talk! Don't you get it? Bad things happen
when I talk! Really bad things!

NIKKA

What do you mean? (LUKE and NIKKA exchange a
meaningful glance)

HARRIET

(crying)

It's . . . it's my fault Tunde's dead. I was fighting with him
and I said "I wish you were dead"—I literally said those
words—and then, well, we all know what happened next.

LUKE

(pause) What?

HARRIET

He died, idiot! (LAUGH TRACK) It was the last thing
I said to him. So . . . it's my fault.

NIKKA

You can't believe that, cuzzo.

LUKE

Yeah, who hasn't wished someone dead?

MOMMA

(raises hand)

Me. (hums) That's some bad juju right there! (LAUGH TRACK)
(she goes back to singing) Many waters to cross . . .

HARRIET

Lyrics, Momma. Still wrong.

NIKKA

What I'm saying is, what was the first thing you said to him?

HARRIET

What? How should I know?

NIKKA

The hundred forty-seventh?

(HARRIET stares)

NIKKA

The eight-hundred and two thousand,
three hundred sixty-fifth?

LUKE

(stares at camera)

This is a profound moment.

NIKKA

It's not about the last thing you said, or the first thing—
it's not even about the fact that he's dead.

MOMMA

It's very sad, though. (goes back to singing) "If you make your
heart free, baybee, maybe you'll understand . . ."

LUKE

The last thing I said to him was "OK, dawg."
(looks worried) Was that bad?

NIKKA

This thing is, what are we going to do *now*?

MOMMA

EAT!

(singing)

All of me I've left behind . . . I will love you allllwayys

Let me make you some food. I'm learning Jamaican
food next. (fake accent) Wah Gwaan? Ital only, mon!
(LAUGH TRACK)

HARRIET

Momma, you're getting Stevie Wonder wrong.

You love Stevie Wonder.

MOMMA

I love YOU. (They hug. AUDIENCE: Awwww!)

HARRIET & MOMMA

(simultaneously)

Can you forgive me?

HARRIET

(pulling away)

Forgive YOU? For what?

MOMMA

I haven't been there for you. I haven't been there for me.

I didn't think I could . . .

LUKE

Be there? (LAUGH TRACK)

HARRIET

I thought you didn't love me anymore. That you couldn't
love me without Tunde.

MOMMA

But . . . I made all this food! (LAUGH TRACK) I'm almost there, Harriet. (praise and worship music returns at very low volume)

LITTLE GIRL

(returns, dripping)

I'm back from running away.

HARRIET

You ran away? I thought you just went swimming.
(LAUGH TRACK)

LUKE

This is a *Very Special Episode*. They always have someone running away.

MOMMA

And a stern but loving momma who welcomes them home.

HARRIET

Always?

MOMMA

(holds out her arms for another hug, and Harriet runs into them)

I'm almost there.

HARRIET

Well . . . (to LITTLE GIRL) I'm glad you're back.

LITTLE GIRL

Me too. (Now they hug. AUDIENCE: "Awwwwwwww")
Will you tell me a new story?

HARRIET

Sure, but I don't remember the old one.

LITTLE GIRL

That's OK, I know you have a lot of them to choose from.

MOMMA

How about a game of chess?

HARRIET

(incredulous)

Really?!

MOMMA

(wise nodding)

Really.

(pause for all-around loving look exchanges)

NIKKA

And *that*, cuzzo, is how a story goes. Group hug!

LUKE

That's right, a love story. (AUDIENCE oooooohs, LUKE
is flustered.) I didn't mean it like that! (LUKE &
HARRIET exchange a meaningful look. NIKKA &
MOMMA smile knowingly.)

HARRIET

(shy)

Uh, why do you keep calling me cuzzo?
I thought it was cuzzee.

NIKKA

(shrugs)

Tomato, tomahto. (LAUGH TRACK)

LUKE

Ooh, that reminds me—I'm hungry! Who wants pizza?

(the three exchange warm smiles, link arms, and stand)

But first, we save that little girl! Unless . . . we ran out of time?
Did we run out of time?

LITTLE GIRL

(taps him on the shoulder)

I'm back already, remember? (LAUGH TRACK) But I might go swimming again. If you all come with me.

NIKKA
(starts to answer, HARRIET holds her back)

HARRIET
I got this, cuz. Of course we will. (to LUKE, smiling) And if there's one thing I learned today, is that there's always time for a second chance. *(puts her fist out, gesturing for the others to join her, all for one/one for all style)*

Let's do this . . . *together!*

(APPLAUSE)

(CREDITS ROLL)

"What—how—why?" I look around in a panic, expecting BRats, the Three Boys, and Alisia to burst in. "Are you OK?"

"Yeah, but . . ." says Luke, slowly standing up, "I don't think your friend is." He points to BenoiX's legs sticking out from under the bed, like Wicked Wizard of the (Very) South. "Nice kicks, though." He grimaces. "That really had to hurt."

"That's not the point," says Nikka, rolling her eyes. "The pain is not the point. That's never how it works."

"You have to get out of here!! What am I going to do?" *How am I going to get to another Me now?* I want to stop, drop, and cry. I tried to save them and now they've ruined everything. "You couldn't just listen to me and leave me alone, could you? Do you understand what you've done?"

"Why did you say that?" asks Nikka.

"Because you've just messed up my chance to save—"

"I mean what you said about Tunde," she interrupts. "That you killed him."

Oh. That.

It's so absurd that I feel like I'm in a sitcom and the laugh track should be starting.

"Yeah," she pounds the spot on the bed next to her. "That. How could you say something like that? You know what happened. We all know . . . that kid shot him." She holds up a hand as Luke opens his mouth. "I'm sorry, I'm not ready to say that person's name." She turns back to me. "So why would you say something so horrible and wrong?"

"If you think that, why do you sound angry at *me*?" I mutter, looking down at my hands. The purple manicure she'd given me is raggedy now, almost completely chipped away. My dress is filthy, and torn; I look worse than the kids who were serving us at the Prom, and I wonder if that's what's next. Maybe this is all BenoiX's warped reality show, "From Princess to Peasant," and everyone's in on it. Maybe in another life, I'm watching myself, and cringing while I laugh. *It's funny because it's true.*

It doesn't matter now. I can't trade places now. Ben-oiX is lying underneath that bed and I'm stuck in this self— in this life. I look around. I hear a faint, distant *drip drip*, but the tunnel walls and floor are bone dry, and I realize how cold it is. I look up at the hole made by the bed crashing down.

Nothing and no one has come running. I don't know how to get up or out. Instead of saving them, I've brought Nikka and Luke to a place they can't leave. They *should* be angry. They should hate me.

So why can't they just hate me and make me feel better? I put a hand in the remaining pocket; the gum wrapper the Little Girl had given me is still there.

"You've lost it," says Luke. He starts to pick up the larger pieces of mirror on the floor. "You have really lost it and that's why we're here. You need to—"

"I—we were fighting that day—" I start, and Luke tries to say something, but Nikka shushes him. She knows it doesn't matter now. This is what Something Serious means. "We were having a stupid, stupid fight and I said it. I said, 'I wish . . . I wish you were dead.' And then he went to school and died." I stop, and the *drip drip* is a little louder, the only sound in this cold, dark hole.

"So, do you think it was . . . bad magic?" Nikka asks softly. I look at her, but her face is serious.

"I think it was me, that's what I think," I say.

And then she starts crying, sobbing so hard that I'm afraid she'll hurt herself.

"Nikka—"

"I'm sorry," she wails. "I'm so, so sorry. I—" She is crying so hard, she's struggling to breathe, and I put one hand, then two, around her shoulders. I turn to Luke for help, and see that he's standing there, silently crying himself. When he catches my eye, he lets out a roar, an inhuman, excruciating sound (and for a minute this reminds me of the Nollywood movie we'd all watched, the last movie night we'd had together, when the main character had had acid thrown on her right before her wedding and the funeral service was interrupted by aunties wailing).

Why are you like this? They are going through the worst pain, and you—

"I'm so sorry we let you live in that kind of pain," says Nikka at last. "I'm so, so sorry. I should have reached out, I should have seen, I should have known . . ."

"He literally asked me to look out for you whenever he wasn't around," says Luke. "I'm the one who let you down. Who let him . . . Tunde . . . down."

In a red flash, the old bile and rage rises in my throat. "Why do you both have to make everything about you? It's sick, you know, it's *sick, sick, sick*. I said it—I *did* it—do you hear me? I SAID IT, I DID IT!" Now I'm crying, but there aren't any tears, just dry, choked sobs, and I double over holding my stomach, squeezing my eyes shut. I feel them come to either side of me, but I can't stop dry-heaving.

And then I hear my own voice screaming, "I SAID IT I DID IT!" over and over; I don't feel my mouth moving—

But that's me

That's *me*

And she won't stop.

I cover my ears.

ISAIDITIDIDITISAIDITIDIDITISAIDITIDIDIT

Shut up shut up shut UP SHUT UP

Wait, who's that? It sounds like me

And it sounds like the Voice

And it sounds like Luke and Nikka

ISAIDITIDIDITISAIDITIDIDITISAIDITIDIDIT

I open my eyes, and they are saying it too, yelling it with me. And then the tears flow,

and flow

and flow.

They're crying too.

My mouth opens to ask again *why*

They are making this about them

again

But I'm tired

and I don't

want to hold this
Because it's too much it's too big it's too heavy
it'stoomuchit'stoobigit'stooheavy
No matter how many selves I am
None of me can hold this.
None of this makes sense.

So we cry
and cry
and cry

And Ever Since Then

Sometimes people talk about needing/having/wanting a good cry. There's nothing *good* about it. My body feels like I've been fighting my way through sludge and being punched and kicked every step of the way. My eyes and nose are raw; when I reach up to wipe them, it stings. Slowly I lift my head; Nikka is gently sniffing on one side of me, and Luke's eyes are closed as he breathes deep, hard breaths.

The bed is rocking gently—swaying, dipping, and rising, almost as if . . .

The bed is a wet raft, floating on a sea of water. Everywhere I look, there's water.

And it's rising.

372 RHUDAY - PERKOVICH

"This thing is sinking," says Luke. He's right; the water isn't rising, the bed is taking on water, slowly, but definitely. "Where did all of this water come from?"

"It's . . . our tears," Nikka says softly.

We look at each other for a long while, saying nothing, and everything, at the same time. Pieces of mirror float by. I try to see ahead, but it's too dark. I look up, but the hole they fell through has closed, and it occurs to me, Nikka-style, that maybe time's up. The ticking clock in every story like this has run out. The portal has closed.

I'm left with myself. I unfold the Little Girl's gum wrapper to make a futile attempt to wipe my face again. There are traces of writing on it; it's not a gum wrapper at all. It's the piece of paper, from the bathroom at school. The Troll Tunnel. The portal.

You missed out on the magic. The way out has closed.
But I'm not alone.

I grab Nikka and Luke's hands. "We're going to have to swim out of here," I say. "There's got to be a way out through the other end of this tunnel. But the only way to find out is to swim."

Luke points to the murky water, the bits of glass. "Through that?"

Nikka moves around the bed slowly, trying to prolong our buoyancy. "Where . . . what happened to . . . him?"

We can't see BenoiX's legs anymore.

"Are you serious right now?" says Luke.

The water is not so calm now, churning and turning over. I can almost *hear* it.

"I can't," says Luke. "I don't think I can do this. My leg. It's . . . bad. Y'all go on ahead. I don't want to hold you back."

Nikka rolls her eyes. "Are *you* serious right now?"

"Just hold onto me," I say quickly. "I got you." *I'm so scared.*

"But I was supposed to be—"

I interrupt him. "You did. You are." I force a smile. "I'm all that in the water, remember?" He starts to speak again, then he smiles a half-smile. "Look at that, it's like the sun coming out," I say, grabbing his hand and squeezing it.

"This is all really sweet, but we've got a situation here, y'all," says Nikka. "Something's coming." We all look ahead to where's she's pointing. A dark shape approaches, moving swiftly over the angry waters.

It's Alisia, rowing a boat.

Dreams Really Do Come True

"Déjà vu all over again!" Alisia calls out. "You really messed up, Harriet." Light flashes behind her, and I can see maybe a mirror—or a door—in the distance.

"Stay back, Alisia," I say. I whisper to Luke and Nikka: "She's dangerous."

"No, really?" says Nikka, putting all the *I told you so* she can in her voice.

"It's over, Alisia," I say. "We just want to go home."

"You *were* home," she replies curtly, coming up next to us. "We welcomed you to the Underground, and you had the opportunity to go Beyond. To be more. To forget what you did and who you are. But you threw it away. For what?" she barks now, pointing to Nikka and Luke. "That?"

"For them," I say, "And me. I don't need to be anyone else. I don't even need to forget."

She spits into the water, and it sizzles. "Don't you, though? You can't do anything right anymore. You don't have the capacity to *be* anything right anymore. You proved that when you wished your own brother dead. And that gave you so much power to do all kinds of beautiful wrong, but now . . . you'll live in your mistakes. Literally *swimming* in your failure."

Steam rises from the water, and the sounds of the Prom, faint and burbling, are just below the surface.

"Oh, you can hear them?" says Alisia. "Those kids that cheered for you, that were here for you?"

I stay perfectly still, and she laughs a loud, empty laugh.

"Yep, you *drowned* them, Harriet. You killed them too. It's like your superpower."

I remember Harley Quinn and those empty eyes. I think of the Little Girl, and my heart hurts. I remember that translucent skin, the joyless dancing, the cheerless cheers. The waves get bigger, and as the salty water splashes against our bed-raft, I know it's not going to last much longer.

"You're a liar," I say to Alisia, in a clear, high voice that I don't recognize. "A lying, lonely, loveless liar." I look straight into her eyes. She doesn't flinch.

"Do you see that?" whispers Nikka next to me. "Like a door made out of a mirror?"

"A mirror that looks like a door," whispers Luke. She shushes him.

"They were already dying," I say. "They were dying as soon as I—as *we*—came down here." I draw in a deep breath, like the ones I used to take when I first learned to dive. "I'm sorry about what I said to Tunde," I say. "I'm so, so sorry." Nikka squeezes my hand. "But you're wrong. I'm not going to just live in that. It's more important what I do next. Who I *can* be. How I *can* love." Now Luke squeezes my hand on the other side.

Alisia snorts. "How cute. It's like the very special episode of a stupid, corny show. Anyway, I don't care anymore. You do you and see how far that takes you." She gestures to her boat. "You got one last favor. Get in."

I shake my head. "Forget it, Alisia."

Many waters to cross . . . I hear Momma singing her song in my head. *I'm almost there*, she says. *Just a little more to go.*

"What do you think you're going to do?" laughs Alisia. "You can't get out of here without my help. I'm not taking them anywhere, but if you want, I'll take you to the exit, and then you can go get help or whatever and come back for them." She smiles. "You have my word I won't touch them. I wouldn't dream of it. Contamination and all, you know. And there's no one else left. Oh, except her."

My Little Girl? My heart leaps.

"Which her?"

Alisia shrugs and doesn't answer.

"What happened to BenoiX?" I ask. "He was . . . here."

"Yeah, we squashed him like a roach," says Luke bluntly.

Alisia grins. "You really think you did something, don't you?" She sighs dramatically. "He's the one who sent me for you. Just now."

Nikka gasps.

Alisia goes on, relishing in our shock. "He's not gonna go away, Harriet. He'll *always* be here. He'll rebuild, and I'm here for it. There will always be an Underground."

"You think we're not going to tell everybody about this?" I say. "You think we won't stop other kids from becoming monsters like you?"

"I'm sure you'll try," says Alisia. "For a little while. But even you may not recognize us when we return. He's not Night Man or BenoiX anymore."

"You might not recognize me either, when I come back," I answer, holding her stare. We stay like that for a moment, then she looks away. "Because I will be back."

Luke coughs.

"So . . . what . . . what's his name now?" I ask, even though I already know.

"Oh . . . this is so good," Alisia says, giggling. "It's . . . the UnderToad! Get it? *The UnderToad*!"

"That's not even original," says Nikka. "He stole it from a book."

Alisia stops laughing abruptly. "But it's true," she says slowly. "It's very true. So you might want to get in the boat, Harriet. Now."

You could have been all those other Selves.

Remember the alligators?

Or were they crocodiles?

Either/Or

Why not both?

You chose None.

I look at Nikka. "Do you remember that part when she said she must go soon?" We'd read *The People Could Fly* over and over again, the whole story aloud in unison, both dropping to a whisper when we got to the line about being the ones who fly.

"And they joined hands . . ." Nikka continues, because of course she remembers.

"On the count of three," I whisper.

"One," says Luke.

"JUMP!" I yell, and we do.

I choose everything.

And I hear a flushing sound

And the water is cold and thick, and swirls round and round like a vortex

I choose all of Me.

And Nikka and Luke are holding onto me, and I'm holding onto them, and I start swimming, and I keep swimming, toward that door-shaped mirror,

(or mirror-looking door)
toward Momma,
and chess
and pepper soup and French fries and pizza
toward wardrobe lions and roller coasters
toward *that movie about the pig*
and singing off-key
toward the park and the Peace Fountain
and *hanging out with me and my girls*
toward the stories and the songs
and dumplings and laughing
and crying
together
toward my big brother
and memories
toward the Little Girl
who gave me the map to find my way home.
I've got many waters to cross.

I keep swimming.

ACKNOWLEDGMENTS

To Adedayo: Your thoughtful reading is a blessing; you are infinitely gifted. Most of all, thank you for being my ring of endless light.

To Renée, Kelly, Dhonielle, Lamar, Anne, Karina, Rebecca, and Linda: Thank you for the loving listening, reading, consoling, and listening again over the YEARS it took me to eke this one out,

To Laura, who lifts me, and so many of us, up to share her shine,

To Kikelomo, whose light inspires, and who reminds me every day to keep moving toward the stories and songs,

To Joe, who knows what it means to wait till we have faces,

To Marietta, an incredible agent and blessing of a friend, who asked me "What is real?" at exactly the right moment,

To my amazing gift of an editor Nick Thomas, who "got" this story after just a few words of conversation, and didn't give up on it even when I did, who challenged and cheered me on through every variation and universe of this book, who gave me the room to tell this weird, messy story,

To the brilliant Briana Mukodiri Uchendu, who took my breath away from the moment I saw that gorgeous, moody, perfect cover art,

To Suzanne Lander, whose thoughtful and precise copyedits were a gift,

Thank you.

ABOUT THE AUTHOR

Olugbemisola Rhuday-Perkovich is the award-winning author of several books for children, including *Operation Sisterhood*, *It Doesn't Take a Genius*, and *Two Naomis* (as co-author). She is a member of the Brown Bookshelf, and editor of the We Need Diverse Books anthology *The Hero Next Door*. Olugbemisola lives with her family in NYC where she writes, makes things, and needs to get more sleep.

Please visit her on IG @olugbemisolarhudayperkovich and at http://olugbemisolabooks.com.

SOME NOTES ON THIS BOOK'S PRODUCTION

Art for jacket was created by Briana Mukodiri Uchendu, using Procreate on her iPad. The text and display were set by Westchester Publishing Services, in Danbury, CT, using variations of Avenir. A sans serif made by Swiss designer Adrian Frutiger in 1988, the word Avenir means "future" in French, perhaps giving homage to a notable past sans serif, Futura. The book was printed on FSC™-certified 78gsm Yunshidai Ivory paper and bound in China.

Production supervised by Freesia Blizard
Book designed by Jade Broomfield
Assistant Managing Editor: Danielle Maldonado
Editor: Nick Thomas